Celtic Myths and Legends

CELTIC MYTHS AND LEGENDS

EOIN NEESON

MERCIER PRESS

MERCIER PRESS

Trade enquiries to CMD DISTRIBUTION,
55a Spruce Avenue, Stillorgan Industrial Park, Blackrock, Dublin

Originally published as *The First Book of Irish Myths and Legends* in 1965 and *The Second Book of Irish Myths and Legends* in 1966.
This edition 1998.

ISBN 1 85635 222 6

10 9 8 7 6 5 4

Printed in Ireland by Colour Books Ltd.

CONTENTS

INTRODUCTION

ALTHOUGH THE IRISH ARE ONE of the oldest and most homogeneous people in the world, certainly in Europe, their origins are unclear. For the most part the oldest records of Celtic settlements in Ireland are found in compilations such as the *Leabhar Gabhala (The Book of Invasions)*, and other works dating from the eighth century AD. These are evidently based on popular tradition, but probably also on earlier written accounts now lost.

Of those who preceded the Celts only their archaeological remains survive, some of them – like the Newgrange complex, predating (c.3,000 BC) the pyramids of Egypt, with which it shares many symbols and mathematical precision – are mysterious and awe-inspiring. Who these people were has not, so far, been decided.

Ireland was peopled quite late, not before the ice receded after the last ice-age and the ice-bridge with Britain and the Continent had melted or been inundated between 9,000 and 10,000 years ago. That the earliest people to reach Ireland's shores were skilled and advanced in thought is clear, but as to who or what these pre-Celtic people might have been is hidden by time. They were, it is believed, late mesolithic hunter-fishers (though there is some evidence of very early agricultural activity) and were capable of building boats that could cross the intervening sea and that could carry people, animals and supplies.

They also already had a long tradition behind them. By becoming an island people they became essentially homogeneous. In contrast to their co-mingling Continental cousins this insularity also provided, for them and the Celts who followed, the circumstances essential to the development of enduring cultural characteristics.

The earliest settlers lived here for some 3,000 years before being absorbed by neolithic farmers who remained here until the first arrival of the Celts, and it is to them that we must ascribe Newgrange and other ancient buildings, many of which – though long pre-dating them – would become important features of Celtic mythology.

So far as is known the first Celtic settlers arrived about 800

BC bringing with them an entirely new culture and one that was itself curiously divided.

The dominent Celts who settled in Ireland (and there were probably others, both before and contemporaneously) brought with them aspects of cultural development that differed considerably from those of their cousins in Britain and on the Continental land mass. One of the most notable differences, which has come to be labelled 'P Celts' and 'Q Celts', was in the use of language. But there were social and philosophical differences too, although contact with Britain – much of which became an Irish Celtic colony – and Europe was strong.

Many of these differences may be accounted for by the (probably correct) inference and tradition that, over several hundred years, the Irish dominent Celts came, progressively, from the Celtic heartland of *Mittel Europa*, south about via the Danube, Phrygia (Turkey), Egypt, Etruria and Tartessia and Galicia (both in Spain) and so to Ireland, bringing with them the cultural influences they had acquired *en route*, while the Bretonic Celts made their way through the forested and undeveloped north-west overland to the English Channel and Britain.

Much of what we know about our Celtic forbears has come down to us in the form of mythological tales and since this book concerns myths and mythical figures, perhaps mythology is a good point at which to start. Most dictionaries define a myth as a purely fictitious narrative often involving supernatural or supranatural persons and embodying popular ideas on natural phenomena. But historians, archaeologists and ethnologists are putting a new interpretation on myths, particularly since the German, Von Schliemann, discovered the site of so-called 'mythical' Troy at the beginning of the century, and so upset the notion that it was all a figment of Homer's imagination.

Scientific archaeology proved that a city existed on the site of Troy – in fact that several cities preceded it – and that it was great and walled; that it was destroyed by fire about the time in which Homer set the Trojan wars. The question is where does myth end and truth begin?

It can easily be overlooked that Irish literature, deriving directly from mythological sources, is – apart from that of ancient Greece and Rome – the oldest literature in Europe, which effectively means in the world. There is an unfortunate tendency to dismiss the idea that myths have any significant meaning. When the word 'myth' is used today it is generally to suggest one of three things, all of them inaccurate. These are (1) an arena the exclusive province of scholars; (2) fairy tales for children; (3) a synonym for what is untrue. These give an inaccurate and pejorative meaning to the word. With regard to (1), the truth is that if myth is based on anything at all, it is on reasoning. The second common error is to dismiss myths as stories fit only for children. It is, of course, true that mythological stories appeal to children. They are, after all, intended to impress and be awe-inspiring. But – appalling 'fairy tale' versions notwithstanding – to suggest that myths are suitable *only* for children is nonsense. Mythology, demonstrates our forefathers' awe before the 'unknown and supernatural'. If this has been superseded it is not because it is the province of children, but because new explanations have displaced the old.

Finally, mythology is, in fact, a repository of the self-image of a people. It provides a revealing, even authoritative, blueprint of former human outlook and man's early search for truth. Myths relate events and states of affairs basic to, yet surpassing, both the mortal world and its people, presenting, as Kees W. Bolle (*The Freedom of Man in Myth*, 1981) put it: 'extraordinary events without trying to justify them'.

EUROPE HAS INHERITED THREE main streams of mythology, subdivided, in turn, roughly in two. They are the dark, sombre, brooding mythological cycle of Scandinavia and Germany; the bright, sun-filled (irrespective of how much blood was spilled) Graeco-Roman tradition. So far as Ireland is concerned and in spite of her geographical location, she shares in her myths the sunshine and brightness of the Greek and Roman tales.

Isolated on the very fringe of Europe, lapped by the nethermost ocean of the period, and a good deal closer – in the physical sense at least – to the hairy primitives of Britain, Germany and Scandinavia and their bloody sagas of immolation and savage despair, why were the Irish evidently of a considerably more advanced social and ethnological stage of development, and why are their myths and stories permeated with the same light and brilliance to be found in the Greek and Roman tales? Perhaps in seeking the answer to these questions we may also find a clue to the origin of the people themselves.

To begin with a people called the Milesians lived, somewhere about 2,000 to 3,000 BC – and possibly earlier – in Ionia and were, according to Herodotus, an Hellenic and Phoenician people speaking a distinctive language of their own and, it is thought, with even older Scythian connections. They were a strong, independent people of distinctive characteristics, so much so that they were the only ones of that region – roughly the western coastline of modern Turkey – from whom neither Croesus the Lydian nor Cyrus the Persian exacted tribute when they overran the area about 1,000 BC. Both Herodotus and Xenophon mention the Milesians as being good at both commerce and war. They were also natural colonisers. They lived in three cities, the chief of which was called Miletus, but they represented only a portion of the race. The remainder were nomads – sea nomads at that – and settlers. It was, in fact, the Milesian command of the sea that enabled them to survive when their neighbours were destroyed by the Lydians, the Medes and the Persians; and it was their command of the sea that enabled them to establish trading colonies and permanent settlements in Sicily, Sardinia, Italy and Spain.

In the *Leabhar Gabhala,* the Milesians are represented as coming directly from Spain to Ireland, which is consistent with the Ionic Milesian colonisation of Sicily, Sardinia, Italy and Spain – Tartessia. What more natural places for westward probing colonists following the paths of (or it may be the stories about) earlier travellers such as Nemed and the Tuatha de Danaan to use as bases?

Although the Milesians, like the Macedonians, were Hellenes though not necessarily Greeks, with the same religious tradition, they lived in Asia among nations that to them were barbaric and, in the pantheistic climate of the period, undoubtedly came under the influence of Asiatic mystical beliefs (as indeed Herodotus remarks), a point which will become significant in a moment. Furthermore it is known that both the Milesians and the Lydians had a common tongue, like that of the Macedonians of Hyperborean – or barbaric – origin, which could, indeed, have been a Celtic tongue. That it was Indo-European is undisputed.

A simple definition of mythology is impossible. Created by

mankind to give shape and meaning to otherwise inexplicable wonders and unseen gods, it is something of fact; something of fiction, but entirely of neither.

From late medieval times onwards the accumulated mysteries of mythology and folk wisdom began to conflict with that rigid axiom of many disciplines, the doctrine that nothing has validity that cannot be scientifically proven. For mythology this inflexible doctrine proved very hostile. As when (later) it was also applied to history – one brigade of historians seeking to encase the subject in a straight jacket of 'scientific revision' – sometimes producing some very peculiar results.

Like superstition mythology came to be an 'unsophisticated' (what today might be termed unenlightened) casualty. In reality it is absurd to exclude oral historical tradition on the grounds that it is irrelevant to historical knowledge – particularly where it concerns belief. To suppose that it was of interest only to children and old people before verifiable written documentation became common is a ludicrous, but by no means unknown, conclusion.

It is nonsense to assert that countless generations responded to the fundamental mysteries of life and death with what they perceived as essentially false. Their myths enshrined what they believed was, for them, the truth. Mythology is a repository of old truths and beliefs and, so, contains – even if only in symbolic form – the history, records and beliefs of the ancients. By describing what can never be determined by reason and observation alone, mythology offered an explanation for what was otherwise inexplicable.

If today the word 'myth' is corrupted it is because it concerns patterns of belief so ancient that we lack the appropriate means to discern them; which is not to say that such patterns – even beliefs – may not have been misconceived, but that is a different question. By expressing the anxiety of man through the ages to define and understand perceived mysteries, mythology may be said to represent elusive truths envisaged by societies – usually remote in time – and perhaps, but not necessarily, in thinking. Unlike history, mythology does not purport to provide concrete answers. On the other hand where else should one look to know what the peoples of past civilisations believed?

MYTHOLOGY PROVIDED ANSWERS TO natural, social, cultural and biological phenomena. For us myths illuminate the nature of ancient ritual and religious custom, demonstrating patterns that can never be determined by reason alone.

Mythology is really a name used for a form of religious symbolism, and indicates the self-image of a people in a given civilisation. While relating to it, myths concern gods and extraordinary events outside ordinary human experience, and are a source of knowledge and have an authoritative, revelatory function, about human existence. They are, accordingly, understood to be both religious phenomena and narrative literature. Diminished and debased by time or not, mythology nevertheless represents a vast accumulation of religious significance and perceived belief.

The time is overdue when the inherent dignity of mythology was restored and it is no longer considered merely as an adulterated province of childhood, a remote one of scholars, or, worst of all, a mere synonym for falsehood.

Mythology sought enlightenment. Since the profoundest mystery is death, the association between it and religion is clear. There is everywhere evidence of religious activity, belief in the supernatural and awe before death in prehistoric tombs.

We would be foolish to assume that people down through the ages were not also moved towards enlightenment, or, as we so often seem to be instructed in spite of our assembled wisdom, that mankind acquired souls only when they learned to write. Surely our remote ancestors lived in a world vastly peopled with spirits, and brought these spirits and their mysteries with them through many ages?

It is no accident that religion and mythology bind together some of the most compelling civilisations of history. On the heels of religion came the concept of justice, which pervades mythology.

Without doubt the Celtic druids practised a religion that even then contained very ancient elements, no less than influences from Mediterranean and Asiatic cultures. It is even reasonable to assume that some surviving traditions and characteristics which are rooted in Celtic patterns, in turn inherited traditions going back thousands of years.

The early waves of immigration to Ireland – from various

but, in the main, probably related sources – contributed to Celtic homogeneity. The early Celtic settlers were the inheritors of Indo-European traditions already very ancient. Behind these lay the obscure religions of the Neolithic agriculturalists; and underlying all were the beliefs and rites of the hunting people ... a pedigree which might stretch 20,000 years, or more, into the remote past. Blinded by science or not, we are an extension of that pedigree.

Celtic mythology, the oldest in Europe apart from the Graeco-Roman, has helped preserve ancient European traditions of the only Celtic people not conquered by Rome. Is it because it is so difficult to interpret that mythology is so often dismissed as being unworthy of serious historical or literary consideration?

After the battle of Mycale, in which the confederate Hellenic states defeated the invading army of Xerxes, the Milesians, who had been an occupied people under Persian domination at this time, attacked their enemies from the rear during the battle and 'proved their bitterest enemies' (Herodotus; *Histories*, Book 9).

Subsequently the Hellenes held a council on the future of the people of Ionia and decided to abandon the indefensible coast to the Persians, and remove the Ionians for re-settlement elsewhere. The plan was eventually abandoned (after pressure from the Athenians who had no wish to see this forward area of defence fall into the hands of the enemy) but not before two things happened; a confederation of Peloponnesians was formed for Ionian defence, and many of the Milesians – the most prosperous and adventurous of the Ionians – decided to ship westward and settle in their new colonies elsewhere. One wonders if they did not by this time have a colony beyond the Hesperides too?

We are told in addition that the Milesians came to Ireland after the Tuatha de Danaan who, in turn, had followed the Nemedians and either conquered or absorbed the, more or less, indigenous Firbolg/Fomorian inhabitants. We are told that the Firbolgs were uncouth, savage and altogether unfit specimens for association with the mystical and visionary Tuatha de Danaan; in effect that they were very much like the Picts who flourished until much later in the neighbouring island, succumbing finally to the resources of civilisation in the guise, on one hand, of the Roman legions and, on the other, of Irish settlers who conquered Argyle and subsequently most of Scotland.

References to Scythia in the old Irish tales have generally been dismissed as mere intrusive embellishments of later scribes letting their imaginations run wild, or have been passed over without comment; a few scholars, such as Mary Hutton, have paid them serious attention. Miscellaneous, but contributory, pieces of evidence may be found scattered throughout various works by different authorities. *The Four Masters,* for example, mention that after the Gaels (Celts) had arrived in Spain from Scythia, one of them, Bregan, built a tower and a city called after himself, Bregantia. From the tower his son, Ith, saw Ireland in the distance. Red Hugh O'Donnell is alleged to have visited the site of the tower in 1602 AD. Incidentally Ith, according to Padraic Colum, was the brother of one Mil or Mileadh, and the father of Eber and Eremon; this information is given with a slight variation in the *Leabhar Gabhala*. Colum adds, with it seems to me several centuries of anticipation, that Mil equates with the Latin 'miles' soldier, and that Eber and Eremon both mean Irishman in Latin.

We already know that the Milesians and the Celts flourished simultaneously in several parts of the world – Asia Minor, Italy and Spain. The point is, could the Ionic Milesians have been Celts? The answer would appear to be that they could. They could certainly have been Scythians. It is established that the Scythians entered Asia in pursuit of the Cimmerians *whom they expelled from Europe*. In other words the Scythians drove these Cimmerians, as the Greeks called them, eastwards from the very area dominated by the Celts, who are also known to have gone eastwards and established a substantial colony in Asia. Is it possible that the Scythians and the Celts are one and the same, or at all events that the Scythians are of Celtic origin? Furthermore, having dealt with the Cimmerians and established themselves on the shores of the Caspian Sea (to which many references also appear in the Irish legends and traditions), the Scythians drove southwards and subjugated the Medes, dominating the very territory in which the Milesians and Lydians were to flourish. The Scythians maintained their supremacy in that part of Asia for twenty-eight years, until the Medes again expelled them from it. But during that time Scythian customs, manners and traditions, not to mention blood, would have become firmly established – particularly as the vast tract of land known as Scythia was just north of Macedonia and its neighbour in Asia Minor, Ionia. It is only right to point out here that the Scythians, or Scoloti, originated according to one account of Herodotus (*Hist.* 4.7) when Hercules came to the region from his home on an island, *near Gades in the ocean beyond the Pillars of Hercules,* called Erythea, and cohabited with a snake woman who bore three sons who were the forerunners of the Scythians.

On the grounds that the Ionic Celts (perhaps inhabitants of Miletus in what is now the west coast of Turkey where, in Galatia, a Celtic language was spoken down to the fourth century AD) can be directly linked with their common Celtic heartland and with Irish folk tradition, there is a substantial basis for the tradition that the dominant Celts who came to Ireland (about 800 BC) did so from Spain, having traversed the Mediterranean from end to end – as did the Milesians from Miletus about the same time, give or take a hundred years or so. For example the proper name of the Greeks, Danaos, and its similarity to De Danaan may not be totally without significance in this context; but even more to the point would appear to be a race mentioned by Xenophon, and possessing the same mystical, awe inspiring, wizard-like characteristics as the Tuatha de Danaan; they were called the Dana. And, as is well known, the proper title of Lugh Lamh Fada, son of the De Danaan hero Cian and of a royal Firbolg mother, was the Il-Dana. Tradition holds that the Fomorians and the Firbolgs were defeated at the first and second battle of Moytura.

According to the *Leabhar Gabhala* the first to lead a colony to Ireland, immediately after the flood, was one Partholon, who, like those determined settlers who followed him, came from the cradle of the world, Asia Minor. Partholon apparently suffered his fate at the hands of the Fomorians or some other indigenous people, for nothing more is heard of him. Then came Nemed and his people, who once again were absorbed by the Fomorians – a sort of race of Calibans, it seems, who never took to anyone except the next arrivals, similar to, and possibly related to, them in nearly every known particular. These are, of course, the doughty Firbolgs who seem to have taken over the country from the Fomorians without any difficulty. This is of some importance as we'll see in a minute, and again points to the fact that the other invaders were alien to both Fomorian and Firbolg alike.

The next to arrive were the Tuatha de Danaan, the magicians from the east. (P. W. Joyce, by the way, states categorically that the Tuatha de Danaan 'spent some time in Greece where they learned magic and other curious arts.' It is far more likely that their magic hailed from their own traditions and way of life in Scythia and among the Persians.) They surpassed, according to the *Leabhar Gabhala*, the sages of the arts of heathendom *(sic)* in learning lore and magic and druidism and cunning. They learned their arts in four cities – Falias, Gorias, Murias and Findias – which I have not been able to identify, but which have the singular Persian S-ending in common, which was applied only to persons or places of uncommon attributes. Out of Falias came the stone of Fal *(Liath Fail)* which was at Tara, and on which the kings of Ireland were crowned. Out of Gorias came the spear of Lugh Lamh Fada (the spear thrower?). Out of Findias was brought the sword of Nuada, another Danaan hero, and out of Murias came the Dagda's cauldron, from which no one ever went hungry. The Dagda was a great warrior king of the Danaan, who is said to have reigned from AM 3370 to 3450.

The De Danaan defeated the Firbolgs at the two battles of Moytura, a place near Cong in County Mayo. The first of these battles, which according to Joyce lasted four days, was fought AM 3303, and the Firbolgs were defeated with great slaughter and their king killed. Afterwards the De Danaan took possession of the country, but, with characteristic improvidence for the future, allowed a powerful nation of Firbolgs to live in Connacht. This was nearly their undoing for, some 27 years later, in AM 3330 – on the eve of Samhain, or 31 October according to Joyce – the second battle of Moytura took place.

It is hardly too far-fetched to read into this the intermingling, on the eastern – or most readily settled – coast, of established Firbolg and incoming Tuatha de Danaan communities ... the Il-Dana, product of a De Danaan king and a Firbolg queen. Clearly the sophisticated, mystical, but not necessarily excessively warlike Tuatha de Danaan would expand across the country.

The tradition of the *Leabhar Gabhala* is that Nemed and his followers hailed from the region of the Caspian Sea, where the Scythians and the Milesians had settlements. It is there, too, that

Xenophon places a people named the Dana. One cannot avoid the connection with Tuatha de Danaan, literally People of Dana (n). One of the names for the Greeks, Danaos, may not be without significance. Xenophon's description of the Dana who lived by the Caspian closely resembles the classic traditional image of the Tuatha de Danaan. He says that they possessed awe-inspiring wizard-like characteristics. And in that context the proper title of Lugh Lamh Fada, the demi-god son of a Tuatha de Danaan father, Cian, and a Fomorian mother, Ethlenn, was the Ildanach (pronounced Ill-Dawnuck, Man of Enlightenment). The Ildanach is said to have brought with him to Ireland a light, generally supposed to have come from his forehead. Was it the brightness of fire? Of intellect? Of knowledge and technology? An early bronze or iron helmet, perhaps? Was the 'lamh-fada' – the long hand – a spear thrower (as was used almost exclusively, according to Xenophon, by the Asiatic communities of which the Dana were one), like a thong-wrapped javelin – the 'weaver's beam' of the Phoenicians – such as was used exclusively in western Europe by the Irish from the earliest times until the seventeenth century.

'IS MYTH FACT OR FANCY?' is a meaningless question except in a minor relative and comparative sense. Euhemerism – attributing to a myth a factual, historically accurate basis, is fanciful nonsense. But we should be careful of the baby when throwing out the bath water; it is just as foolish to reject mythology holus-bolus simply because we don't understand it and because those who did are beyond reach.

Nemed found the country, or the inhabited part of it, occupied by Fomorians, a nomadic race of sea rovers indigenous to the northern world, rather like the Vikings some thousands of years later. The Nemedians were absorbed by these wild men. It is accepted by the Greeks and their historians, notably Herodotus, that the Scythians – known generally as Scoloti, by no means excessively removed from the Scoti by which the Irish became known – and the Celts, while undoubtedly to their minds Hyperboreans, or barbarians (so, we must remember, were all others except Greeks, including the Persians), were of a social and intellectual order much more advanced than their Germanic, Helvetian and Asiatic neighbours; they spoke, it is emphasised, an Indo-European language and maintained a large colony in Asia Minor.

In the main, hitherto, Celtic scholars and historians have worked on the assumption that, if the Nemedians, the Tuatha de Danaan and the Milesians existed at all, they had widely different and separate origins. This is surely wrong if the De Danaans, with many similar characteristics to the mysterious and magically inclined Dana, are, like the Nemedians who preceded them, reputed to have come from Asia Minor, as did the Milesians who followed them. And it is an historic fact, as many historical examples show, that colonisation from one source tends to attract successive waves of colonists from the same source rather than from alternative sources. Of the Fomorians and the Firbolgs, little is said or conjectured, particularly of the former; and for a very good reason. They were nomads, but not settlers. The Firbolgs who were not absorbed by the learned and scientifically minded Tuatha de Danaan perished; the Milesians, practical, hard-headed merchants, colons par excellence and warriors to boot, had little difficulty in supplanting the esoterically inclined De Danaan and taking the conduct of affairs out of their hands, leaving them their superstitions, their mysteries and their magic, all of which the Milesians would have held in some awe. Nevertheless it is hardly surprising that tradition holds, perhaps of this very situation, that the Tuatha de Danaan vanished, with their mysteries, under the earth where they still survive (or did at the time of earliest recorded history anyway) in the form of Sidhe, or fairy people. It is not hard to equate this belief with the gradual absorption of mystics like the De Danaan by a more vigorous and pragmatic people, who in turn must have benefited from their forerunners by a great heightening of the imaginative and creative faculties.

The De Danaan occupied the country more or less peaceably, so far as one knows, until the coming of the Milesians. And here again the Nemedians, the De Danaans and the Milesians very likely had a common origin, a common tongue and were very much kith if not indeed kin.

The Milesians were the final and lasting settlers. It does not follow that if the Nemedians, the Tuatha de Danaan and the Milesians displayed different characteristics that they must have had separate racial origins. Time, particularly in a period of rapid change, emphasises contradictory facets, conditions and influences could have produced widely different characteristics in people of the same ethnic and linguistic group.

Finally, on this point, there is a school of thought which holds that the name Ireland – Éire – is derived from Piera, a name with an Indo-European root expressing fertility or fecundity. It is known, of course, that the rich countryside of Ireland was regarded with something amounting to awe by the Greeks because of its fruitfulness. The Greek home of the Muses is also Piera. From this word, it is argued, is derived Eiru, Hibernia and Juvernia – all names for Ireland.

THE CELTS ATTRIBUTED TWO SIGNIFICANT personas to Ireland, both of them female. They were that of a beautiful, fecund, queen and that of an ancient and malevolent hag, the Cailleach. An agricultural/pastoral people the Celtic dependence on crops and fodder made them aware of rotation and of cyclic events. This idea was so basic that, in an important ritual, the king 'married' the earth (presumably as the young queen). Presumably it was believed that as the king grew older and less potent his consort also aged, becoming the old, barren, and therefore infertile Cailleach. *She* might be rejuvenated or retain her youth and remain fit for marriage; but for a mortal king that was impossible. Hence the idea of ritual murder/sacrifice of the king at an appropriate juncture and the vast mythology fabricated around that event.

That might help explain why the Celts, like some of the Hellenes with whom they had much in common, practised ritual murder of their kings, rejuvenating and making once again nubile the very land itself.

Above the entrance to Newgrange is an aperture that, at the winter and summer solstices, admits the sun's rays so that they penetrate a long passageway and in a marvellous and uncanny fashion, illuminate the circular chamber deep within – a construction also found in some of the Egyptian temples, as are many of the carvings at Newgrange.

Here are many mysteries – of the Celts and of Newgrange and its prehistoric builders – complicated by the fact that the people with whose active mythology Newgrange is most associated – the Celts – did not come to Ireland until almost three thousand years after Newgrange was built. On what repository of belief and tradition did the Celts superimpose or build their own?

It is held that Newgrange is (primarily) a ritual burial ground. One assumption is that these abiding monuments are some kind of vast mausoleum in which multitudes were cremated and buried from time to time. Of course nothing could be further from the truth. If they were ritual burial chambers – and there is little doubt about that – they were primarily the temples of a ritual. There is not space enough for such a ritual to have included large numbers of people. But many who were not directly involved may have been outside onlookers.

They were not, like the pyramids of Egypt (which they predate), simply elaborate burial chambers constructed to commemorate individual kings. They were used over and over, presumably for the same, a derived or a substituted, ritual. This can only have meant their being a focus for some spiritual activity or cult which clearly involved both an elite priesthood and the participation of a large population.

The Newgrange tumuli were, therefore, places of living and long-standing ritual. The question that arises is what kind (or kinds) of ritual might have been involved? Tara – Cathair Cro-Fhind, the Crimson City, to the Tuatha de Dannan – is close to Newgrange. It was, from beyond the mists of time, the 'mystical fifth' centre of Ireland and the seat of its kings. The standing pillar-stone known as the Bud Fhearghus, or the Standing Member of Fergus (now moved from its original position), is supposed to have cried out when the true (new) king drove his chariot round it. It still bears scars held to be from chariot bosses.

From the air the Newgrange complex – the mounds, Knowth, Dowth and Newgrange – form a triangle of hemispheres. Two are about the same size and the third is larger. They resemble an outsize representation of a pregnant Mediterranean fertility goddess. Moreover the Newgrange chamber is shaped precisely like a womb. And what happens on the solstice? The life-giving rays of the sun penetrate this 'womb'. And for what conceivable purpose other than to fertilise the earth and bring forth a new, vital king?

Are we here looking at the 'womb of the world'? That the old king was brought to Newgrange where he was ritually murdered (an important archaeological find at Newgrange was a carved stone mace-head, of clear ritualistic significance) and then cremated; and that the new king sprang forth from this womb, possibly smeared with the blood of his predecessor, leaped on a chariot, drove to Tara and whirled his chariot round the 'Standing Member' so that it screamed, finally completing the mystical and cyclic ritual by 'marrying' the earth?

BY DEFINITION THE SOCIAL importance of mythology lies in the period before recorded history began. And in Ireland, so far as we know, written records came quite late. Mythological literature, therefore, presumably lingered late as well.

There is little evidence of an Irish script or form of writing before the arrival of Christianity in the mid fifth century. If earlier records were kept, they have not survived. Accordingly it is claimed that Celtic mythology was entirely oral, the argument being that writing did not exist in Ireland before it was introduced by Christian missionaries. However there was continuous known contact over a long period with Rome and Roman Britain. It seems unlikely that an advanced people like the Irish Celts would ignore the benefits of literacy, even if they did not develop it themselves. Sedulius (Saigheal), contemporary of Patrick and writer of the first great Christian poem, was Irish; as was another contemporary, the heretic Pelagius. Aethius came to Ireland before Patrick seeking books to replenish the restored library at Alexandria, and the druids are said to have had a secret writing made on books of thin, wedge-shaped, plates of wood, held together at the bottom, by a peg so that they could be spread like a fan. Because examples have not survived does not mean that they never existed.

The earliest written versions of the mythologies are from the ninth and tenth centuries and are copies of earlier examples. Where, now, are those earlier writings? The perishable materials that were almost certainly used are more likely to account for their non-existence today, rather than the non-literacy of the peoples concerned. It stretches credibility to assume that intelligent people capable of formulating a complex legal and civil code and with a highly developed social order and who, for hundreds of years, traded with literate and powerful neighbouring nations, would not have used something as fundamentally important – and available – as writing.

Apart from that of Greece and Rome, Irish literature (much of it based on myth and legend) is by far the oldest in Europe. The earliest surviving copies of older chronicles from Ireland date from between the sixth and eight centuries AD. Before that there were older – possibly, but by no means certainly, oral – chronologies from which these later models were drawn.

The explosion of written literature in Ireland from the sixth century may, however unlikely, have been spontaneous; it certainly predates any other in western Europe. It is therefore not just the oldest, it also forms a direct link between later European and Classical literature.

With the devastation of western civilisation after the fall of the Roman empire learning, literature and religion went into decline all over Europe except in Ireland, the only European nation-state never part of the empire. Within eighty years of the establishment of Christianity about the middle of the fifth century, monastic townships of up to three thousand students proliferated and missionaries were going from Ireland to Europe with their new-found faith to re-illumine the darkness there, and also the literature of Ireland.

The Gaelic tradition that lasted for over fifteen hundred years hardly materialised fully sophisticated without records. Nor was its culture the isolated product of unknown imaginations boiling on the westernmost island of Europe when the Continent slept after the fall of Rome.

The impact of Christianity in the fifth century was dynamic, and much was recorded under its influence in both Latin and Old Irish, and were probably not the first recensions. Whether the use of Latin followed the coming of Christianity or not, is not known. But, interestingly, even the prehistoric linear carved script – ogham – found mainly on Irish mesoliths, is in Latin alphabetical form.

It is a remarkable thing that so much of the original vitality and psychological insight survived. For this we are in debt to those early clerics and scribes who recognised the importance of what they dealt with and preserved this 'pagan' literature for posterity.

Through the annals and such accounts as those of the *Leabhar Gabhala* and the *Book of Invasions* (copies dating only from the eighth century onwards), the heroic period, as it is called in Ireland (dated with reasonable accuracy to between 200 BC and 250-350 AD) lives on in its literature.

The rediscovery of Celtic pre-history towards the end of the last century (native traditions and mythology having been virtually lost under alien rule since 1601) was undertaken by – mainly German – scholars steeped in the philosophy of the Greek and Roman world and in nineteenth century romanticism. They may, for such reasons, have further excluded much of what seemed shocking or immoral to Victorian eyes, just as their view of the Celts would also have been coloured by such dubious authorities as Julius Caesar and would, in any case, tend to have been influenced by their knowledge of the Celts of northern Europe rather than by those of Ireland or Scotland, who, ironically, were the purest reservoirs of surviving Celtic folklore, culture and traditions, which differed in some important respects from northern European Celticism.

It is worth noting that the influence of this 'heroic age' survives to this day – for instance in the more than 2,000 years of the spoken language, the oldest vernacular in Europe, now – sadly in decline!

Nuada of the Silver Hand, who was, according to the *Four Masters*, king of Ireland from AM 3311 to 3330, lost his hand during the first battle of Moytura during which he commanded the De Danaan. A new arm was made for him by the great De Danaan artificer Creidne and attached to the stump by the great physician Diancecht, but the cure took seven years (3303–3311) during which time Bres, like Lugh of mixed blood, half De Danaan and half Fomorian, ruled Ireland as regent. At the end of seven years, however, he had to retire in favour of Nuada. Whereupon he promptly went to the land of the Fomorians, variously given as Lochlann (Scandinavia) and Alba (Scotland), and instigated an invasion of Ireland with a Fomorian army which would be aided by the disaffected Firbolgs, and which was to be commanded by the Fomorian, Balor of the Evil Eye. During the battle Balor killed Nuada but was himself slain by Lugh with his far-reaching weapon. The entire story surrounding these battles, the motives, the actions and the outcomes, is typically Hellenic in structure, for it begins with a dream in which Balor was warned that his grandson would kill him; he thereupon had Lugh sent to be drowned when he was born, but Lugh survived through the kindness of those given the task of his destruction, to fulfil the prophecy that he would kill his grandfather. It is very reminiscent of the story of Astyages, the Median king, who tried to kill the young Cyrus in much the same way, and with similar results.

The battle in which the Milesians are said to have defeated the De Danaan decisively was the Battle of Taillteann, in Meath.

The Lydians, a contiguous people to the Ionians on the Asia Minor coast and who intermarried and formed alliances with them, were also an Hellenic people, living in what had been Scythian dominated territory, as seafarers and colonists. They were the first known people to use gold and silver coinage and introduce retail trade (and let it be noted that many authorities hold that it was the search for gold that brought these Mediterranean settlers across the world to Ireland in the first place). They also claimed to have invented the games popularly played all over Attica and reaching their climax during the Olympic games at Corinth. The story goes that the games were invented at the time they first sent a colony to Tyrrhenia during the reign of Atys, son of Manes. During this time Lydia suffered a famine and, to alleviate the suffering somewhat, they invented games which they would play all day on alternate days, and eat on the days in between. After eighteen years when there was no improvement in their famine condition, the king decided to divide the population into two lots, one of which should emigrate and the other remain at home. Those who sailed away were commanded by the king's son, Tyrrhenus, and they sailed until they came to northern Italy where they settled, changing their name when they landed to Tyrrhenians and calling their county Tyrrhenia – which areas some authorities have claimed as the sole birthplace of the Irish Milesians. This, however, is clearly wrong. But it was undoubtedly the colony of their friends and neighbours in Asia Minor, the Lydians, who were so fond of games.

Now it is a tradition that Lugh, son of a De Danaan father and a Firbolg mother, instituted at Taillteann a series of games on the Olympic model *in honour of his foster-mother,* Taillte, who was, of course, a De Danaan.

It is conceivable that the defeat of the De Danaan at Taillteann by the Milesians was not a military defeat, but a bloodless victory on the sports field, which would be more in accord with the veneration and awe in which the Milesians subsequently held their De Danaan forerunners because of their magic rites and practices. It may be too conjectural. It may be that the Battle of Taillteann, the home of the games, was a bloody affair; but it is a relevant factor in this hypothesis that these games were initiated on the Lydian pattern by a leader whose people might very well have hailed from a Lydian settlement.

In explanation of the origin of Lugh and Nuada, it was accepted practice, particularly by the Lydians and Milesians, to breed with the women of the people they conquered.

According to M. A. Hutton, who devoted considerable time and study to the Celtic mythologies towards the end of the last century, the version of Cuchulain's training found in the *Foghlaimh Conchulaind*, an unedited tract at the time, gives in detail the story of his training which is presupposed in the versions contained in the *Leabhar na h-Uidre* and in the *Book of Leinster*, the accepted sources of the Táin Bó Cuailgne. In this work Cuchulain is trained by Scatha, the warrior-queen-teacher, in Scythia and in Great Greece. The name Scythia occurs frequently in old Irish literature, Scythia being 'a vague term for a region extending from what is now Hungary, eastward far into Asia.' In other words in what was utterly a Celtic country. That there should have been frequent intercourse between the Celts of Ireland and the Celts of Europe, and that young Irish nobles should have gone from Ireland to get warlike training among the Celts of the Continent, seems only what one might expect. In Kuno Meyer's edited version of the Wooing of Emer by Cuchulain one finds that Cuchulain went to Scatha, *'fri Alpi allaanoir'*, 'eastward from the Alpi'. This has been argued as meaning that he went to Albyn, in fact to the Isle of Skye, and that it was there that Scatha had her warlike school. But eastward from Alpi would not answer the position of Skye relative to Scotland; but it would very well answer the position of Scythia relative to the Alps. Furthermore, the *Book of Leinster* refers to Cuchulain's training in Armenia and to his wars with – significantly, perhaps in the light of the fact that his teacher was also a woman – the *Cichloiste*, or Amazons. There appears to be no reason why Amazons should otherwise find themselves in an Irish legend than that they came into contact with its hero.

And there is one final point worthy of mention which is that the religion of the early Irish was neither pantheistic like that of later European neighbours, nor anthropomorphic like that of the Greeks, but was similar to that of the Asiatic Milesians and the Lydians, which was a rather harmonious and sophisticated blend of the two ... so far as any information is available on the subject at all. This might explain the ease with which Christianity established itself in Ireland in the fifth century.

Perhaps the most significant thing about the Irish myths for the student of letters is that they were written when the literatures of modern Europe had not yet been born and the literary energies of the ancient world were dead. These Irish legends are the connecting link between the two and were first written down in early Christian Ireland, which had not felt the direct influence of Rome, among a people for whom the tales were still vivid and who, perhaps, inherited a rudimentary literature drawn from ancient Celtic sources. At all events, now began to emerge men who, because of their work on these tales, became the earliest classical scholars in the modern world.

It is maintained by a number of authorities that the influence of the literary works familiar to the Irish emigrant scholars of the sixth to the tenth centuries bore a singular influence on the development of the literatures of France, Germany and Italy. The form of the twelfth century French romance 'Aucassin and Nicolette', according to A. H. Leahy, is that of the chief Irish romances and may, he maintains, have been suggested by them.

'It is as hard,' he writes, 'to suppose that the beautiful literature of Ireland had absolutely no influence upon nations known to be in contact with it, as it would be to hold the belief that the ancient Cretan civilisation had no effect upon the literary development that culminated in the poems of Homer.'

The Celtic mythological tales have a literary merit of their own, a style and character of their own, which would, surely, have been lost and dissipated in the process of constant mutation of the order implied by those who maintain that they have grown solely from the minds of bards. Furthermore, the sophistication of the tales, like the sophistication of the great tales of Greece, is that of art brought to bear on ideas, however bald and ancient the idea itself.

To take a classical illustration, which Leahy used in a similar context, the barbarity shown by Aeneas in *Aeneid* X in sacrificing four young men on the funeral pyre of Pallas was an act which, if it occurred in Virgil's day, would have caused utter horror. Nor does it prove that there was an ancient tale of Pallas in which victims were sacrificed like that, nor even that such victims were sacrificed in Latium at that time. But it does suggest that Virgil was familiar with the idea of such sacrifices, and his sense of drama impelled him to use it in the Pallas episode, for he would hardly have invented it.

THE TALES GIVEN BELOW are chosen for several reasons, but principally because they represent all that is best and different in the myths of Ireland.

The first, and one of the oldest, is set in the earliest period, that closest to the Hellenic fatherland, it may be, and is one of the Three Great Tragedies of the Gael, *The Fate of the Children of Tuireann.* Its similarity to the story of Jason and the Argonauts is too obvious to need much comment. The other two tragedies of the Gael are, of course, *The Children of Lir,* and *Deirdre and the Sons of Usna* which is one of the finest stories of its kind in the world.

It is as great and as moving in concept, both of incident and of character, as the *Iliad;* the story is fast moving and is told with a great deal of deliberate art, for example in the restraint shown in the tragic death of Deirdre and in the remarkable and well-sustained lament of hers before she is killed.

The Wooing of Etain, with its strong supernatural flavour, its observation of nature and its insistence on the idea of regeneration, its mystical quality, is an important story.*

The Combat at the Ford is perhaps the finest example of the genre that has survived to us.

The Children of Lir is a fanciful, half other world, tale that besides great poignancy and considerable literary merit demonstrates a linking of the old tradition with Christianity. But it has been debased by being used as a children's fairy tale for generations. There is also the great epic of the Fenian cycle, *Diarmuid and Graine,* which is to its time and place what *Deirdre and the Sons of Usna* is to the Red Branch cycle and what *Helen and Paris* is to the *Iliad.* The Fenian cycle is of considerably later date than the Red Branch tales and deals, one is well-satisfied, with undisputedly historical characters. The stories, while transcending human limitations in many respects, cling tenaciously – almost self-consciously – to an everyday context and exaggeratedly recognisable human traits. To draw an extreme example the difference between the two cycles is – to me at any rate – as if one had been written under the influence of a strict, all-powerful, but fatherly monarchical society in which all the noble virtues (and all the noble vices) played a large and intrinsic part, and the other written by the same people some hundreds of years later after they had come under the influence of a considerably, and consciously, more socialised community in which the voice of the lesser blood (not, perhaps, that exactly of the common people, but certainly that of the un-aristocratic middle-class) was loud and powerful.

The time element alone hardly seems reason enough for such a profound change in approach and it may be that the Fenian cycle was, indeed, the product of some revolutionary change in the social system which required a body of literature of its own. Like many of the myths and legends of both cycles, the story of *Diarmuid and Graine* has more than one version, but the principal source is the *Book of Leinster*.

The Sickbed of Cuchulain comes also from the Red Branch cycle and is another tale about its great hero, Cuchulain, probably the greatest symbol of heroism associated with Ireland. However, in this particular venture, his honour (as the word would probably be interpreted today; but notions of honour, whatever about honourableness, like notions of fashion change with the passage of time and what is acceptable today may be scandalous tomorrow) in this story emerges today in a doubtful light because of the manner in which he treats the women who love him. The one, his wife, he lies to blandly; and the other, his mistress, he abandons – albeit with a show of profound grief. However, it is the man and not the women who is of importance in this story. Nevertheless, in common with other tales from the same cycle, the sophisticated concepts of human behaviour painted with such skill and acute observations are far ahead of their time in Western Europe.

Again, of course, there are several versions of the tale to choose from and there is a discrepancy in the two principal versions, that of the eleventh century *Leabhar na h-Uidri* which has been taken from the earlier and lost *Yellow Book of Slane* which, in turn, had two versions to draw on; and a fifteenth century manuscript in Trinity College, Dublin. The versions differ in many respects. The eleventh century version, for example appears to begin abruptly after the story had already advanced considerably, while the other version does not supply a full conclusion to the tale. The significance, to my mind, of these discrepancies and of the variety of versions of many of these legends lies not in any scholarly detection in trying to trace the 'true' original; but in the fact that so early, which is yet quite late in the literary traditions associated with the tales (we are given to understand), there were many versions, clearly indicating that there *must* have been several oral versions at an even earlier date. The inference to be drawn from this within the context of my argument is that it supports, not the retelling of an artificial composition (so much less likely than literary mutation), but the transmitting of something far more personal, and in which the listeners could be far more personally involved, the histories of their ancestors. In the telling and retelling of something believed, or half believed, and based on fact the room for expansion; for glorification; for heroic dimension is clearly far more readily available than in the case of mere fiction. Any parent knows that a slip in the retelling of a favourite fairy tale, be it just a matter of a word, and all hell breaks loose; but the tendency to aggrandise the feats and stature of our ancestors is inherent in all of us, and the more of us there are telling the stories about them, the more variations of the stories there will be.

In *The Sickbed of Cuchulain*, the row of asterisks signifies the point at which the two versions coincide in the tale.

However, the principal purpose of these myths and legends is enjoyment and enrichment and, I hope, some little additional knowledge into the lives and customs of the people who lived in Ireland between four and one thousand years ago. Apart from the Greek and Roman myths there is not a literature in Europe so old on which to draw, nor one nearly as old which is the product of so advanced a society – barbaric though that society may appear to us in many respects now.

EOIN NEESON

* *There are two versions of this legend, the details of both being combined in the one given here.*

The Fate of the Children of Tuireann

At the first great battle of Moytura the Tuatha de Danaan routed and killed great multitudes of Firbolgs in four bloody days, driving the remainder west into Connacht – so-called because of a great king and magician there called Conn, who showed his power by covering the province one day with snow, so that ever after it was called Conn-sneachta or Conn's snow. And the De Danaan were happy enough with this arrangement, because they had suffered enough in the battle themselves, and not the least of their hardships and tribulations was the fact that their king, Nuada, had his right arm cut off at the shoulder by a hairy Firbolg champion called Sreng. And after that he was in great pain and torment and nearly died. But Diancecht, the great De Danaan physician, healed the stump and made for Nuada an arm of silver which he set in its place, so that the king forever afterwards was called Nuada of the Silver Hand. And still and all he was sick and troubled with his arm and unfit for the cares of the kingdom of Éire, so that he made Bres regent for him in the interim.

But Bres was only half a De Danaan, and that on his mother's side. For his father was Balor, king of the Formorians. And while it might have been good politics to give the regency to Bres had Bres been an honourable man, Bres was not an honourable man. He laid the race of the De Danaan under a tribute to his father's people, and exacted it with great severity. And all this time Nuada was in great pain and suffering and was unable to help his people.

Then one day Nuada's steward, who was a one eyed man – having lost the other in the same battle in which his king lost an arm – was standing in the sun on the ramparts of Royal Tara looking across the golden and the green plain around it with his one eye, when he saw approaching the palace two fine looking young men who greeted him as they came closer. The steward returned the greeting.

'Who are ye,' he asked, 'and where might ye be from?'

'We are Miach and Omiach,' they replied, 'sons of Diancecht and good physicians ourselves.'

'Well, if ye are,' said the steward, 'maybe ye could put an eye back where my own eye used to be.'

'I could put,' said one of them, 'the eye of that cat in your lap where your eye was.'

'Fair enough,' said the steward, and without more ado it was done. But it was a mixed blessing for the steward, although he was delighted at the time, for as sure as he wanted to rest or to sleep, the eye would leap at the squeak of a mouse; at the flight of a bird or a rustling in the reeds; and when he wanted to look at a banquet or a great assembly of warriors, that is the very time it chose to close and go to sleep.

But none of this worried him at the time he got it and he ran forthwith in to Nuada and told him that great physicians had come to Tara: 'For,' he said, 'they have put the eye of a cat into the place of my own eye.'

'Bring them in,' said Nuada.

Now, as Miach and Omiach entered the palace, they heard a great and pitiful sigh.

'That is the sigh of a warrior,' said Miach.

'It could be the sigh of a warrior with a daol, blackening him on one side,' said Omiach.

Now it should be explained that a daol, or darbh-daol, is not a good thing to have with you; for it is a thing in the form of a chafer or cockchafer, like a beetle or cockroach; but a daol will fasten on a man, or a woman for that matter, and suck the life and the goodness out of him. So it was that Omiach said what he said.

The king was brought to the physicians, the sons of that Diancecht who made the silver arm for him, and they examined him. They drew out the arm from his side and out of it there bounded a daol through the palace, and the whole household followed it and killed it.

Then Miach searched for an arm of equal length and thickness as his own to give the king, but among all the Tuatha de Danaan not an arm could be found that would suit him except that of Modhan the swineherd. This the king could not have, of course, because of what Modhan was.

'Would the bones of the king's own arm suit you?' Miach was asked.

'That is what we would prefer,' he replied.

And so a man was sent for the arm to the battlefield of Moytura and he brought it with him to Tara and the disinterred arm was given to Miach.

Then Miach said to Omiach: 'Would you prefer to set the arm or to go for the herbs that will put flesh on it when 'tis set?'

And Omiach replied: 'I would prefer to set the arm.'

So Miach went for the herbs and brought them back, and then the arm was set and clothed with new flesh by them.

Now, although it is not properly part of this story, it is no harm to know the result of this. Because Miach was a better doctor than his father Diancecht, and substituted for the silver arm a real one of flesh and bone, set joint to joint and sinew to sinew and clothed in flesh in 'three moments', his father Diancecht was so enraged at this damaging competition that he took a sword, when he learned of what Miach had done, and slew him. Where he buried the body, however, there grew, up through the soil of the grave, three hundred and sixty-five healing herbs, one for every sinew and joint of the young physician's body – each herb to cure a disease in that part of the body from which it grew. These were plucked and gathered in their proper order into her cloak by Miach's sister Airmed, also more skilled than Diancecht; but he, when he heard of it and with his anger still unappeased, came and mixed them all on her so that their separate and great virtues were lost forever.

Now, sometime after these events and yet before the second battle of Moytura, Nuada and the principal people of the Tuatha de Danaan were assembled at the Hill of Uisneach, one of the Royal residences, for a bitter purpose. And that was to pay the annual taxes to the Fomorians that Bres had imposed upon them. This tax was a tax upon each kneading trough, a tax upon the quern or grindstone, a tax on the baking flags and an ounce of gold for each person of the Tuatha de Danaan who could be stood upon the Hill of Uisneach. If this tax, equally hard upon a man's pocket and on his stomach, was not paid, then the man who refused had his nose cut off by the Fomorian tyrants.

Now, as Nuada and his chieftains stood waiting uneasily on the Hill of Uisneach for the Fomorian tax-gatherers, across the plain towards them they saw coming from the east a band of armed men led by a young man of great command and, as they say, with a radiance about him like the sunset. They were Lugh Lamh Fada and his foster-brothers, the Clan Mananaan – the sons of Mananaan Mac Lir whose real name was Oirbsen the Navigator and who lived at Emain Abhlach, the Palace of the Apple Trees and which is now known as the Isle of Arran in the Firth of Clyde. And Lugh, the Il-Dana or man of sciences, was the son of Cian and a grandson of Balor, but he had no love for his grandfather's people who oppressed the De Danaan.

And not alone was Lugh a man of great science and knowledge; a man of proud and noble bearing, but he was equipped as such a man should be. The horse he rode was Mananaan's Aonvarr, as swift as the winds of spring and equally so whether she raced over land or sea. And, so 'tis said, no rider could be killed from her back. He wore Mananaan's armour which protected him well, for he could not be wounded under it, over it or through it; and across his breast he had the torque of Mananaan, which no weapon could pierce. He wore a jewelled helmet to protect his head, and when he took it off his eager face was as bright as a sun-filled summer's day. At his left side hung the Freagra, the Answerer, the sword of Mananaan, from whose wound no one could survive and which, when it was drawn from its scabbard, melted the strength of hostile warriors, when they saw it, to that of women.

And so, led by this mighty leader, these troops from the east rode to where Nuada and his people stood on the hill who welcomed them. But hardly were the friendly greetings over when they all saw coming towards them another group of armed men, but different to the first in every way. They were a heavily armed band of eighty-one surly and evil-looking men on whom was marked the stamp of cruelty, and they were the Fomorian taxgatherers, led by Eine, Eithfath, Coran and Cokpar who had the reputation of being the cruellest and fiercest of them all. When Nuada and his people saw them coming each one of them stood up before them, much to the surprise of Lugh, who asked: 'Why do you stand for these savages when you didn't stand for us?'

'Because,' said Nuada, 'we dare not do otherwise, for if there was one of us, even a child a month old, who stayed sitting in their presence, that would be excuse enough for them to kill us all.'

Lugh said nothing for a moment. Then: 'By God,' he said,

'they should be killed themselves.'

For another moment he stayed silent, and still the king and all his people remained standing before the Fomorians.

'By God,' said Lugh then, 'I'll kill them myself.'

'And if you do,' said the king, 'it will only do more harm than good, for the Fomorians would bring an army and destroy us completely.'

But Lugh ignored him, crying: 'This oppression has gone on long enough,' and with that he drew the Answerer and attacked the Fomorians until all but nine of them were dead, and they escaped only because they ran, while Lugh was slaughtering their comrades, to Nuada and put themselves under his protection against the rage of Lugh.

Then Lugh turned to them: 'I would kill you also,' he said, 'but I'm sparing you so that you can go back and tell your foreign king what you have seen.'

So the nine tax-gatherers returned across the sea to Lochlann, or Scandinavia, where the Fomorians were and told them what had happened, that the only reason Lugh had spared them was that they might tell it to their king Balor.

When he had heard everything, Balor turned to his chiefs and said: 'Who is he?'

But they did not know who he was until Caitlin, Balor's queen, said: 'I know who he is; he is the Il-Dana, our grandson, our own daughter's son. And it is prophesied that when he comes to Eire our power there will end.'

But Balor did not believe her because he had also heard this prophecy and had taken steps to avoid it. For it had also been prophesied that Balor would be killed by his grandson. So, when his daughter, Ethlenn, who had married the De Danaan nobleman Cian, was pregnant he made his plans. When the child was born and turned out to be a boy, Balor had the infant taken away. He gave it to one of his retainers, who lived by the sea, with instructions to see that the child was drowned. But because he did not say why, the infant survived and this is how he did so. The wife of the retainer was also pregnant, and gave birth to a stillborn child just at that time. She was so distressed that the retainer, seeing no harm in it, substituted the living infant for the dead one, which he disposed of in the sea. Lugh survived and eventually came under the patronage of Mananaan, who recognised him for what he was.

But all this Balor did not know, therefore he did not believe his wife, who was a sorceress among the Fomorians, when she told him that this hero was the Il-Dana.

So Balor and his chiefs, Caitlin and the druids and poets and philosophers of the Fomorians, and Balor's twelve sons went into council. After they had discussed the situation for a while, Bres, whose authority it was that had been flouted in Éire by Lugh and the De Danaan, stood up and said: 'I'll take an army of seven great brigades of horsemen of the Fomorian army and find this Il-Dana and destroy him, and I'll bring his head to you at our palace of Berva in Éire.'

This proposal was agreed to by Balor and the Fomorian chiefs, and they began to make detailed plans.

Warships and transports were prepared for Bres and his men; their seams were freshly caulked with pitch and they were loaded with provisions and weapons. Meanwhile Luath the Long and Lugh the Storyteller were sent throughout Lochlann to summon the cavalry soldiers that Bres wanted. When they were all assembled they checked their weapons and equipment and sailed for Éire.

Balor stood beside the ships in the harbour before they sailed and said: 'Find the Il-Dana and destroy him and cut off his head. And when you have that done, make fast your cables to the island of Éire, which gives us nothing but trouble, and tow it far to the north of Lochlann letting the great ocean fill its place. Leave it there in the cold north where none of the Tuatha de Danaan will ever follow it.'

Then, with blazing sails filling the sky over them, and with one, concerted stroke, the newly rigged fleet moved out from the harbour upon the moving sea, over the mighty sea and the awful and cold abyss, mounting the ridges of the waves and the treacherous mountains of the bottomless ocean until they made harbour in Eas-Dara, or Ballysodare as it is now, in Sligo. And they were quick to disembark and let their fury loose on the western part of Connacht, which they devastated.

Now the king of that part of Éire, where the Fomorians were aided by their kinsmen and allies, the Firbolgs, was the Bodbh Dearg, son of the Dagda More, or Great Dagda, Eochaid Ollav, mighty king and oracle of the Tuatha de Danaan, whose palace was at the Boyne, near Tara.

The Bodbh Dearg immediately sent to Tara for help from Lugh, who was still there with Nuada because Lugh had routed and slain a pocket of Fomorians in Eas-Dara while the Fomorians had been planning the invasion. It was dawn when the news reached him, with the spearpoint of day striking at the night, and he immediately prepared Aonvarr of the Flowing Mane. Then he went and asked Nuada for his help.

'I'll meet them,' said Lugh, 'as quickly as I can, but I need more men. I'd like to ask you for them so that they may come with me now.'

But Nuada refused. 'I will not give my men,' he said, 'to avenge a deed that has not been done against myself.'

Lugh, when he heard this, could hardly contain his anger and, turning on his heel, he strode from the king's presence and mounting his steed, rode westward from Tara.

LUGH HADN'T GONE VERY far when he saw three fully armed warriors riding towards him. When he got closer he recognised them as his father, Cian, and his two uncles Cu and Cethan, the sons of his grandfather, Cainte. He greeted them and they asked him: 'What has you up so early?'

'Trouble enough,' said Lugh, 'for the Fomorians have landed and are destroying Bodbh Dearg, the Dagda's son. I'm on my way to help him and give them battle and I'm wondering what help I can expect from you?'

'We're with you,' they said, 'and there's not a man of us but will keep a hundred Fomorians from you in the battle.'

'Good enough,' said Lugh, 'but there is something else I'd prefer you to do first, and that is to ride through the country and summon the warriors of the Sidhe, the spirit world, to me from wherever they are.'

And with that they separated. Cu and Cethan went southward, Lugh continued his journey to the west, and Cian, Lugh's father, made his way northward through the plain of Muirthemne, which is in the centre of Éire.

And it is at this point that our story proper begins, for Cian had not gone very far when he, in his turn, saw three fully armed warriors coming towards him and he recognised them as three

De Danaan chiefs, the sons of Tuireann, Brian, Uar and Uraca. Now it so happened that there was a feud of great bitterness between the three sons of Cainte – that is Cian and his brothers who had gone south to rouse the Spirit army for Lugh – and the sons of Tuireann, so much so that, if they chanced to meet, it was a foregone conclusion that none would survive the encounter but the stronger party.

No sooner did Cian see the three sons of Tuireann than he said to himself: 'Now if only Cu and Cethan were here it would be a wonderful fight; but since they are not, and I am only one against three, I would be well advised to fly.'

Near him was a herd of swine rooting in the rich soil of Muirthemne and Cian promptly changed himself into the appearance of one of them with a druidical wand, and joined the herd, rooting at the soil like the others.

But he had no sooner done so than Brian, eldest of the Sons of Tuireann, said: 'Brothers, did ye see a warrior crossing the plain a moment ago?'

'We did,' they replied.

'And where has he gone?' asked Brian.

'Damned if we know,' they replied, and Brian admonished them for their carelessness.

'It is foolish and careless of you,' he said, 'not to be more alert in open country in time of war. Now I know what has happened to him; he has changed himself, with a druid's wand, into the shape of a pig and is now rooting with that herd there. And you can take it,' he added, 'that whatever else he is, he is no friend of ours, for if he was why would he do it?'

'That's bad enough,' said Uar and Uraca, 'but what's worse is that you know as well as we do that the man who owns that herd would have the three of us killed if we hurt any of his pigs, and how are we to know our enemy unless we kill them all?'

'Ye're a bright pair,' said Brian, 'when for all your schooling you can't distinguish a druidical pig from a real one, and if you'd paid attention to what you were being taught you could. But I can,' he said, and as he said it he touched his two brothers with a druidical wand of his own and turned them into a pair of fleet, slender, eager hounds which straightaway put their keen noses to the scent and made for the herd giving tongue ravenously.

When they came near the herd, Cian, still in the shape of the pig, made a break for a nearby wood where he sought to find shelter, but Brian who had cut across his path hurled his spear through his chest.

Immediately the pig screamed out in a human voice: 'Why did you do this evil, knowing who I am?'

'Your voice,' said Brian, 'is the voice of a man, but your shape is the shape of a pig, and I do not know you by either your voice or your shape.'

And the pig answered: 'I am Cian, son of Cainte, and I ask quarter.'

To this Uar and Uraca, who had resumed their human forms and joined them, said: 'Indeed we will grant it, and we regret what has happened.'

But Brian said: 'Indeed, and I swear it by the gods of the sky, if you had seven lives I would take them all.'

'Well,' said Cian, 'if you would, you would. But grant me one last request.'

'What is it?' asked Brian.

'Allow me to resume my proper form before you kill me,' said Cian.

'Very well,' said Brian, 'for,' he added, fiercely, 'in some cases I think less of killing the man than the pig.'

Cian accordingly took his own shape and said: 'Will you grant me quarter now?'

'We will not,' answered Brian.

'Indeed,' he said, 'ye are the sons of Tuireann, and are about to kill me; but even so I have circumvented ye, for had I been killed as a pig, there would only have been due on me the eric of a pig, but now that I am a man again you will pay the eric of a man. And moreover,' he said, 'never was there killed and never shall there be killed a man for whom a greater fine shall be paid than you will have to pay for me, for even the weapons with which I am killed will cry abroad the killing to my son.'

'In that case,' said Brian, 'it is not with weapons that you will be killed, but with the stones of the earth.' And with that he and his brothers threw aside their arms and seizing the boulders that lay scattered about, hurled them at the wretched Cian with hatred and violence, until he was reduced to a frightful and disfigured mass. Then they dug a grave six feet deep and buried him. But the very earth itself, angry at this fratricide – for the sons of Cainte and the sons of Tuireann were blood relatives – refused the body from them and cast it back again to the surface. And six times the sons of Tuireann buried the battered body of their kinsman Cian in the earth, and six times the earth refused it; but on the seventh time the earth refused no longer and the body remained where it was buried. Then the sons of Tuireann, who had been on their way to join Lugh in battle with the Fomorians, took up their arms again and prepared to resume their journey. But as they did so from the very soil beneath their feet, they thought they heard a voice, faint and muffled, crying:

> The blood upon your hands, Oh sons of Tuireann,
> Will there remain until we meet again.

Meanwhile Lugh had continued westward through Athlone and Roscommon and over Moylurg and the Curlew Mountains until he reached the great plain where the Fomorians had their camp, filled now with their plunder of Connacht.

As he approached Bres stood up and looked towards where Lugh, who had circled the camp, was coming through the night.

'There,' said Bres, 'is a strange and remarkable thing, for the sun that rises every other day in the east is rising now out of the west.'

'And better for us, perhaps,' said his druids, 'that it should stay where it ought to be.'

'What else could it be but the sun?' asked Bres.

'The light you see,' said the druids, 'is the flashing of his weapons and the radiance of the Il-Dana himself; the man whose head you seek, who killed our tax-collectors and is now on his way here.'

And shortly afterwards, true enough, Lugh came up and greeted them.

'What are you doing here,' they said, 'since you are, as we know well, our enemy.'

'And why wouldn't I be here,' asked Lugh who knew what he was about, 'for isn't only one half of me De Danaan, while the other half is from you; am I not the son of the daughter of Balor himself? And now I come in peace to ask you for the milch cows you have taken from the people of Connacht.'

And then an angry and bad-tempered Fomorian chief, shouted: 'May the light of day abandon you until you get a single one of them.'

And all the others shouted at Lugh in much the same strain.

But Lugh, who was the Il-Dana or man of science, cast a spell upon the cattle so that the milch cows were returned to their owners and the dry cows were left behind to encumber the Fomorians and tie them to their camp until the warriors Lugh had sent for arrived to give them battle.

For three days and three nights Lugh harried the Fomorians until the army he had sent for arrived. Shortly afterwards Bodbh Dearg arrived also, bringing with him an army of three thousand men.

'What's the delay,' he shouted to Lugh as he rode up on his sweating horse, the sun glinting from his armour.

'Waiting for you,' shouted Lugh back at him with a grin, and with that he sprang to arm himself with the arms and armour he wore when he first saw Nuada of the Silver Hand on the Hill of Uisneach. In addition he slung about him a great, dark-blue shield and his two, heavy socketed, thick handled, deadly spears that were said to have been tempered in the blood of poisonous snakes. Then the entire army, kings, heroes and warriors, made a battle phalanx; before and above them they raised a bulwark of glittering spears protruding through their locked shields as they advanced.

The Fomorians were ready and, when the advancing phalanx of the men of Éire was within range, they hurled flight after flight of javelins so that the air became thick with them, like flights of birds homing in the evening, and the same rush was in the air with their passage; and underneath the screams of wounded men and blood where they fell on the saturated ground. But still the phalanx advanced on the Fomorian camp, and now it was the great, broad-bladed spears that did their deadly work, and the clash and the noise were awful; and when the spears broke and were lost in the bodies of men, then they drew their wide grooved, golden crossed swords and fought foot to foot and shield to shield; and over them and above them rose forests of leaping flame from the din and the wrath of battle.

Then Lugh, standing in the middle of the great carnage, looked around him for the battle-pen or headquarters of Bres, from which he would direct the battle. Standing there, tall among the blood-mad warriors, Lugh sought through the smoke and the confusion for Bres. Across the writhing bodies of men pinned to the ground with broken spear shafts, the piled corpses of men who fell by the sword, the naked and headless bodies of those who had already been stripped of their armour, he searched until he saw the battle-pen of Bres. And then he rushed towards it in so great a fury that a countless number of Fomorians fell before him until he drove himself right to the son of Balor whose bodyguard now lay dead around him.

But even as Lugh prepared to kill Bres, the other appealed to him, saying: 'Don't kill me, Lugh. We are, after all, related, so let there be peace between us, since nothing can withstand your blows. Let there be peace now and I will undertake, by the sun and the moon, by the sea and the land and by all the elements, to bring my Fomorians to your assistance at Moytura where you will surely face my father, Balor of the Evil Eye, provided they do not desert me.'

Then, when the Fomorians saw their chieftain captured by Lugh, they too dropped their arms and asked for peace; and next the druids of the Fomorians and their men of learning came to Lugh and asked him to spare their lives, and Lugh answered them: 'So far from wanting to kill you,' he said, 'I swear that had the whole Fomorian tribe gone under your protection, I would have spared them.'

And after they had acknowledged Lugh and returned their spoils, Bres and what remained of his army returned to Lochlann with their druids.

WHEN THE DAY WAS over and the last of the Fomorians had gone from the field, Lugh saw two of his kinsmen among the host of exhausted warriors, resting now after the battle. He asked them if they had seen his father, Cian, anywhere. 'We did not,' they said.

'Was he killed by the Fomorians?' asked Lugh.

'He was not,' they replied, 'for there was no sign of him in the battle.'

'Then,' said Lugh, 'he is dead, for if he was alive nothing would have prevented him from coming. I know he's dead,' he went on, 'and until I know how he died and who killed him neither food nor drink will pass my lips.'

Then, with a small band of companions, he retraced the way he had come until he reached the place where he had parted from his father a few days previously. From there he travelled north to the plain of Muirthemne where Cian was forced to turn himself into the shape of a pig when he saw the sons of Tuireann.

And when Lugh reached this place, he stopped and dismounted and walked across the earth without knowing why he did so. And as he walked the very stones of the earth beneath his feet spoke with a single voice and said: 'Here lies the body of your father Cian, Lugh, forced to take the shape of a pig when he saw the three sons of Tuireann; but killed by them in his own form; the blood upon the hands of the Tuireann, there will remain till they meet Cian again.'

Lugh listened to these words silently. Then, calling his own people to him, he went directly to the spot where the sons of Tuireann had buried his father and disinterred the body so that they might see how the murder was committed. When they saw it, and the dreadful condition it was in, Lugh remained silent for a long while.

Then, giving his father three kisses, he said: 'A cruel and vicious murder have the sons of Tuireann given to my father. My God, I am sick to think of it. I can't see, or hear or feel in my heart for grief. Oh God, why wasn't I here? Oh God, Oh God, that's bad enough, but that a De Danaan should kill another and a relative. I swear to you that because of this fratricide, the curse of brother against brother will be the curse of Éire for countless generations.'

And having made this prophecy, he made the following lament above the body of his father:

Frightful only can be called the evil done to Cian
The mangling of whose body has crippled my own;
And eastward by all her roads
And westward by all her soil
For a great while will Éire be filled with evil.

The death of Cian, the great champion,
Has left me like a walking corpse,
Without strength, without power, without a feeling of life.
The Tuireann have killed him and I say,

With the knowledge of my hatred,
It will come against them and theirs to the ends of the world.

Then, when Cian was buried again and a monument with his name engraved on it erected above him, Lugh said: 'This hill here on which he died will be called after Cian from this on. Now, let us go back to Tara where Nuada sits with the De Danaan chiefs around him. But say nothing of all this until I myself have mentioned it first.'

So they returned to Tara, Lugh following them. And when he reached there he was received with great honour and ceremony, being put to sit at the right hand of the king, for news of his great success over the Fomorians had long preceded him to Tara where they were already celebrating the victory when he arrived.

Lugh said nothing as he sat down and appeared calm and composed. But he looked about the great hall until he saw the sons of Tuireann among the throng. And it was clear who they were and what they were, for in all things they excelled any of the champions there assembled. In fleetness of foot there was none to compare with them; in feats of arms the same, and in addition they were by far the handsomest. And only Lugh himself had surpassed their deeds and courage in the battle with the Fomorians. Therefore the king had honoured them too above anyone except Lugh. Then Lugh asked that the gong of silence be rung, and when it was struck and the notes had died away and with them the hum and clatter of conversation and all were listening, he said: 'Men of the Tuatha de Danaan, now that I have your attention, I wish only to ask one question. It is this; what vengeance would each of you take on those who knowingly killed your father?'

For a moment there was a stunned silence; and then Nuada said, 'What do you mean? Surely it is not your father, Cian, who has been killed?'

'I regret,' said Lugh, 'to tell you that it is indeed my father who has been killed and here, in this hall, I see those who slew him, and they know better than I the manner in which they did it.'

The sons of Tuireann said nothing; but Nuada jumping to his feet said: 'Not one day, or two days, would it take the man who killed my father to die; but as many days as it would take him if I lopped off a member from his body each day until he cried for death from the torment under my hands.'

At this there was a great shout of acclamation and angry agreement from those present, in which the sons of Tuireann joined like the rest. And Lugh, who had been watching them closely, said, when the clamour had died down: 'The murderers here have passed judgement upon themselves, for they joined with the rest of you in your agreement. And as you are here to bear witness, men of the De Danaan, I claim the right to put an eric on them for my father. If they refuse it, I will not violate the sanctuary of the king's palace, but, by God, they will not leave this hall without settling accounts with me at the doorway.'

Then Nuada said: 'If it was I had killed your father, Lugh, I would be well satisfied if you were willing to accept an eric fine from me.'

Then the sons of Tuireann whispered among themselves: 'He's talking for our benefit,' said Uar and Uraca, 'it's obvious that he knows it all, however he does, and it seems better that we should confess now rather than try to hide it and have him condemn us.'

Brian, however, had his doubts. 'Maybe he's only trying to get a confession out of us,' he said, 'because he's not sure, and then he would not accept the eric fine when he knows for sure.'

But Uar and Uraca persisted and said: 'It is your right to confess, since you are the eldest,' they said, 'but if you don't we'll do it ourselves.'

Then Brian stood up at his place and said: 'What you are saying is directed at us, Lugh, because it is well known that there is enmity between your father and his brothers and us, and if one of them is dead, who is most likely to have killed him in your opinion, but ourselves. Yet Cian was not killed by any weapon of the sons of Tuireann. But because of what I said, we therefore will give an eric to you as if it was so.'

'Very well,' said Lugh, 'and I will accept an eric from you even though you doubt my word on this, and I will say here and now what it is, and if you think any part of it is too great then I am willing to remit that part of it.'

'That seems fair enough to us,'; said Brian, 'what is the eric?'

Then, looking closely at them, Lugh said: 'Here it is; first, three apples; second, the skin of a pig; third, a spear; fourth, two horses and a chariot; fifth, seven pigs; sixth, a hound-pup; seventh, a cooking spit and eighth, three shouts on a hill.'

The assembly had been looking at him in astonishment as he said this, and it was easy to see the look of relief and perplexity mingled that stood out on the faces of the sons of Tuireann. Uar and Uraca were visibly relieved, but only Brian frowned in doubt.

'Now,' said Lugh, 'that is the eric I ask from you, and say so, and I will redeem part of it now; and if you do not think it is too heavy, then you had better see about fulfilling it.'

'So far,' said Brian, 'we do not consider it too heavy. In fact it seems so ridiculous that I suspect some treachery from you. We would not consider it heavy if you multiplied it by a hundred times ...'

'Well, I do not think my eric too small,' said Lugh, 'and I will guarantee as a De Danaan and before the De Danaan to ask no more and to seek no further vengeance once it is paid. Now, as I have guaranteed this before the De Danaan, I demand the same guarantee from you that you will faithfully complete this eric.'

'Are we not ourselves, and our word, sufficient guarantee,' asked Brian, suddenly angry.

'No,' said Lugh, 'you are not, for it would not be the first time that the like of you went back on the promise of a fine.'

So, unwillingly, because their word had been doubted, the sons of Tuireann agreed to be bound by solemn oath and sureties, and offered as security that they would complete their part of the fine, provided Lugh did not increase his claims. And they did this before the great assembly of the Tuatha de Danaan chiefs and princes in the Hall of Moycorta in Tara.

The Lugh said: 'Now that is agreed and there is no going back on it, it is time to give you more detailed knowledge of the eric.'

'It is,' replied the sons of Tuireann.

'Very well,' said Lugh, 'the three apples must come from the Garden of the Hesperides in the eastern world, and none other will I have. There are no apples in all the world like them, for they are the colour of gold and have immense power and virtue. They are as big as the head of a month old child, and never grow less no matter how much is eaten from one of them. They have the taste of honey, and if a wounded man or one in deadly sickness takes a bite from one he is cured immediately. Moreover, if a warrior has one of them, he can perform with it whatever feat he will, by casting it from him, and it will return to his hand. And brave though you are, Brian and Uar and Uraca, I do not think you have the ability – a matter I have no regrets about – to take these apples from those who guard them, for it has been prophesied that three young knights from the west would come to take these apples, and the king who owns them has set great guards upon them.'

He paused a moment and looked about him. The faces of everyone in the room were grim.

'The skin of the pig,' he went on, 'is that of Tuis, the king of Greece. And when this pig lived every stream through which she walked became wine thereafter for nine days, and the wound or sickness with which it would come in contact would become well. Now the druids of Greece said that it was not in the pig, but in the pig's skin, that the virtue was so they had it flayed and preserved the skin. And that is the second part of my fine, nor do I think you will have any success in getting that. And do you know what spear I want from you?'

'We do not,' answered the Tuireann, grimly.

'It is the venomed spear of Pisear, king of Persia, and the Slaughterer it is called. And in time of peace it must be kept in a great cauldron of water to prevent it destroying the palace, and whoever carries it in wartime can do what he will with it. And that is the spear I want, and I doubt if you will get it.

'The steeds and the chariot I want are those of Dobar, king of Sicily,' said Lugh, 'the chariot that excels those anywhere in the world and the horses that, no matter how often they are killed, will come to life again if their bones are brought together in the same place. You will not get these easily, if at all.

'The seven pigs I demand,' he went on, 'are the pigs of Easal, king of the Golden Pillars which, though killed every day, will be found alive again the following day; and the hound-pup is the property of the king of Iora. Failinis is the name of the pup and so great is her power that the wild beasts of the forests fall down helpless before her. And the cooking spit I require is one from the island of Fiancara, protected by the warlike women of the island, any one of whom is able for three champions such as you. And the hill on which you must give the three shouts is the Hill of Mokeen in Lochlann; and Mokeen and his family are solemnly bound not to permit a shout to be given on the hill, and are constantly on guard against it. It was with them, moreover, that my father received his education and, even if I were to forgive you, you may be sure that they would not. And even if you were to succeed in all the rest of the eric, then they will make sure to avenge my father's death.

'And this, sons of Tuireann, is the eric I ask of you.'

ASTONISHMENT AND DESPAIR SETTLED on the children of Tuireann when they heard the terms of the eric. But, together and silent, they stood up and, without saying a word left the great hall of Moycuarta and went to their father's house and told him what had happened.

Tuireann was worried and upset, but he gave the following advice to his sons.

'Your news is dreadful,' he said, 'and I cannot see how you can escape death and destruction in carrying out this eric-fine; but, hard as it is for me to say it, it seems that your punishment is a just one for it was an evil thing to kill Cian. Now as far as the fine itself is concerned, no living man can get it without the help of either Lugh himself or of Mananaan. Therefore go to Lugh now and ask him to lend you Mananaan's horse, Aonvarr of the Flowing Mane, and he will not give it to you; what he will say is that it does not belong to him and that he would not give the loan of a loan away. Then ask him for Mananaan's boat, the Wave-Sweeper – which will be of more use to you anyway – and he will not refuse you that, for he is solemnly forbidden to refuse a second request.'

So the sons of Tuireann went to Lugh and asked him for the steed, and Lugh replied as their father had said he would: 'The horse is not my own,' said Lugh, 'and I cannot lend what I only have on loan myself.'

'In that case,' said Brian, 'lend us the Wave-Sweeper of Mananaan.'

Lugh was angry when he saw how he had been tricked, but there was nothing he could do about it.

'Very well,' he said, 'she lies at Brugh na Boinne, the harbour of the Boyne, and you have my permission to take her.'

So the sons of Tuireann returned once more to their father's castle where Tuireann and their sister Eithne were waiting for them, and told them that Lugh had given them the boat.

'Much good it will do you, I'm afraid,' said Tuireann, 'except that it is better than nothing at all. Clearly Lugh wants as much of the eric as will be of use to him at the coming battle of Moytura, otherwise he would have found ways of thwarting you in your second request also. He may help you in getting those things for him. But for the things that are of no use to him, and much danger to you, he will give you no help and be all the more satisfied if ye get killed while attempting them.'

The three young warriors took their leave of their father and went to the Boyne harbour where the boat lay moored. Their sister Eithne went to bid them farewell.

When Brian saw the boat, he was horrified, for instead of the large seagoing ship he had expected, he found it was no more than a quite small currach, or open canoe.

Bitterly he kicked at it and said: 'What use is this to us, even if more than two of us would fit in it?'

But his words alarmed Eithne, who warned him that the currach was a magic one and would adapt itself to suit whatever was necessary to be carried in it; furthermore it was forbidden to grumble at it. And she went on to say: 'You had no right, my brothers, much as I love you, to do what you did, and I am afraid that nothing but evil will come of it.'

Then they exchanged the following verses:

Eithne: It was an evil thing to do
For you three, fair and generous.
The noble father of the noble Lugh
To kill: and the evil on all of us.

The Sons: Oh Eithne do not say that,
Keen our hearts, brave our deeds:
Rather death a hundredfold
Than to live like cowardly weeds.

Eithne: Search the lands and islands
To the limits of the Red Sea;

Your banishment from Ireland
Is a great sadness for me.

After this the three brothers entered the canoe, which, as Eithne had said, grew as large as was necessary to accommodate them and their gear, and bidding a last farewell to their grief-stricken sister, sailed out on the open sea.

'Now,' said Uar and Uraca, 'what course will we take first?'

'The apples,' said Brian, 'for they are what Lugh asked for first. And so,' he said addressing the currach, 'we command you, Wave-Sweeper of Mananaan, take us without delay to the Garden of the Hesperides.'

And, as always, the currach responded directly to the voice of whoever commanded it, and it bounded forward across the bosom of the green-crested waves, more swiftly than the winds of spring, it took the shortest sea route and did not stop until it reached harbour near the Garden of the Hesperides.

Then Brian said: 'Now, how do you think we ought to go to the Garden of the Hesperides, for it seems to me that it is bound to be well guarded and probably with the king himself at the head of the guards?'

'Since we are bound to be killed sooner or later in paying this eric,' said his brothers, 'perhaps it would be best to get it over and done with now. Therefore maybe the best way would be to go forward and attack them and if we succeed well and good, and if not we might be just as well off to die here.'

'Brave, but foolish words,' said Brian, 'and soldiers should be wise and intelligent as well as brave. Let us do this so that people can say afterwards of us that we were prudent and skilful as well as valiant, so that they will respect our cunning and not despise our stupidity. It seems to me that the most sensible thing for us to do in this case is to turn ourselves into the appearance of hawks and sweep into the garden. The guards will only be able to use their light weapons against us, and let you make sure to avoid them and be prepared for them. Then, when they have fired all they have at us, let us sweep down and carry off an apple each, and I will try to take two if I can.'

So that is what they did. Brian struck each of them with his druid's wand and transformed them into the appearance of hawks of incomparable beauty and speed, which made off towards the garden immediately. When they reached it they circled and hovered high in the sky for a moment, and then began to descend in spirals. But the guards spotted them and attacked them with great showers of missiles, which the three brothers dodged and evaded until all the guards' ammunition was gone. Then, swooping suddenly down on the glittering trees, the two younger brothers carried off an apple each and Brian took one in his talons and one in his beak, and they rose again into the air without having been wounded or touched. Then they turned westward again and raced for the place where they had left the Wave-Sweeper.

But the news had already reached the court of the king who had three daughters who were cunning sorceresses. They immediately transformed themselves into three griffins and pursued the hawks out to sea, and they threw great tongues of fire after them and around them from their open screeching mouths, which overtook the hawks and burnt and blinded them so that they could bear the heat no longer.

'We're finished now,' said Uar and Uraca, 'unless we can get out of this.'

'I'll see what I can do,' said Brian, and tapped his brothers and himself with the druid's wand which this time turned them into three swans and they flew below to the sea. When the griffins found that the hawks were gone they gave up the pursuit, for they were not very intelligent, and the sons of Tuireann made their way back to the Wave-Sweeper.

AFTER RESTING AWHILE THEY decided that, since it was not too far away, they would go to Greece to seek the skin of the pig and bring it away either by guile or by force. So they commanded the currach to take them to a harbour close to the palace of Tuis, the king of Greece.

When they reached landfall Brian asked: 'In what form do you think it best that we should go to this court?'

'In what other form would we go there,' replied Uar and Uraca, 'but in our own.'

'I disagree,' said Brian, 'it seems to me that the wisest thing to do here would be to disguise ourselves as poets and learned men from Éire, for poets and scholars are held in high honour by the noble Greeks.'

'That's all very well,' replied Uar and Uraca, 'but where are we if we're asked to show our skill? We haven't a poem between us, and still less do we know how to compose one.'

'More fools you,' said Brian, 'for not learning both when you had the opportunity.'

Nevertheless he persuaded them and, putting the knots of poets in their hair, they approached the palace gates. The guards asked what they wanted.

'We are poets from Éire,' replied Brian, 'who have come with a poem for the king.'

One of the guards reported this to King Tuis, who said: 'Bring them in, for if they have come so far in search of a patron then they may have found him.'

Now the king commanded that the court should be made even more splendid than it already was to receive these foreign poets so that when they left they could tell the world that it exceeded anything they knew for grandeur. And so, when all was ready, the three sons of Tuireann, in the guise of poets, were admitted to where the king sat, surrounded by his nobles, in the glittering banqueting hall. Bowing low the three warriors greeted the king, who saluted them in return and welcomed them. The king invited them to join the feast, which they did, and never had they seen a household so full of merriment, a banquet so splendid or a palace more magnificent.

Then, according to custom, the king's own poets arose to recite their poems for the king and the guests and when they were finished, Brian, speaking low, said to his brothers: 'We must make a poem for the king also.'

'We have no poems,' they replied, 'therefore how can we recite one for the king? Ask us to fight like warriors, as you have taught us, or to fall if they are stronger than we are, but to make a poem ...'

So Brian, giving them a look of disgust, said: 'That is not the way to compose a poem.' Then he stood up himself and asked for attention while he sang his own poem, which was this:

> Your fame we sing of, Oh Tuis,
> Great as an oak among kings,
> A pigskin, reward without meanness,

We claim in return for our songs.

In the war of a neighbour, an ear,
And the ear of a neighbour shall clash
But he who gives without fear
Shall lose nothing, not having been rash.

A hot host and tempestuous sea
Are weapons that one would oppose;
A pigskin, reward given free,
Is what we claim from you, Tuis.

'That,' said the king, 'is a very good poem, I daresay, but I don't understand one word of it.'

'I will interpret it for you,' said Brian.

'Your fame we sing of, Oh Tuis, great as an oak among trees ... that means that you excel all other kings in nobleness, generosity and greatness just as the oak excels the other trees of the forest. A pigskin, reward without meanness, we claim in return for our songs ... that means what it says, that you have the skin of a pig that I want to get from you as a reward for my poem, and in the war of a neighbour an ear, and the ear of a neighbour shall clash ... means that, unless you give it to me willingly, you and I will be about each other's ears. And that is what my poem means,' concluded Brian.

The king sat back and looked at him in wonder at what he said. For there was Brian with his two brothers, while the king was surrounded by a host of nobles, friends and soldiers.

'I would praise your poem,' he said, 'if you had not mentioned my pigskin. And you seem to be a very foolish man, oh poet, to ask for that skin, for, if all the poets and scholars of Éire, and all the chiefs and nobles of the whirling world were to demand it of me, I would refuse them, unless they took it from me by force. Nevertheless, you will not go unrewarded, and I will give you three times that skin full of red gold in payment for your poem.'

'You are generous, oh king,' said Brian, 'and good luck and good health to you for it. I knew I would get something worthwhile if I asked for what I did boldly. But I am a suspicious man by nature and will not accept your offer, lest your servants cheat me in the measuring, unless I see them measuring the gold from the skin with my own eyes.'

The king agreed to this and so his servants took the three sons of Tuireann to the treasure house to measure the gold, and one of them brought the skin from its special place to be filled.

'Measure the two skinfuls for my brothers first,' said Brian to the man with the pigskin, 'and give me the last measure, for it was I who made the poem.' And satisfied with what he said the man turned to do as Brian told him, but as he turned Brian grabbed the skin with his left hand and drawing his sword with his right hand, knocked the man senseless with a blow from the flat of it. He wrapped the skin about himself and turning with his brothers rushed back through the palace attacking everyone they met on their way until they reached the banqueting hall again. There the nobles, seeing how things were, surrounded and attacked them. The sons of Tuireann were hard put to it to defend themselves without killing them, but, as it was not a noble, nor a champion nor a warrior escaped being injured.

At last Brian fought his way to where King Tuis was, and the king attacked him with great courage and strength. But brave though he was, and strong though he was he was no match for Brian, and he eventually gave up to the eldest son of Tuireann.

As for Uar and Uraca, they wounded and stunned all round them until none were left save the women and the servants, the senseless and the wounded. Then the three sons of Tuireann rested there in the palace before continuing their journey in the Wave-Sweeper.

While they rested they considered the next best step to take in accomplishing their eric, and it seemed to them wisest to go to the kingdom of Pisear, the Persian king, for the blazing spear.

So, they left the blue-washed shores of Greece and commanded the currach to take them eastward into Persia. And as they went Brian reminded his brothers that now that they had the apples from the Garden of the Hesperides and the pigskin from Tuis, it might not be so difficult to acquire the spear. Furthermore, although Uar and Uraca were not all that happy about it, they agreed that the disguise of poets had served them well and they proposed to remain in that disguise at Pisear's court.

And, just as happened when they came to the palace of Tuis, they were welcomed and admitted to the banqueting hall where King Pisear was celebrating with his nobles and chief people. They were seated with distinction and after a time the king's poets arose and began to recite their poems for the assembly. When they had finished Brian again said to his brothers, sarcastically: 'Get up now and make a poem for Pisear.'

But they said no, that they could not, but that they would fight if he asked them to.

'That would be a queer way of making a poem,' said Brian, 'but never mind, since I have my own poem for the king, I'll sing it for him now.' And he spoke this poem.

> Pisear has little value on spears
> For his enemy's battles are broken.
> Pisear has little cause for tears
> Since it is others who receive the wounds.
>
> The yew is the finest tree in the wood
> Called king without opposition.
> May the great spear shafts make their way
> Through the wounds of those they slay.

'That is not a bad poem,' said the king, 'but I don't understand the reference to a spear in it.'

'Because,' said Brian, 'I want to get your spear as a reward for my poem.'

'You are a foolish man,' said the king, 'to make that request, for no man has ever escaped punishment who asked me for my spear and the greatest gift I could give you, or the greatest favour these nobles here could obtain for you, is that I should spare your life.'

When Brian heard this, he remembered about the apple he had in his hand, so he threw it at Pisear and rattled the king's brains in his head so that he fell down senseless. Then Brian and his two brothers drew their swords and began to slay all around them until all fled in terror and there was no one left in the banqueting hall except the three sons of Tuireann.

Then they searched the palace until they came to the room, in its deep recesses, where the blazing spear was kept with its head down in a great, deep cauldron of hissing and bubbling water. Then, taking up the lot, they left the palace and went back to their currach.

THEY RESTED FOR A few days after their battle, and while they were resting decided that they would next go to take the horses and the chariot of Dobar, the king of Sicily. So, in high spirits after the success of their first three ventures, they commanded the Wave-Sweeper to take them westwards to Sicily. There they landed, and Brian, carrying the great, venomed and blazing spear of Pisear in his hand, asked his brothers in what guise they should present themselves to Dobar.

'What other way but as ourselves,' they replied, 'three champions of Éire who have come to take his steeds and his chariot by force or by any other way that comes handy?'

'No,' said Brian, 'that does not seem to me the best way to go about this. But let us represent ourselves as three mercenary soldiers from Éire, willing to serve him for his money. In that way we will learn how and where the horses and chariot are kept and guarded.'

So, having agreed to this, the three of them set out for the palace.

Now it so happened that the king and all his subjects were attending a great fair on the plain before the palace, and when the three warriors came near the crowds drew back and made way for them so that they were able to walk straight up to the king. They bowed and paid homage to him and he asked them who they were and where they came from.

'We are soldiers from Éire,' replied Brian, 'seeking service and pay among the kings of the world.'

'And will you serve me for a while?' asked Dobar.

'We will,' said Brian, and so they made a covenant and compact with the king ... the king to place them in a post of honour and they to serve him faithfully and ask their own reward. They remained in the palace for a month and a fortnight, getting what information they could and familiarising themselves with the places of the island, but they saw or heard nothing of the steeds and the chariot. And after that time Brian said: 'This isn't so good, brothers. We know no more about the horses and the chariot now than we did when we came here first.'

'Then what will we do?' they asked.

'I think,' said Brian, 'the way to deal with it is this; we will arm ourselves fully for travelling and go before the king and tell him that unless he shows us the steeds and the chariot we will leave his service.'

This they did, and when they went to the king he asked them what was wrong and why they were dressed for travelling.

'I will tell you, Dobar,' said Brian, 'soldiers of Éire, such as we are, are accustomed to be the most trusted guards and champions of the kings they serve, and their most precious possessions; and in addition they are counsellors and advisors as well. But you did not treat us like that, Dobar, for we have learned that you have a chariot and two steeds which are the best in the world, and yet we have not even seen them.'

'If that is all that bothers you,' said the king, 'it is an easy matter to adjust, and there is no need for you to leave my service. Indeed I would have shown them to you on the first day if I had known that you wanted to see them, but I shall show them to you now. For I never had in this court or in my service soldiers in whom I had greater trust.'

Then he sent for the steeds and for the chariot and yoked them to it, those steeds that were faster than the winds of March and equally swift across land or water. And Brian, who was eyeing them carefully, said: 'Now listen to me, Dobar, King of Sicily. We have served you faithfully up to now, and now we wish to name our pay according to the covenant that we made with you; and it is this that we demand, those steeds and chariot, these we mean to have, and nothing else.'

Then the king in terrible anger said: 'Foolish and luckless men! You shall certainly die because of your presumption.' And the king and all his men turned towards the three sons of Tuireann to kill them.

But Brian, watching his opportunity, sprang into the chariot, hurled the charioteer to the ground, and took up the reins in his left hand. Then, raising the blazing spear of Pisear in his right hand, he drove through the hosts of Dobar so that the king and his men were scattered by himself and Uar and Uraca. Then, taking their prize with them, they returned again to the Wave-Sweeper.

After resting awhile until their wounds were healed, they decided that next they would go to Asal, king of the Golden Pillars, to search for the seven pigs which were the next part of the fine that the Il-Dana had put upon them.

And so they sailed forthwith towards the land of the Golden

Pillars in the Wave-Sweeper, but as they came towards the shore they saw that it was lined with armed men, and every harbour was strongly fortified, for the fame and the news of the great deeds of the sons of Tuireann had travelled before them throughout the countries of the world; of their being banished from Éire and of their seeking and carrying off the gifted jewels of the world. And it was because of this that Asal's men guarded his shores so thoroughly.

Asal himself came down to the harbour to meet them as they sailed in and when they were close enough he told them to stay their course; and then he asked them sadly if what he heard of their exploits was true. Brian replied that it was true.

'What reason have you for it?' asked Asal.

Then Brian told him that they had no choice in the matter. 'It is the fault of the Il-Dana,' he said, 'and of the unjust sentence which he has imposed on us and which we are bound to pay. If the kings to whom he had sent us had given freely the precious things we sought we would have departed in peace; but as they did not, we fought against them, unwillingly it is true, and overthrew them, for none was able to stand against us.'

'And why have you come here?' asked Asal.

'If we get the seven pigs in token of your kindness and friendship, then we will take them thankfully; but if not, then we will fight for them and either bring them with us by force, or we will fall ourselves in the attempt.'

'If that were to be our fate, like that of Greece and Persia and Sicily,' said Asal, 'then it would be unfortunate indeed for us to give battle.'

'Indeed,' said Brian, 'it might.'

Then the king went into council with his chiefs, and, having debated the situation at length, they decided to give the pigs to the sons of Tuireann of their own free will since no king, however powerful, had as yet been able to withstand them.

When the three champions heard this they were overcome with wonder and amazement at the wisdom of the decision, and gave gratitude and thanks to Asal, as much for his wisdom in granting them the pigs without battle and bloodshed, as in relief for getting one part of the fine without losing a great deal of their own blood in the process.

That night Asal entertained them in his palace where they

were welcomed and feasted and provided with comfortable beds to rest in. On the following day they were escorted to the kings' presence and the pigs were handed over to them. Then Brian sang a poem in praise of Asal's wisdom and generosity.

'And where,' asked Asal, 'do you propose to go next, sons of Tuireann?'

'We'll go,' said Brian, 'to Iora for the hound-pup, Failinis, which is another part of the eric that the Il-Dana has put on us.'

'Then do me a favour,' said Asal, 'take me with you to Iora, for my daughter is the king's wife and I will do what I can to persuade him to give you the pup without battle.'

The sons of Tuireann agreed to this, but King Asal, being the prudent man he had shown himself to be, didn't much care for the look of Mananaan's frail currach for such a journey in spite of its marvellous qualities, and he insisted on going in his own ship. This was prepared and with great pomp and ceremony the great ship and the small currach moved together out of the harbour of the land of the Golden Pillars and sailed for Iora, and their adventures on that journey, if any, are not related.

But when they reached Iora their fame and prowess had again gone before them and the entire shore was lined with fiercely armed men who shouted at them warning them to come no further, because they knew the sons of Tuireann and what they had come for.

Asal advised the three warriors to remain at anchor where they were and said that he would go ashore and try to persuade his son-in-law, the King of Iora, to be sensible. So Asal himself went peacefully ashore and was taken respectfully to the palace of the king of Iora. This king asked him what brought the sons of Tuireann to his country.

'They want the hound-pup that you have,' replied Asal.

'You showed little sense in accompanying them then,' said the king to Asal, 'for there aren't three warriors in the entire world to whom the gods have given enough strength or good luck as to take that pup, either by force or goodwill.'

This attitude upset Asal, and he pointed out that wherever the three sons had been, they had been successful and left destruction behind them no matter what the opposition, except in his own land, and that was because he had given the seven pigs freely.

'They have overpowered great kings,' he said, 'for they have arms that no warrior, however powerful, can withstand; and I urge you to take my advice and give them the hound-pup in peace.'

But his words were wasted on the King of Iora who was full of fiery words and anger, and the troubled Asal went and told the sons of Tuireann how matters stood.

Then Brian and his brothers armed themselves and declared war on the king and warriors of Iora and a terrible and bloody battle began on the shore as they landed from the currach.

For, though nothing could stand against the sons of Tuireann, the army of the Iora was great and its warriors brave. And the battle became so fierce and confused that the three brothers became separated from one another, Uar and Uraca being driven away from Brian where he wielded tremendous wrath and destruction on all who crossed his path with the blazing spear of Pisear. At last, through the din and the smoke of the battle, Brian spied the battle-pen of the King of Iora surrounded by his guards, and he fought his way towards it and no man in his path could stand against him so great was his battle-fury. When he reached the battle-pen he burst in upon it like a thunderbolt and, although the king put up a powerful and venomous defence, Brian, though by far the more wrathful and the stronger, held back so as not to slay his enemy, but prolonged the combat to tire him. When he then had an opportunity he seized the king and bound him with his arms and carried him aloft to where Asal was. Throwing the king down at Asal's feet, Brian said: 'There is your son-in-law for you and I swear, by my weapons, it would have been easier to kill him three times over than to bring him alive to you like this.'

When the army of Iora saw their king defeated and a prisoner they threw down their arms. Peace was made between them and the sons of Tuireann, and the hound-pup was handed over to the three warriors from Éire. Then they took their leave of Iora in friendship with its king and people and Asal, to whom they bade farewell with kindness and regret.

LUGH, MEANWHILE, HAD BEEN following the successes of the sons of Tuireann with mixed feelings. He was kept closely informed of all that happened through his own mystical powers and now he was aware that they had acquired all those parts of the eric he had put on them which would be of use to him in the forthcoming battle of Moytura, but that they had not yet got the cooking-spit or given the three shouts on the Hill of Mokeen. Accordingly he wove a spell and sent it after them which, falling on them as they sailed from Iora in the Wave-Sweeper, made them forget the remaining part of the fine and filled then with an immense homesickness. Therefore, satisfied that they had fulfilled the eric, they commanded the currach to return to Éire with all possible speed.

Now it so happened that when the Wave-Sweeper reached the shore of Éire at Brugh na Boinne, Lugh was with Nuada at a great fair on the plain before the city of Tara. It was revealed to him through his extraordinary powers that the sons of Tuireann had landed on the Boyne, and he immediately left the fair and, telling no one, went to the fort of Cathair Crofinn, closing the mighty gates and doors after him. There he armed himself fully in the armour of Mananaan and the magical cloak of the daughter of Fleas and waited.

Soon afterwards the sons of Tuireann were seen approaching the fair and as they did so the great multitude flocked out to meet them, gazing in wonder at the things they brought and to welcome them home. Nuada himself greeted them warmly and asked them if they had fulfilled the eric.

'We have,' they replied, 'and where is Lugh that we may give it to him?'

'He was here a little while ago,' said Nuada. But the fair was searched for Lugh without success.

Then Brian said: 'I know what has happened. He has learned that we have returned with these great weapons against which even he himself could not stand, and he has barricaded himself in one of the strongholds of Tara for fear we might turn them on him.'

Messengers were then sent to search for Lugh to tell him that the sons of Tuireann had the eric he demanded and were ready to give him the fine. But Lugh still did not trust the sons of Tuireann, and the answer he sent back was that the fine should be given to Nuada for him.

The sons of Tuireann did as Lugh demanded, and turned

their marvellous spoils over to the king there on the lawn before the palace, keeping only their own arms. When Lugh had been satisfied that things had been done as he required, he came out and inspected the eric narrowly.

'Here indeed,' he said, 'is eric fine enough to pay for anyone who ever has been killed and anyone who ever will be killed to the end of time; but nevertheless and notwithstanding that it is great, and many times great, there is one kind of fine that must be paid in full to the last iota, and that is an eric-fine, for of this it is not lawful to hold back even the smallest part. And moreover, King Nuada and King Bodbh Dearg, and you people of the De Danaan, you are guarantee for my full eric fine; therefore while I see here the three apples, the skin of the pig, the blazing spear, the chariot and the steeds, the seven pigs and the hound pup – where, sons of Tuireann, is the cooking spit of Fincara? And I did not hear that you gave the three shouts on the hill of Mokeen.'

When they heard this a great weakness overcame the sons of Tuireann and they fell to the ground as if they were dead. They lay in this stupor for a while and when they recovered they spoke no word, but left the fair and went straight to their father's castle at Howth. To him and to Eithne they told what had happened and that, having thought they were safe and rid of the eric, they now had to set off on another voyage to complete it.

Having spent the night with their father and sister, the three sons prepared to set sail in their ship next day – for they no longer had the benefit of the Wave-Sweeper to take them wherever they wished to go. They sailed out of Dublin Bay, with the Hill of Howth on one hand, and Wicklow Head on the other, and made across the loud-murmuring sea in search of the Island of Fiancara. For three months they searched the ocean, landing at this country and that and on one island and another one, but could not get the least information about Fiancara. At last they met an old, old man; toothless and almost eyeless, for they were hidden in his head with folds of flesh about them like the shell of a walnut, and he told them that in his youth he had heard of this Island of Fiancara, but that it lay not on the surface of the sea, but down deep in the seething waters where it was sunk because of a spell put on it in times long past.

Then Brian put on his diving suit with its helmet of clear glass and, telling his brothers to wait his return, he leaped over the side of the ship and sank from sight. It is said that he was a whole fortnight walking the bed of the salt water seeking the Island of Fiancara before he found it.

When he did so he discovered it to have many houses, but one great palace more noble than all the rest and to this he immediately went. When he reached it he found that its doors stood open so he entered and found inside nothing but a group of women, all very beautiful, engaged at needlework and embroidery; and among them, lying on a table, was a cooking spit.

When Brian saw it he said not a word, but walked straight to the table, seized the spit and turned and walked towards the door. The women neither spoke nor moved, but each had her eyes fixed on him from the moment he entered admiring his manly bearing and fearlessness; but when they saw him walking off with the spit they burst out laughing, and one of them said: 'You are a brave man, Brian, to attempt what you are. But, even if your two brothers were with you, the weakest of us – and there are a hundred and fifty of us here – could by herself prevent the three of you from taking the spit. Nevertheless, you are brave and courageous to make the attempt knowing the danger and, for thy boldness and valour, and the manliness you show, we will let you take this one for we have many more besides.'

So Brian, having thanked them and made his farewells, left them and went to find his brothers. Uar and Uraca had stayed anchored in the one place while Brian was away, fearing that if they moved they might lose him for good. At last they began to be afraid that he was lost and were about to draw anchor and set their sails when they saw the glitter of his helmet rising towards them from the bosom of the waves. Brian himself followed up through the sea and they were overjoyed when they saw him clutching the cooking spit in his hand.

When Brian had told them all that had happened he rested awhile before setting out for the Hill of Mokeen, for they knew that here they would be likely to have their most difficult task. They turned the prow of their ship northwards and sailed in that direction until at last they saw the green hill rising smooth and lofty from the shore. When Mokeen saw them approaching he knew at once who they were and, wading into the sea, he shouted at them: 'It was you who killed my friend and foster-brother Cian; and now you come here to shout upon this hill; well, come out of your ship for you will not leave these shores alive.'

When Brian heard this he was consumed with an almighty rage and he leaped ashore and the two great warriors attacked each other ferociously; so great, indeed was their onslaught on each other that it can be compared only to the fury of two bears, or the laceration of lions or the savagery of great beasts, until at length Mokeen fell dead.

And then the three sons of Mokeen came out to fight the three sons of Tuireann. And so a fight began that surpassed all the fights that ever were or were ever told of; so great was the noise of it that the waves receded from the edge of the mountain and curled back in terror; the very mountain itself, across whose face they struggled and let flow each other's blood, split and sundered and poured forth the fire of its heart, and the sky blackened with smoke and reddened with flame, so that if a man were in the east as far as the Hesperides, or in the west as far as the world's end, then he would come in awe and wonder to see such mighty blows being given and received.

Finally, after three days of great combat and shaking the mountain with their stamping feet, the three sons of Mokeen put their three spears through the bodies of the three sons of Tuireann. But neither fear nor weakness did this bring to the heroes, for they in turn put their three spears through the bodies of the sons of Mokeen, who fell dead before them on the battle-field.

But now that the combat was over and their battle-fury had passed off, the three sons of Tuireann fell to the ground themselves, lying on the blood-stained grass, and remained there for three days without moving or speaking a word as if they were dead; a heavy curtain of darkness veiling their eyes.

At last Brian revived and, seeing his brothers lying where they had fallen, said feebly: 'Brothers, how are you?'

'We are dead,' they replied, 'or as near it as makes no difference.'

'Get up,' said Brian, 'my poor brothers, and make the three shouts on the hill before death claims us.'

But they were unable to do it. So Brian, gathering together all his remaining strength, lifted one of them in each arm even while the life's blood flowed in rivers from him, and they raised three feeble shouts on the Hill of Mokeen.

Then Brian, still supporting the other two, staggered to the ship and they fell on board and turned her prow towards Éire. For days the ship moved across the ocean without guidance save its own, but drifted all the time towards Éire. And, while they were still far off, Brian lifted his head and gazed across the sea to the west and suddenly cried: 'I see Ben Eadair, the Hill of Howth, and the fort of Tuireann, rising from the waters.'

And Uar, from where he lay, for he had not the strength to lift himself, said: 'Oh Brian, if only we could see them; and on your honour and from your love for us, raise our heads on your breast that we can and after that it makes no difference if we live or die.'

Then they sang this lament:

Lift our heads, Brian, on your breast,
Son of Tuireann, generous and red-armed:
Oh torch of valour without deceit,
That we may see Éire again
Raise to your breast and your shoulder
These heads, oh soldier hero,
That we may see before us from the water
Usna, and Tailteann and Tara,
Dublin and the smooth Boyne with you:
If we should see Howth before us
With Castle Tuireann to the north
We would welcome death from that onward,
Even if it were a suffering death.

Brian:
It is a tragedy, sons of brave Tuireann;
Birds could fly through my two sides
Yet it is not my sides that make me suffer,
But that you both have fallen.

We would prefer death to take us
Brian, son of Tuireann,
Than to see the wounds on your body
Without doctors to cure you.

And since there are none here to cure us –
Miach, Omiach or Diancecht–
It is tragic, Brian, who suspected no deceit,
To have parted with the healing pigskin.

So Brian lifted them in his arms so that they could see Howth hill as the ship drifted into the harbour under its craggy slopes. Slowly and in great pain they made their way to Castle Tuireann and Brian called out as soon as he was near enough: 'Father, take the spit and go to Lugh as quickly as possible and tell him that we have given the three shouts on Mokeen's hill. Tell him that we have now paid the full eric price and bring back from him the apples of the Garden of the Hesperides, otherwise we will surely die.'

But Tuireann answered sadly:

If all the jewels of the world, south and north,
Were given to Lugh to ease his wrath
It would not be enough to save
You from the sepulchre and the grave.

We are one in flesh and blood
To the son of Cian, son of just Cainte;
He will not deal us blood for blood
Even though we killed his father.
Oh father do not delay in going,
Or be long in returning,
For if you are you will not find us
Alive when you get back.

So Tuireann mounted his chariot and drove at a gallop to Tara so that his horses were covered in lather that flew about him like foam as he went, and the sods of the earth rose high behind him like a flock of birds. He found Lugh and gave him the cooking spit and said: 'My sons have now paid the full fine, having given the three shouts on Mokeen's hill. But they are mortally wounded and will die unless you give me the magic apples to cure them with.'

But Lugh refused him coldly and turned away.

So Tuireann returned sadly to his three sons and told them what had happened. Then Brian, for all his weakness, said: 'Take me with you to Tara, and I will see him, and maybe then he will relent and save us.'

So Tuireann laid him in his chariot and returned to Tara where they found Lugh. But when Brian begged for the apples to save himself and his brothers, Lugh said: 'I will not give them. If you offered me the breadth of the entire world of red gold, I would not give them, unless I thought your death would follow. You killed my father cruelly and with nothing less than your own death will I be satisfied.'

So, having done what he could to persuade the Il-Dana to relent, Brian returned to his dying brothers and lay down between them and as he did so the three of them gave a united sigh, and their lives departed from them at the same instant.

Then Tuireann and his daughter Eithne stood hand in hand over the dead heroes, and sang a lament for their dead.

Having done so, Tuireann and Eithne were so grief-stricken, that they fell beside the bodies of the three young men and died with them, so that they were all interred in the one grave.

That, then, is the tragedy of the Sons of Tuireann.

The Wooing of Etain

MANY THOUSANDS OF YEARS ago, after the Milesians had come to Ireland and the Tuatha de Danaan had retired to their mystic forts from their domination, Etain of the Horses was the wife of Midhir, the mystic lord of Bri Leith. Now Midhir also had another wife, which was the custom in those days, called Fuamnach, who was consumed with jealousy of the beautiful Etain and who was constantly belittling her and finding fault with her until the jealousy grew to such a canker that Fuamnach could not rest night or day until she found some means to drive Etain out of her husband's house. So she went to the unprincipled druid, Breisle Etarlamh, and between her hate and his sorcery they changed Etain into the shape of a dragon-fly that finds its pleasure among the flowers of the countryside. And when she had been changed Fuamnach raised a great wind that swept her up and out of Midhir's palace and carried her for seven years above the world, until she came to the palace of Aengus Óg, son of the Dagda Mór.

Now it so happened that, although he had been fostered by Midhir, Aengus Óg was ill-disposed towards him. So, although he recognised Etain even in her transformed shape, he did not inform her husband when she was borne to him on the enchanted wind. Instead he made a crystal bower for her and filled it with flowers and fruits, with windows through which she might come and go, and he laid a purple veil in it for her and wherever he went, Aengus Óg took the bower with him.

And there, each night, she slept beside him by a means that he devised, so that she became well nourished and fairer than before; for the bower was filled with wonderfully scented shrubs, and it was upon these that she thrived, upon the scent and the blossom of the finest of precious flowers.

But Fuamnach's jealousy was still unabated and, through her witchcraft, she learned of the love that Aengus Óg had for Etain. So she went to Midhir and, with great cunning, said to him: 'Why don't you ask Aengus Óg to visit you, so that I may make peace between you again, and you may both then go and seek for Etain?' She knew well, of course, that Aengus Óg could not bring Etain with him on this visit. So Midhir invited Aengus Óg, who could not refuse such an invitation, and he came, leaving Etain behind him. And while he was with Midhir, Fuamnach, still boiling with hatred for her enemy, searched until she found the place where Aengus Óg had left Etain. And when she had found her she raised another wind like the previous one, that carried Etain out of the bower and across the face of Ireland for seven years without touching the earth, in sorrow and in danger. Finally that great wind carried her above the fort of Etar the Warrior, where the men of Ulster sat at a banquet. And it so happened that Etain fell through the roof into a golden cup from which Etar's wife was drinking. And, unknown to the woman, she swallowed Etain together with the milk that was in the cup. And it so happened that as a result of this she fertilised her womb and in the course of time gave birth to an earthly child, a girl, who was given the name of Etain, daughter of Etar. And it was one thousand years in time since Etain of the Horses, who married Midhir, was born, until she was born again as the daughter of Etar.

Etain was brought up at Etar's house, and she had fifty handmaidens who were chiefs' daughters constantly with her, clothed and maintained by Etar so that they would be companions for his daughter. And one day when they had gone to bathe in the river where it joins the sea, they saw a horseman riding across the plain towards them. He rode right to the water's edge and stopped to look at them bathing. The horse he rode was a great brown stallion that pranced and curvetted about the beach shaking its curly, creamy mane and tail. The horseman wore a long, flowing green cloak and a gold embroidered shirt across which the cloak was fastened with a great, golden torque that reached from shoulder to shoulder. On his back he carried a round, silver shield with a golden rim and a golden boss and in his free hand he carried a five pointed spear with bands of gold along the shaft from haft to head. His long, fair hair was swept back from his face and held in place by a circlet of gold and his eyes were calm and grey.

He sat on his dancing steed for a while gazing at the maidens, who were all filled with love for him, and then he said: 'Etain, the most beautiful of women, you are found who have been lost for many ages; wife of a king, you were swallowed by the wife of another; a heavy draught. For you a king shall wage great wars, bring destruction to the spirit world of the Sidhe and raise thousands in battle-rage; but for all your adventures and trials, Etain, you shall come to live with our folk evermore.'

And having said this, much to the wonder of the young women and their greater wonder, he went away from that place and they did not know either where he had come from or where he departed to.

Now, when Aengus Óg returned to where he had left Etain and found her gone, he realised what had happened, and told Midhir: 'Fuamnach has deceived us,' said Midhir, 'and if she finds Etain she will do evil to her.'

'Indeed,' said Aengus Óg, 'she may have already done so, but I will see to it that she does not escape my vengeance.'

So Aengus Óg pursued Fuamnach across the broad face of Ireland until he eventually found her in the retreat of the druid Breisle Etarlamh, and he took his sword and, with the one blow, struck off the heads of both of them.

When the reborn Etain was a young woman Eoai Airemon was the supreme sovereign in Ireland, for the five provinces of Ireland were obedient to him and the king of each province paid him tribute. And about a year after he became high king he announced throughout the length and breadth of Ireland that a great festival would be held again at Tara as had been customary in the past, and he issued a royal request, which was the same as a command, that the men of Ireland should attend it bringing with them their due tributes and customs. But the answer from the men of Ireland to this summons was: 'We will not attend the festival of Tara during such time, whether it be long or short, that the king of Ireland remains without a wife who is worthy of him.'

For there was no noble of distinction in Ireland who was without a wife; nor, they said, could any king be without a queen; nor did any man go to the festival of Tara without his wife, or any wife go without her husband.

And so, when he received this answer, Eoai sent forth his horsemen and his scribes, his officers who commanded the roads of Ireland and the couriers and stewards of the borders of his provinces to search the country for a wife who, in her form and her grace and her countenance and her birth, would be fitting for their king. And in addition there was another condition and it was that she should not have been the wife of any other man before him.

And the horsemen and the scribes and the officers and couriers and stewards searched the country until, at last, they found a woman worthy to be the wife of Eoai, and she was Etain, daughter of Etar the Warrior who was king of Echradh. When they told Eoai about her, he went to see her for himself and bring her back with him.

But as he came near to the castle of Etar he saw a young maiden sitting beside a stream combing her hair. The comb itself was of silver chased with gold and beside her was a silver basin also chased and embossed with golden birds, flying and sitting, and seemingly carrying in their beaks the bright beads of carbuncle with which the rim was set. She wore a beautiful purple mantle above another, a white one, ornamented with silver fringes, both clasped at her throat with a golden brooch. A green and red and golden tunic of silk with a long hood she wore as well, clasped above her breasts with clasps of gold and silver, so that men saw the bright gold and the green silk flash against the sun. On her head were two heavy tresses of flashing hair and even as Eoai saw her she was undoing it so that she could wash it, raising her arms in a graceful gesture as she did so, and bending her head sideways.

Her arms were as white as the snow of a single night, and her cheeks like the glow of a foxglove; her teeth were even and small, and gleamed like pearls between her lips, delicate and crimson. Her eyes were like the hyacinth and her shoulders high and soft and white. Tender and smooth were her wrists and her fingers long and of great whiteness with beautiful, pink nails crowning them. White as the foam of the wave her long, slender, silken-soft flanks, and her thighs smooth and white; her knees were round and her ankles straight with slim feet to set them off, and her breasts tip-tilted and firm were glorious to behold. Her eyebrows were blue-black and gently curved, and never was seen a more beautiful maiden or one more worthy of love by the eyes of man.

When Eoai saw her he was struck with a tremendous desire and love for her and he rode up to her crying: 'Who are you, young woman, and where are you from?'

'That is easy to answer,' she replied, 'I am Etain, the daughter of the king of Echradh.'

When Eoai heard this he was overjoyed and immediately told her who he was and why he had come.

'I know,' said Etain, 'and for twenty years I have waited for you, ever since I was born; and, although many men have wooed me and wished to marry me, not one of them has taken me because I have waited for you since I was a little child.'

And after that Eoai went to Etar the Warrior and paid him a great bridal price for Etain whom he brought with him back to Tara where she was welcomed like a queen.

Now Eoai had two brothers, one of whom was called Aillil and, together with all the other nobles of Ireland, he came to the Festival of Tara to meet the king's new wife. But as soon as he saw her he could not take his eyes off her for the immense love that suddenly descended on him for her. But, because she was his brother's wife, he kept his secret to himself. But, in spite of that it raged and tore and tormented him so that he became sick and weak and had to remain in Tara in one of his brother's palaces where he was looked after as well as possible, but without effect for none knew what was wrong with him. And he lay like that for a year without any indication that he was improving.

One day Eoai, who was worried about Aillil, came to see him and, putting his hand on his forehead, and said: 'How do you feel today?'

But Aillil only sighed.

Then Eoai said: 'Surely you must be improving by now.'

But Aillil replied: 'On my oath, as each day passes into night, it's worse I get.'

Then Eoai brought a skilled druid and physician called Fachtna to see Aillil and when he examined him, Aillil heaved another great sigh.

Then Fachtna said: 'One of two great sicknesses that kill a man and for which there is no cure is here; either the sickness of love or the sickness of envy.'

But Aillil refused to confess the reason for his illness to the physician for he was ashamed, and he was left there to die as no hope was held out for him. And he was left because Eoai had to make the royal progress throughout Ireland at that time, even though he was reluctant to leave his brother in that condition. So he said to Etain:

'While I am away take whatever care needs to be taken of Aillil. If he dies then see that he is properly mourned, that his grave mound is built and a monument put up with his name and record engraved on it.'

And Etain said that she would do this. And when Eoai was gone, Etain went every day to the room where Aillil lay and talked kindly to him and this eased his sickness as all who looked after him saw, and as long as she came to visit him he did not get worse.

Etain, of course, noticed this too and she determined to find out what it was that was wrong with him, so one day, when they were alone together, she asked him what was the cause of his sickness.

'My sickness,' he said, 'comes from my love for you.'

'And why,' she asked, 'didn't you say so before when you could have been cured long ago?'

'I could be cured even now,' he said, 'if only you would be kind to me.'

'Indeed,' she said, 'and I will be kindness itself.'

And so every day she came to visit him, bathing his head, bringing him food, and talking with him until at the end of three weeks Aillil was much better.

Then he said to her: 'You have proven your kindness to me, Etain, and I am whole again in body; but the completion of my cure at your hands is still missing; when may I have that?'

And she was greatly upset by this and by the illness that he had been through and afraid that it might strike again, so she said: 'All that you ask you shall be given; but not in the palace of the king. Meet me at dawn tomorrow in the little wood on that hill and there your sickness will be completely cured.'

Aillil lay awake all that night in a fever of anticipation and love, but as dawn approached and the hour when he should have met Etain he fell into a deep, trancelike sleep from which he didn't waken for over three hours.

Meanwhile Etain had gone to the hill to keep the rendezvous and when she was there she saw a man approaching who looked, and spoke, and answered as if he were Aillil and so she remained with him. But when she returned to the palace and discovered Aillil in the depths of misery, she asked him what was wrong, and he told her how he had been asleep at the time of their appointment.

She said nothing to him about what had happened, though it was a great shock to her, but said: 'Tomorrow is another day.'

And that night Aillil made a great fire and sat beside it so that he would not sleep, but again, as on the previous day, he fell into a trancelike sleep just before dawn from which he did not wake for several hours.

And Etain kept her rendezvous the second time, and again came the man who had the appearance and the speech of Aillil. But when she returned to the palace she found him again sorrowful because he had failed her. And three times Etain came, and three times Aillil failed to arrive, but that same man was there on each occasion. And on the third day she said to him: 'It was not to meet you that I came here, then why have you come? And as for Aillil, who was to meet me, it was not for sin or evil desire that I came to meet him, but it was just that the wife of the king of Ireland should rescue him from the sickness which oppressed him for so long.'

Then the stranger looked at her and said: 'It was more suitable for you to meet me, for when you were Etain of the Horses, it was I, Midhir, who was your husband.'

'And what caused us to be parted?' asked Etain.

'The witchcraft of Fuamnach and Breisle Etarlamh,' said Midhir, and then he made a great poem of surpassing loveliness, which described the country of the Sidhe in which there is no secret and no sorrow, where all is beauty and there is no sin and where love is everywhere, and he asked her to come back with him to it. But she refused.

'I will not give up the kingdom of Ireland for you,' she said, 'a man who knows not his clan nor his kindred.'

Then Midhir told her that it was he who, long before, had put the sickness of love on Aillil, so that his blood ceased to run and his flesh fell away from him; and that it was he also who closed his eyes with sleep so that no dishonour would fall on Etain.

'But will you come with me,' he asked, 'if Eoai should consent?'

'If such a thing happened,' said Etain in disdain, 'I would go.'

When she left Midhir she returned immediately to the room where Aillil had been, and met him outside in the lawn.

'Oh Etain,' he said, 'even though I was unable to meet you, our rendezvous has worked a wonder, for I am cured of my sickness and, moreover, your honour has not been stained.'

'It is glorious to have happened like that,' said Etain, but she said nothing of her meeting with Midhir.

In due course Eoai returned from his royal progress and was delighted to find that Aillil was fit and well again, and he particularly thanked Etain for her share in the cure, since it was well known how Aillil had improved under her care and attention.

Then one day some time later, Eoai, went out very early in the morning to watch the dawn come up over the plain of Bregia, which was a most wonderful thing to see – and still is if you should chance to see it from the royal hill of Tara – beautiful with the bloom of the yellow furze, and the multicoloured hues of the different blossoms glowing in the first light. Now while he was there he saw a strange warrior close beside him on the high ground. He was a tall, straight young man, wearing a purple tunic; his long, golden hair reached to his shoulders and his eyes were lustrous and grey. In his hand he held a five pointed spear and in the other a silver shield with a golden boss. Eoai said nothing, for he knew that this young warrior had not been in Tara the night before, and the gates to the outer wall had not yet been opened except his own private entrance.

Then the warrior came and placed himself under Eoai's protection.

'Welcome,' said Eoai, 'to the hero whose name I do not yet know.'

'Your welcome is no more than I would expect from a king,' said the warrior.

'Yet I still do not know you,' said Eoai.

'But I know you well,' replied the warrior.

'What is your name?' asked Eoai.

'My name,' said the warrior, 'is not famous. I am Midhir of the Sidhe.'

'And what do you want?' asked Eoai.

'I came,' said Midhir, 'to play a game of chess with yourself.'

'Well indeed,' said Eoai, 'I'm a fair hand at the chess.'

'Well, then,' said Midhir, 'let's see how good you are.'

'No,' said the king, 'because the queen is still asleep and my chessboard is in her room.'

'I have here,' said Midhir, 'a chessboard which is not inferior to your own.'

And that was true, for the chessboard was of silver and the men to play it two kinds of gold, red and white; and the board itself was divided into squares by costly jewels. So Midhir then set out the board and asked Eoai to play.

'I will not,' said Eoai, 'unless we play for a stake.'

'Well, what stake to you suggest?' asked Midhir.

'It's indifferent to me,' said Eoai.

'Very well then,' said Midhir, 'if I lose I will give you fifty dark grey horses, with chestnut dappled heads; high eared and broad chested; wide nostrilled and slender hooved, strong, eager and spirited, but well broken for all that.'

They played several games, but since Midhir did not put forth his great skill, all the victories went to Eoai. But instead of the horses which Midhir had offered, Eoai demanded that Midhir and his people should perform services which would benefit his realm; that they should clear away the rocks and stones from the plains of Meath, remove the bogs from his fortress of Teave, cut down the forest of Bregia and finally make a road across the bog of Lamhrach. And all these things Midhir agreed to do under the supervision of one of Eoai's stewards. And, that evening, the steward came and saw that Midhir and all his people were at this work with oxen, and that it was nearly completed.

And it is a fact that it is from this thing that Eoai is most remembered, for when the steward went to see Midhir and his people at work he noticed that the oxen were harnessed about the shoulders.

Now it was the custom in Ireland at that time for the men of the country to harness their oxen with a strap over their foreheads so that the pull might be against their heads. But when it was seen that the Sidhe people placed the yoke upon the shoulders of the oxen so that the pull might be there, Eoai commanded that his oxen should be yoked in the same way, and that is how he got his full name, Eoai Airemnech, or Eoai the Ploughman.

The people of the Sidhe laboured all that day at the tasks

Eoai had demanded of them and, at nightfall, they were completed and the steward went in great wonder to Eoai and told him so and that not alone was the work completed, but that it was incomparable. And as he was speaking Midhir came before them and his face was angry and as black and scowling as a thunder-cloud.

Eoai greeted him.

'Cruel and senseless is what you asked, Eoai,' said Midhir, 'and you have caused much hardship and suffering to my people to make them work like this. All that you asked I have done, but you have made me angry with your requests.'

'Well,' said Eoai, 'I have no anger against you.'

'Very well then,' said Midhir, 'let us play another game of chess.'

'What stakes will we play for?' said Eoai.

'Let the winner decide,' said Midhir.

'Very well,' said Eoai, confident that he would win again.

But this time Midhir used his full skill and defeated Eoai decisively.

'My stake is forfeit to you,' said Eoai.

'And would have been long ago if I wished it,' said Midhir.

'What is it that you want?' asked Eoai.

'To hold Etain in my arms and get a kiss from her,' said Midhir.

Eoai was outraged; but he kept silent for a while, while he was thinking.

'Very well,' he said then, 'a month from today come to Tara and you will get what you ask.'

Now Midhir had allowed Eoai to win at first so that Eoai might be in his debt, and that was why he had paid the great stakes that Eoai had demanded from him, and it was because of this that he had been able to insist that this game be played in ignorance of the stakes.

During the month that elapsed before Midhir was to claim his reward, Eoai called the armies and the heroes of Ireland together at Tara and placed them, ring upon ring, in defence around the entire city. And within the city itself he kept the most famous warriors of all so that the city was guarded within and without. And the king and queen were in the innermost stronghold of all which was locked and barred, for Eoai feared that a great army would come against him.

And, feeling safe and secure within this stronghold, on the appointed night he gave a great banquet to all the principal chief kings who were there. Etain was pouring wine, as was her custom, when suddenly Midhir stood alone among them. Always fair and handsome, he seemed fairer and handsomer than ever that night standing in the banqueting hall surrounded by his enemies. So noble were his looks and bearing that, instead of rushing upon him, the assembled chiefs and nobles fell silent in amazement. The king, who was the first to recover, welcomed Midhir with a mixture of irony and respect.

'Your welcome is what I expected from a king,' said Midhir, 'now let you give me what you promised. It is a debt you owe me, and I, for my part, paid what I owed you.'

'I have not yet considered the matter,' said Eoai.

'You promised Etain herself to me,' said Midhir, 'and that is what I came for.' And Etain hearing these words blushed for shame.

'There is no need to blush,' said Midhir gently, 'for your marriage vows have in no way been disgraced. You resisted me when I asked you to come, and I have not come for you until Eoai permitted it. It is not any fault of yours that I am here.'

'I myself told you,' said Etain, 'that I would not give you anything unless Eoai allowed it.'

'But I will not allow you to go,' said Eoai, 'nevertheless he may put his arms around you on the floor of this house and kiss you as you are. But he will not leave here alive after ...'

'Very well,' said Midhir.

Then, taking his weapons in his left hand and Etain beneath his right shoulder, he carried her off through the skylight of the palace, straight upwards.

And the hosts rose up about the king, for they felt they had been disgraced, seized their arms, and rushed outside to where the banquet hall was surrounded by the warriors. But all they saw above were two white swans circling Tara in the night, which then turned and flew off towards the Sidhe fort of Femun.

And Eoai, with an army of the men of Ireland, went to the fort of Femun and attacked it and dug it from the ground and destroyed it so that he might get Etain back again. And Midhir and his army opposed him and the men of Ireland in a long and bitter war; again and again the trenches and the battle works that Eoai threw up around the fort were destroyed by the sorties of the Sidhe, and again and again they were rebuilt. For nine long and bitter years the war continued, before Eoai's armies made their way into the fort. And when at last the inner defences fell, Midhir sent sixty women forth, all in the shape of Etain, so that none could tell which was the queen. And Eoai himself was deceived and chose, instead of Etain, her daughter Esa. And so Etain returned to Midhir in his Sidhe palace.

But some say that Eoai discovered that he had been deceived and returned again to the siege of Femun, and this time Etain made herself known to Eoai so there could be no mistake, and he carried her back to Tara where she lived from that out with the king.

The Combat at the Ford

That night Maeve summoned a council of war in her great battle tent that dominated the camp. Within, the rich silks and skins of animals, the armour hanging from the tent-poles and the faces of the chieftains glittered in the glow from a dancing fire; but no face was as heavy and brooding as that of the warrior queen Maeve herself, for she was thinking how all her plans and her vast army were held up by this one man, Cuchulain, who had killed day and night her hosts, and then her chief warriors one by one at the ford until he had slain Calatin and his twenty-seven sons, and his grandson, Gleas, and Freach the brave son of Fidech, all of whom he had killed the previous day.

And they sat and stood about her leaning on their spears to hear what she would advise or do.

But she asked them who they should send against Cuchulain on the following day, and, with one voice, they spoke the name they had been waiting to speak for weeks: 'Ferdia!' Even though they knew that he was bound by compact not to give combat to his friend and comrade in arms, Cuchulain.

But they knew, even if it had not been proved to them over the last weeks, that there was only one champion who could meet Cuchulain with any chance of success, and that was Ferdia, the son of Damon, the son of Daire, the great and valiant warrior of the men of Domnann of Iris Domnann; the irresistible force, the battle-rock of destruction, and foster-brother of Cuchulain. They had learned the art of fighting from the same teachers, Aoife and Uathach and Scathach the Scythian warrior queen, and were well matched in skill, in bravery, in valour and in the wielding of their arms. It was well known that to attempt to fight or combat with Ferdia wherever he might be, was like a man trying to knock the oaks of the forest with his fists, or stretching his hand forth into a serpent's lair or walking knowingly into the den of a lion, no matter what hero or champion of the world he might be, except for Cuchulain. And neither of them overmatched the other, except that Cuchulain alone could perform the feat of the Gae-Bolg which Scathach had taught to him in secret. But, to compensate for this, Ferdia was known to have a conganess, or secretly manufactured armour of the toughest horn from the eastern world, which neither arms nor a multitude of edges could pierce, and it was thought that this would protect him and bring him victory eventually in his battle with Cuchulain.

Now all the time that the champions of Connacht had been going each day to try and defeat Cuchulain at the ford, Ferdia had remained somewhat aloof from the rest of the camp. He realised that the other warriors knew that he was the only one in the camp who really stood any chance against the Hound of Ulster, and he also knew that they would begrudge him his refusal to fight Cuchulain, his foster-brother, as the deaths of their own friends mounted.

For, although he would have helped them in a general war against the men of Ulster, he did not intend to fight in single combat against his friend and fellow pupil, with whom he had spent his youth, and with whom he had faced many dangers side by side against foreign enemies, Rormans and Greeks alike.

And every day he sent his servants to watch the combats at the Ford and to tell him how Cuchulain was doing and to bring him word immediately if anything should happen to him, fighting alone against all the mighty men of Maeve. But every evening when his servants returned and told him of Cuchulain's successes, Ferdia was glad and proud because of what the Hound was doing.

And then, after weeks of single combat of this kind, in which Cuchulain systematically slew or disabled her champion warriors, Maeve summoned the council of war at which it was decided to send Ferdia.

So messengers were sent to Ferdia to bring him to Maeve's tent, for she said that she would see him herself to persuade him. But Ferdia denied, declined and refused these messengers, and refused to go with them, for he knew very well what Maeve wanted of him. When Maeve heard this she sent more messengers, but this time the satirists and revilers of Connacht so that they might make three satires against him and three crushing reproaches, to mock at him and revile him and disgrace him, that they might raise three blisters on his face – blame, blemish and disgrace – that he might not find a place to lay his head in the world, if he did not come to Maeve. And that he would be shamed before the hosts of Connacht so that if he did not die of it immediately, he would die of the ignominy within a handful of days.

When Ferdia heard this, that it was proposed to disgrace him before the world, he went with them for the sake of his honour, saying: 'It is better to fall before the shafts of valour, bravery and skill than to fall by the shafts of satire, abuse and reproach.'

So he went with them to the queen's tent, and when he reached it and strode in through the glowing entrance, all who were within, including the king and the queen, great lords and nobles, rose up to receive him and he was conducted with great honour to where Maeve stood beside the king, Aillil, at the head of a banqueting table, beside a richly carved chair. On her other side was a great pile of skins and cushions and when she had greeted Ferdia she placed him sitting at her right hand and spoke kindly to him. But Ferdia resolved to wait and see how the queen might approach the subject.

She entertained him with great dignity and honour, and a great feast was prepared. Choice, well-flavoured liquor – wine from Europe and sweet and dry mead from the cunning distillers of Ireland – were pressed on him by the lovely Finndabar, Maeve's beautiful daughter, who sat beside Ferdia and handed him every goblet that he drank, and gave him three kisses on his mouth with every cup that he took; so that he was not long in falling into an intoxication from the drink and from desire for Finndabar. It was Finndabar who gave him to taste the sweet-smelling apples of her bosom and murmured to him all the time that her darling and her chosen sweetheart of the world's men was Ferdia. And he was so dazzled with her beauty and the rewards she promised him, with the garments of a princess flowing around her, that he was ready to promise anything in life she wished.

And when Maeve saw how intoxicated he was with love for Finndabar, she began to make him great promises in return for what she wanted him to do. 'Do you know, Ferdia,' she said to him, 'why you were summoned here?'

And Ferdia, trying to collect his wits again for he realised that now he would surely need them, looked around the tent and said: 'There are many good chiefs and nobles here ... and where else would I be found, but with them?'

Then Maeve said: 'That is not the only reason I asked you here, Ferdia. But I have a multitude of gifts to offer you if you will take them.'

And she listed the gifts: 'A chariot worth fifty bondmaids with steeds fit for a king, a retinue of twelve fully armed men at arms to accompany you as princes and great chiefs are accompanied; great tracts of land on the broad, fertile plains of Connacht, and a free life at my castle of Cruachan where you will be forever a guest if you so wish; the freedom for you and your descendants from tax or rent, and the right to be exempt from military expeditions for your son and grandson till the end of time; furthermore I will give you Finndabar, my daughter and Aillil's, to be your own wife, and my own most intimate friendship, if you wish it ...'

'That is more than any man could want,' cried the assembled lords and nobles.

'And what do you want of me in return?' asked Ferdia.

'That you will meet Cuchulain at the ford of danger tomorrow,' said Maeve quickly and holding his eye with her own as she spoke.

Ferdia looked back at her for a moment; his head was heavy and his senses reeling and even as he tried to hold his gaze on Maeve it slipped to Finndabar beside him, who was stroking his hand with her own. But he said: 'They are great gifts; vast gifts that any man would crave for. But, as for me, you may take them back again for I will not slay my brother-in-arms, Cuchulain.'

Then Maeve concealed her anger, and smiled at Ferdia again and said: 'Then I will do more.'

And from her queenly robe she took the brooch more precious to her than any gift, for all the kings and queens of Connacht backwards through the cone of time had worn that brooch from the beginning, the sign and symbol of their sovereignty; and with her own royal hands she pinned the glittering jewel on Ferdia's cloak. There was a gasp of amazement from all the chiefs and nobles there assembled, and even Aillil's pale face became still paler.

'Now,' said Maeve, 'Ferdia, golden warrior of the men of Domnann, I have bestowed on you the princely dignity so that you will rank beside the king; go now and fight Cuchulain.'

But, flushed yet determined, Ferdia said: 'I cannot fight my brother-in-arms Cuchulain,'

And Maeve's rage was terrible when she heard this, but she concealed it behind her smiling face, though her whole body beneath her emerald gown quivered with the rage it contained.

'And do you not know, Ferdia,' she said, 'that throughout the camp tonight by every fire you are the subject of joking and mockery; that you, who was trained by Scathach as Cuchulain was, are afraid to meet him?'

Ferdia flushed and then grew pale when he heard this, for it was even harder to endure this taunting than it was to endure the promises she held out and the offer of the bed of Finndabar. He remained silent for a while, and then said: 'I may not fight my brother-in-arms, Cuchulain. Rather than do what you ask and turn my hand upon my friend in bitter combat, I would pick out six of your greatest champions, the best and bravest of all your host, and fight with them; all together or one at a time it would make no difference to me.'

Then Maeve's rage completely overcame her, and she looked at Ferdia for a long time; a cold, calculating malevolent look; seeking best how to bend him to her will.

Then she said in a voice that could be heard through all the tent: 'It was true what Cuchulain said, then?'

'What was it he said, Maeve,' asked Ferdia.

'He said,' she replied, 'that he would not have thought it too great if you had been the first to fall to him at the ford. But now, he says, it would be little honour to kill you after the true heroes he has killed during the last week.'

When Ferdia heard this he became angry; yet if it had not been for the drink he had taken, pressed on him by Finndabar, he would not have believed it. Then he stood up with his great legs spread apart to steady him and his eyes blazing in his head and he shouted: 'It was not right that even Cuchulain should speak of me like that. Never yet has he known cowardice or weariness in me by day or night ... nor have I ever spoken badly of him. And if it is true that he said this, then I swear that I will be the first to be ready for battle at the ford tomorrow, much as I dislike doing it.'

Then he swore to do it and, with Finndabar smiling sweetly in his face and the queen on his other side standing close to him and all around the chiefs and warriors of Connacht, he made the compact; and Maeve in her turn named her six great champions that Ferdia had offered to fight instead of Cuchulain as sureties that all her promises to him would be fulfilled if he killed Cuchulain.

Now Fergus Mac Rí had been standing beside the king and when he heard this he was very worried, for Cuchulain was his foster-son and he became afraid for him if he met Ferdia. For Fergus well knew the great warrior that Ferdia was and the might of his arms and that of all the chiefs of Maeve he was by far the bravest and the best. Furthermore Fergus knew that, with the sole exception of the feat of the Gae-Bolga, everything that Scathach had taught Cuchulain she had also taught to Ferdia who was older than Cuchulain, well-built and powerful, and riper in experience of war. So, when he heard what was happening, Fergus left Maeve's tent and caused men to harness his horses and yoke his chariot even though the night was late and the stars wheeled high in the cold heavens and, springing in, he grabbed up the reins and set off at a gallop to where Cuchulain's little camp was on the other side of the river.

Cuchulain welcomed him warmly, late as it was.

'I am rejoiced at your coming, Fergus,' he said, 'seldom enough we get the opportunity to meet on this expedition.'

'And I accept your welcome gladly, Cuchulain, foster-son and pupil,' said Fergus formally, but hurriedly in his anxiety, 'and I have come to tell you who it is that you will have to face at the ford tomorrow.'

'Who is it?'

'Your own friend, companion and fellow-pupil; your equal in skill and bravery, the great champion of the west, in his impenetrable armour, Ferdia, son of Damon, will meet you tomorrow. And you must beware, for he is not like any of the other champions who have come to battle with you.'

'As my soul lives,' cried Cuchulain, 'I wish that he was not coming here to fight, out of my love and affection for him. And almost would I prefer to fall by his hand than that he should fall by mine.'

'I know that,' said Fergus, 'I know you dislike the thought of it; but he is coming, and of all the warriors who have come to the ford up to now, he is by far the most formidable and best prepared. Therefore, rest well tonight and be prepared.'

'You have mistaken me,' said Cuchulain, 'it is not from any fear of him but from the greatness of my love for him that I think this challenge strange and unwelcome. That is the only reason I regret his coming.'

'Nevertheless, you should not think it any disgrace to fear Ferdia,' said Fergus, 'for he is the equal of ten men in combat and you should be on your guard and prepared. For he is the fury of the lion, the bursting of wrath and the blow of doom and the wave that drowns foes.'

'It's strange that you of all people, Fergus, should warn me to be careful of any man in Ireland,' cried Cuchulain. 'It's well that it was yourself and not another who said those words. From the first Monday of winter until the beginning of spring I have stood here alone,' said Cuchulain, 'checking and withholding the men of four of the five great provinces of Ireland, and not one foot have I gone back before any man in that time nor before a multitude of men, nor shall I retreat before Ferdia, Fergus. For as the rush bows down before the torrent in the middle of the stream, so will Ferdia bow before my sword, if once he shows himself here in combat with the Hound of Ulster.'

Then Fergus returned to where Maeve's army was encamped. And Ferdia, after the banqueting and the feasting and rejoicing were over, returned to his own quarters and told his own people what had happened and that he was bound to meet Cuchulain at the ford in the morning.

When they heard this his troops and servants were far from joy and merriment, in spite of the high spirits of Ferdia who was still half drunk, for they knew that whenever these two great heroes, these two battle-breakers and slayers of hundreds should meet in single combat, one or both of them must fall; and if it was only one who fell, well they knew that it would not be Cuchulain and that they would lose their own great chief, for it now seemed impossible to overthrow Cuchulain on his chosen ground at the ford.

Now during the early part of the night Ferdia slept heavily, being overcome with the liquor he had taken, but towards the middle of the night the sleep left him and his brain cleared and he woke and found that he could not sleep again. He remembered the combat that he had to fight in the morning, and anxiety and care began to worry him; partly it was fear of Cuchulain, but principally it was anger and sorrow that he had promised to fight him at the ford, his foster-brother; and fear of losing Finndabar particularly and Maeve's other great promises gnawed at him, and he began to get angry with himself and churlish towards Cuchulain because his feelings were complex and inexplicable, so he tossed about and could sleep no more.

Finally he rose in the cold, misty morning, and called his charioteer and said: 'Yoke my horses and come with me. I'll sleep better at the ford.'

But the charioteer began to rebuke him, saying, 'You'd be better off to stay where you are. I wish you would not go to meet Cuchulain at the ford.'

'Stay quiet,' said Ferdia, 'and harness the horses.'

Ferdia was angry with himself in the dawn, and the more he thought of what had happened the angrier he became. 'There'll be no turning back,' he said, 'until the Hound's body lies reeking in the ford as offal for the croaking ravens above it.'

'It is not right for you to speak like that about your friend, Cuchulain,' said the charioteer, 'no credit to you for it.'

'Mind your own business,' said Ferdia, 'and get on with your work.'

And so, irritable and with uneasiness between them, they set out for the ford. When they got there Ferdia was overcome with a weariness and a certain kindness, and he said to his charioteer: 'Take the cushions and the skins out of the chariot like a good man, and spread them out for me on the bank till I see would I get a little more sleep before the fighting.'

So the charioteer did as Ferdia asked and, as he lay down, Ferdia said to him: 'Take a look, lad, and see that Cuchulain is not coming.'

'He is not, I'm sure of it,' said the charioteer.

'Look again,' said Ferdia.

'Cuchulain is not such a little speck that we wouldn't see him if he was there,' said the lad.

'True enough,' said Ferdia, 'he's heard that I'm coming to meet him today and has decided to keep away.'

'Oh Ferdia,' said the charioteer, 'that is no way to be going on. It's not right to insult him and be disloyal to him in his absence. Don't you remember when you were fighting in the eastern lands on the borders of the Tyrrhene sea and your sword was wrenched from your grasp; how you would have surely been killed but for Cuchulain rushing forward to recover it for you, killing all round him to get it for you? And do you not remember where we were that same night?'

'I do not,' Ferdia replied angrily.

'We were in the house of Scathach's steward,' said the lad, 'and you crossed words with that giant, half-witted pot boy there. And don't you remember how he struck you in the middle of the back with his great three pronged meat fork and hurled you through the door again? And that it was Cuchulain who rushed in and gave the fellow a blow of his sword that severed the top half of him from the bottom half, and if it was only for that alone, you should not discredit him.'

'What use is it to remind me of these things now?' cried Ferdia in anguish. 'You had right to say them to me last night, and we would not be here at all. However, it's done now, and I'll try to sleep. You keep a good look out.'

'I'll watch,' said the charioteer, 'so that unless a man drop out of the clouds above to fight with you, none shall escape me.'

And saying this he sat beside Ferdia's head, while the warrior dropped into a deep and refreshing sleep.

And at about the same time, in the misty light of the early morning, Maeve, stretched on her couch beside Aillil, nudged him with her elbow and said in a hoarse, half-musing whisper: 'Provided that Cuchulain falls by Ferdia, it will be just as well if he's killed himself too; for it's certain that if he kills his friend, it is we ourselves he'll come after next.'

Meanwhile Cuchulain and his charioteer, Laeg, were talking together after Fergus had left them with the news that Ferdia was to come to the ford next morning.

'How do you intend to spend tonight?' asked Laeg when Fergus had gone.

'The same as every other night,' said Cuchulain, 'why?'

'Because,' said Laeg, 'it crossed my mind that Ferdia won't come to the ford alone tomorrow. For such a fight as this the hosts and chieftains of Ireland will assemble to look on and you may be sure that Ferdia will come to the combat washed and bathed and perfumed, with his hair freshly cut and scented and plaited and in all the great magnificence of a battle-champion. But you are worn out and tired after all these combats, unwashed and uncombed. And it seems to me that you would do yourself honour if you went home to Emer at Slieve Fuad for tonight, and let her attend to you, so that you might not appear dishevelled and ragged tomorrow before the men of Ireland.'

Cuchulain thought that there was sound sense in this advice and went back to Emer, who was gentle and loving to him after their separation from each other. Then, when it was full day, he returned to his camp. And he did this so that the men of Ireland would not say it was from fear or nervousness that he rose early to be at the ford. And, in the broad daylight, refreshed and comforted, he said to Laeg: 'Laeg, harness the horses and yoke our war-chariot and let us go now to the ford, for Ferdia was always an early rising champion and it would not do to keep him waiting.'

'The chariot is yoked and the horses are harnessed,' said Laeg, 'so mount it now, and it will not disgrace your courage or your skill.'

So Cuchulain sprang into the war-chariot and the battle victorious and red-sworded hero grasped the hand-rail, and Laeg cracked his whip and with a leap and a pawing of the air, the two great steeds, the Grey of Macha and the Black Steed of the Glen, bounded forward. And up and around him rose the screeching and the wailing of the Bochawnachs and the Bonawnachs, the spirits of the air and of battle, to strike terror and miserable fear into the souls of his enemies.

And as he came Ferdia's charioteer heard the roar of Cuchulain's approach; the clamour and the hissing and the tramp; and the thunder and the clatter and the scream; for he heard the discs for throwing clanking together as the chariot careered towards them; and he heard the tall spears hiss in the whipping wind, and the swords clash in their scabbards, and the helmet clang and the armour ring; and the arms sawed against one another and the javelins swung, and the ropes strained and the wheels of the chariot clattered, and the chariot creaked and the hooves of the horses thundered on the ground as that warrior and champion, Cuchulain, came forward to the ford, and approached him.

Then he woke Ferdia and said: 'Get up, Ferdia, for he is

coming now ... The Hound of Valour, a noble hawk of battle, the wind of combat in search of victory. A year ago I knew he would come, the hero of Emhain, the Hound of Ulster in his might.'

Then Ferdia sprang up in anger and said: 'For God's sake keep quiet, has he bribed you to praise him to me or what? He's late and I'm tired of waiting here to kill him, so let's get on with it.'

And soon Ferdia's charioteer looking across the ford saw a marvellous sight, Cuchulain's great, green canopied, battle chariot careering towards him with all the swiftness and power of Laeg and the mighty horses. Thin and well-seasoned was the body of it, lofty and long the spears that adorned it, that lithe war chariot. Under the yoke were two great-eared, savage and prancing steeds, bellied like whales and broad chested; they snorted and blew as they charged; high flanked and wide hooved, their pasterns fine, their lines broad and their spirits untameable, the long maned Grey of Macha and the tufted Black of the Glen. Like a hawk on a stormy day, like the gust of a gale in March across the plain; like a stag at the beginning of the chase, such was the pace of the two steeds, touching the soil as if it were on fire, so that the whole earth trembled and shook at the violence of their coming.

And as they travelled Cuchulain instructed Laeg that if he should grow weak in the fight, or seem to be giving way before Ferdia, he was to taunt him with cowardice and fling reproaches and bad names at him, so that his anger would rise and he would fight more bitterly than before. But if he were doing well then Laeg was to praise him to keep his spirits up.

And Laeg laughed and said: 'Is it like this you want me to taunt you: Come on Cuchulain, you're more like a child than a man, that Ferdia throws over as easily as a cat waves its tail? Or like a mother would play with her child?'

'That will do,' said Cuchulain laughing too, 'I should surely fight better after that.'

When they came to the ford Cuchulain drew up on the north side and Ferdia on the south side.

And Ferdia was still full of anger with himself and tried to justify it with sneers, so he said to Cuchulain: 'What brings you here, Cua?'

Now Cu means Hound and would have been welcome indeed, but Cua means 'squint-eyed', and this was how Ferdia insulted Cuchulain. And Ferdia did this because he wanted to appear bold and unconcerned. So he said again: 'Welcome, squint eye.'

But Cuchulain answered seriously: 'Up to today no greeting would have been more welcome than one from you, Ferdia, but today I will not accept it. Indeed, it would be more suitable for me to welcome you than for you to welcome me, since it is you who have invaded my province and pillaged and burned all before you.'

'Ah, little Cuchulain,' said Ferdia, 'what in the world ever persuaded you to come to this fight at all as if you were my equal? Don't you remember how when we were with Scathach you were my attendant whose job it was to whet my spears and make my bed?'

'True enough,' said Cuchulain, 'because I was younger and smaller than you in those days, and it was the custom for juniors to do as much for seniors. But that is not the situation now. There is no champion in the entire world to whom I am not equal, or whom I would refuse to fight.'

And at that each reproached the other bitterly, renouncing their friendship. Each taunted the other that the day's end would see him dead and headless, with his blood strewing the grass or washing away in the stream; but Ferdia was the most bitter. Then Cuchulain said:

> Oh, in days gone by,
> Together you and I
> Fought — 'twas do or die —
> Wherever Scathach taught.
> You, of all who nearest
> Are to me, and dearest;
> Kinsman without peer, this
> Doom your fate has brought.

But Ferdia, indignant rage having laid hold of him, would not listen and taunted Cuchulain again.

Then Cuchulain said again: 'It was not right, Ferdia, for you to have come here because of the meddling of Maeve. I have killed many of her champions and you have been fooled like them and blinded with the promise of gifts. Do you really think that Finndabar loves you? You're not the first she was promised to, yes, or lay with, in order to be persuaded to come here. How could there be anger or enmity between us after all that we shared together? Remember the vow we made never to fight each other. I tell you there is not one in the world who could persuade me to fight you.'

Ferdia paused after this, and was moved by it, for he knew it was the truth that Cuchulain spoke. But he knew too that it was too late for him to turn back. But his chivalrous and noble nature got the better of him then, and he said: 'It is too late, Cuchulain, my true friend, there's no point in talking about the past and we had better get on with what we came for. Let us choose our weapons and begin. What arms shall we select today?'

'The choice of weapons is yours until tonight,' said Cuchulain, 'since you were first to reach the ford.'

'Well, then,' said Ferdia, 'do you remember the missiles that we learned to throw so well with Scathach?'

'I do indeed,' said Cuchulain.

'Very well,' said Ferdia, 'if you remember, let us use them now.'

Then they each took up their two great shields, thick and bossed and heavy for defence, to cover their bodies, and their eight small, razor edged discs to throw horizontally, and their eight light javelins, and their eight ivory handled bolts, and their eight little darts for the fight. Backwards and forward between them flew the weapons, like bees winging on a sunny day, and there was no cast that they threw that did not hit. From early morning until midday they continued to hurl the weapons at each other until they were blunted on the faces of each other's shields. And so good was the aim behind each cast that not one of them missed, yet so skilful was the defence that not a drop of blood was drawn on either side.

'There's no point in fighting with these any longer,' said Ferdia, 'for it's not with them that either of us can win.'

'Very good,' said Cuchulain.

'What arms shall we use now?' asked Ferdia

'The choice is still yours,' said Cuchulain.

'Then let's try our strong, hard spears with the flaxen throwing thongs,' replied Ferdia.

'Right,' said Cuchulain.

So they took their shields again, and the well-balanced throwing spears, and with these they attacked one another from the middle of the day until nightfall. And although the defence was as good as it had been in the morning, so good was the spear casting that each drew red blood from the other.

And at nightfall, they ceased and threw away their weapons into their charioteers' hands and ran towards one another in the middle of the ford and each put his arms around the other and gave him three friendly kisses in remembrance of the past. That night their horses were stabled in the same paddock, and their charioteers warmed themselves at the same fire after they had made for their warriors beds of comfortable rushes and skins with pillows such as wounded men need. And the physicians and surgeons came to heal them and tend their wounds; and of every herb and remedy that was given to Cuchulain, he sent half across the ford to Ferdia so that no man among the hosts of Maeve could have it to say that if Ferdia fell it was because Cuchulain had a better means of healing than he. And of all the food and pleasant drink that the men of Maeve's camp sent to Ferdia, he sent half north across the ford to Cuchulain, for Cuchulain had few to attend to his wants, whereas all the people of Maeve's camp were ready to attend Ferdia.

And so, for that night they rested in peace; but early next morning they rose and met again at the ford.

And this day it was Cuchulain's right to choose the weapons for combat. 'Let us take our great, well-tempered, broad bladed lances then,' said Cuchulain, 'so that the close combat will bring a decision more quickly than the shooting of the light weapons of yesterday. And let us yoke our horses and chariots and fight from them today.'

So they took two great, heavy shields across their shoulders and their broad-bladed lances and charged and wheeled and thrust and struck at one another from the grim light of early morning, to the bloody sinking of the western sun. And if it were customary for the birds of the air to pass through the bodies of men in their daring flight, then they could have passed through the bodies of these two that day through the wounds and the gaps they made in each other, and carried away pieces of their flesh into the clouds and the sky around them.

And by the evening both men and horses and their charioteers were spent and exhausted, and Cuchulain said: 'Let's stop now, Ferdia, for our charioteers and our horses can do no more – we are not like giants from the sea who must be forever destroying each other without rest; let battle cease now, and let us be friends once again.'

'Very well,' said Ferdia, gratefully enough, 'if it is time to stop.'

And again they threw their arms to their charioteers and ran to greet each other in the same manner as they had the previous night. The horses shared the same paddock that night as well, and again their charioteers shared the same fire after seeing to the warriors, for their injuries were so terrible that night that the physicians and surgeons could do little except try to staunch the flow of blood. And, as on the previous night, every remedy and salve that was given to Cuchulain, he sent half across to Ferdia and Ferdia in his turn sent to Cuchulain half of the food that was brought to him.

And they rested as well as they could that night, which was little because of their terrible wounds, and rose early the following morning and went again to the ford.

And that morning Cuchulain saw an evil look and a dark glowering look on Ferdia's face.

'Why are you so mean and evil looking today, Ferdia,' asked Cuchulain, 'and look at me in that vicious way?'

'Not from any fear of you,' snarled Ferdia, 'for there's no man in Ireland I couldn't kill today.'

'Oh Ferdia,' said Cuchulain in sorrow, 'it is a great tragedy for you to come and fight me, your friend and foster-brother, on the word of a woman. Not Finndabar's beauty, nor the coaxing of Maeve, nor all the wealth of the world would have brought me out to fight with you. Why don't you go back while you still can, for a fight to the death it must be between us if we go on, and I have not the heart to fight against you; my strength fails me when I think of the evil that has come between us; turn back, Ferdia, and no disgrace to you because of the false promises made to you by Maeve.'

'I can't, Cuchulain,' cried Ferdia, 'until one of us falls. I know what Maeve is and what her promises are worth, but for all that I cannot withdraw now. My honour at least, Cu, will be avenged, and I have no fear of death. Do not throw it in my face what I have done, my friend, but let us choose our arms, and fight as warriors and men.'

'If that is the way it must be,' said Cuchulain, 'that is the way it will be; what weapons shall we use?'

'Our heavy, two handed, smiting swords,' said Ferdia, 'for they will bring us into closer combat, and nearer to a conclusion, than our spears of yesterday.'

So they took two great, full length shields, and their great, double-edged swords, and all that day they hewed and hacked at each other; striking and trying to lay each other low; to cut and to slaughter and destroy each other until they struck masses and gobbets of flesh, larger than the head of a month old child, from the shoulders and thighs and shoulder blades of each other.

And the battle lasted without respite all that day until in the evening Ferdia cried: 'Let us cease now, Cuchulain.'

'Very well,' replied the other, 'if it is time.'

And they parted then, coldly, and threw their arms to their charioteers. And their horses did not share the same paddock that evening, nor did their charioteers sleep beside the same fire, but Laeg slept with his master on the north side of the ford and Ferdia's charioteer with him on the south side.

In the morning Ferdia rose early and went to the ford alone, for he knew well that the battle would be decided that day, and that on that day and in that place one or both of them would fall. And then he put on his full battle armour for the coming fight; the silken, gold embroidered trews and toughened leather kilt. And on his belly a great flagstone, shallow, of adamantine stone that he had brought from Africa; and over that the solid, twice molten iron skirt about his waist, through fear and dread of the Gae-Bolga on that day. And on his head his crested helmet, studded with forty glittering carbuncles and gleaming with enamel and crystal and rubies and gems from the east. Into his right hand he took his great, death-dealing spear and on his left side he hung his curved battle sword, razor-sharp, and golden hilted. Across his back he hung his massive battle shield, with fifty great bosses on it, each of which would reflect the image of a boar, and with its great central boss of red gold.

And then, when he was fully armed, he prepared himself

for the coming battle by practising a great number of wonderful feats of arms; more than he had ever learned from Scathach, and which he had himself perfected in his years of war.

And when Cuchulain came to the ford he saw Ferdia practising there and said to Laeg: 'You see the wonderful feats that Ferdia is doing. They will all be turned on me today. Then do not forget what I told you; if I look like being bested you must taunt me and deride me to get my anger up.'

'I'll remember,' said Laeg.

Then Cuchulain put on his battle armour, and he in his turn practised many skills and feats he had perfected by himself and Ferdia, watching, knew that they would be tried on himself that day.

'What weapons will we use today?' asked Cuchulain.

'Today the choice is yours,' replied Ferdia.

'Very well then,' said Cuchulain, 'let us try the feat of the ford in which all weapons are allowed.'

'Very well,' replied Ferdia, but even as he said it he was full of sorrow, because he knew that Cuchulain had destroyed every champion and hero who ever fought the feat of the ford with him.

Terribly and mighty were the deeds done that day at the ford by the two mighty champions of Europe; the two great hands of the western world that bestowed gifts and pay and reward on men; the two pillars of the valour of the Gael; the two keys of bravery of the world, brought together in a fight to the death through the lies and trickery of Aillil and Maeve.

From the early morning they hurled their missiles at each other until noon, when their rage became wild and uncontrollable and they drew near one another in blind blood fury.

And then, suddenly, Cuchulain sprang from the bank of the ford and knocked Ferdia backwards and stood upon the boss of his shield, seeking to strike off his head from above with the rim of his own shield. But Ferdia gave his shield a thrust with his left elbow and cast Cuchulain from it like a bird, so that he came down again upon the bank. Again Cuchulain sprang before the other could get up and struck at Ferdia's head, but Ferdia gave his shield a thrust with his left knee and hurled Cuchulain back again.

And Laeg saw what was happening, and began to reproach

Cuchulain as he had been told to do if he saw the warrior being bested: 'Ah, Cuchulain,' he shouted, 'this warrior throws you off like a whore throws away her child; as the river flings its foam; goes through you like an axe through a rotten tree, binds you as woodbine binds the tree; pounces on you like a hawk on a little bird, so that you can never be called a warrior again, you little twisted fairy, you.'

When Cuchulain heard these words he sprang again with the speed of the wind, the swiftness of the swallow, fiery as a dragon and powerful as the lion, and landed on the boss of Ferdia's shield and swung at his head. But Ferdia gave the shield a shake and tossed Cuchulain back as if he had never been there.

And then, for the first time, Cuchulain's great battle rage came on him. His countenance changed and he appeared to grow and swell so great was the rage that overcame him, until he seemed to tower as a terrible giant of the sea until he overtopped Ferdia.

So close was the struggle between them that their heads met above and their feet met below and their arms in the middle around the rims and bosses of their shields. So close was the struggle that their shields burst and split from their centres to their rims, and they turned and bent and twisted and shivered their spears from their points to their hafts. So close were they locked that the Bochawnachs and the Bonawnachs and the demons of war screamed from the rims of their shields and the hilts of their swords and the hafts of their spears. So closely were they locked together that the river was cast out of its bed and dried up beneath them so that a couch could be made in the middle of its course for a king or a queen without a drop of liquid falling on them, except what sprang from the two champions, as they trampled and hewed at each other in the middle of the ford.

Such was the terror of the fight that the horses of the Gael in fear and madness rushed away wildly, bursting their yokes and their chains and their tethers and their traces; and the women and children and the weak and the camp followers among Maeve's hosts fled away south-westwards out of the camp.

Just at that moment Ferdia caught Cuchulain in an unguarded instant and plunged his short-edged sword into his breast, so that Cuchulain's blood streamed to his girdle and the wet soil of the bottom of the ford was streaked and crimsoned with his blood. And Ferdia, seeing his advantage, rained blow after blow on Cuchulain who could barely defend himself against the fierce, slashing hurricane of blows that Ferdia rained on him – even ignoring his own defence – in a frenzied attempt to finish the Hound.

Then Cuchulain, unable to withstand this onslaught, called to Laeg to pass him the Gae-Bolga.

Now the manner of using the Gae-Bolga, a Scythian weapon, was to hurl it with the foot at your enemy. It made the wound of one spear on entering a person's body, but it had thirty barbs to open behind and it could not be cut out of a man's body until he was cut open.

When he heard Cuchulain, Laeg sent the Gae-Bolga floating down the stream and Cuchulain caught it in the fork of his boot.

Now, when Ferdia heard Cuchulain call for the Gae-Bolga, he made a downward stroke of his shield to protect his body and Cuchulain, seeing his opportunity, rammed a short spear with the palm of his hand over the edge of Ferdia's shield and above the edge of his armour so that it pierced him through and emerged the other side. Then Ferdia gave an upward thrust of his shield to protect his upper body, though it was help that came too late, and Cuchulain threw the Gae-Bolga as forcibly as he could cast it underneath at Ferdia, so that it broke through the iron-linked skirt, and broke in three parts the adamantine stone, and cut its way into his body so that every crevice and cavity in him was filled with its barbs.

'Ah!' Ferdia groaned, 'that's the end. But it is not right that it should be by your foot I fell and not your hand.'

Then Cuchulain ran to Ferdia and, lifting him in spite of all his great armour, carried him to the northern bank of the ford in order that he might die on that side and not on the other with the army of Maeve.

And, when he lay him down, a great weakness came over Cuchulain himself and he collapsed beside the body of Ferdia.

But Laeg, who could see the danger, roused him again.

'Cuchulain, Cuchulain,' he cried, splashing water in the warrior's face, 'rise up from there or we are dead men. The army of Connacht is on the move towards us and it is not single combat they'll give us when they reach us, since you have killed Ferdia.'

'What does it matter, now that I've killed my greatest friend,' asked Cuchulain, '... oh Ferdia,' he added, addressing the body of his comrade, 'it was great treachery and desertion of the men of Ireland to bring you to fight here with me, knowing that one of us must die. Oh Ferdia, you are the greatest loss to Ireland; I wish to God it was me who lay there instead of you.'

'Ah,' said Laeg, 'stop that. It is true enough that if he had his way it is you who would be there now. Now hurry, before they come and slaughter us.'

But Cuchulain paid no attention. For a long while he remained silent, bending alone above the body of his friend in great grief. Then he stood up and turned away and, without looking at Ferdia's body, said to Laeg: 'Laeg, remove his armour and let me see that golden brooch which cost him his life here today.'

Then Laeg took off Ferdia's horny armour and took the brooch from the mantle beneath, and handed it to Cuchulain. Cuchulain looked at it lying in his palm, and tears, such as only a strong warrior can weep, poured from his eyes and fell on that ancient brooch.

'Laeg,' he said, without looking up, for indeed if he had looked up he could not have seen, 'Laeg, now cut open the body and take out the Gae-Bolga.'

So Laeg did so and when he drew out the spear, all red with the blood of Ferdia still on it, Cuchulain lamented over his friend 'to whom I have served a draught of blood', and said: 'Now we will go, for every other combat that I ever fought or will fight seems like a game to me compared with this battle with Ferdia, this pillar of gold that I have overthrown.' And as he left he made this lament:

Wars were shared and gay for each
Until Ferdia faced the breach;
Together we had shared the skill
Of Scathach, who had taught us well.
Equal was the praise she gave;
Equal was her praise to each.

Wars were shared and gay for each
Until Ferdia faced the breach,

Well loved pillar of pure gold
Lying now beside the ford, dead; cold!
Who, when on his foes he fell,
Killed as far as eye could reach.

Wars were shared and gay for each
Until Ferdia faced the breach;
Lion fiery, fierce and bright,
Wave whose might nothing withstands,
Sweeping with the shrinking sands,
Destruction on the beach.

Wars were shared and gay for each
Until Ferdia faced the breach;
Gentle Ferdia; dear to me,
Always shall his image be –
Yesterday a mountain looming,
Now a shadow in the gloaming.

DEIRDRE AND THE SONS OF USNA

CONOR MAC NESSA BECAME king of Ulster by a trick. When he was a youngster his mother, a widow called Ness, was ambitious and beautiful. Now she was not highborn enough to consider that Conor could ever become king and the thought never entered the minds of those who knew them, because the king at the time was Fergus Mac Rí, a powerful and noble man whom his people loved. Although Ness knew that Conor was not in line for the throne, she was of sufficient rank to mingle at court and she set out deliberately to attract Fergus, which she did so successfully that he developed a considerable passion for her. But she would not give in to him when he asked her to marry him, and played with him and tantalised him until he was ready to accede to any request.

Then she made it a condition of her marrying Fergus that, for one year, he would leave the sovereignty and that Conor should take his place: 'so that she could have it said that her son sat on the throne and that his children should be called the descendants of a king.'

Fergus didn't like the idea, and his people liked it even less, but she absolutely refused to marry him unless he agreed, so at last he did so and resigned the kingdom to Conor. But as soon as Conor sat on the throne Ness set out to win the hearts and allegiance of the people from Fergus and transfer them to Conor. And she was so successful in this that when Fergus demanded the kingship back he found that there was a league of chiefs and nobles against him who had been won over by her bribes and favours, and the league was so strong that he could do nothing. They said that they liked Conor, who had become their friend and protector, and they were not disposed to part with him; and furthermore that Fergus had abandoned the kingdom for a year only to gain a wife and therefore cared little for it and didn't deserve to get it back, and, while agreeing that he was entitled to keep his wife if he wished, they insisted that the kingship should pass to Conor.

That was the beginning of the serious differences between Fergus and Conor – and Ness, too, for it was then that Fergus began to realise that Ness loved herself and her son more than she loved himself. And this story tells how Fergus eventually, together with his followers, came to leave Ulster – leaving his wife behind – and went into Connacht where he found refuge with Maeve and Aillil.

He swore to be revenged and that is how he came to fight with Maeve and Aillil against Ulster in the Táin Bó Cuailgne when Cuchulain defended Ulster at the ford against the champions of Maeve's army.

But, in the meantime, concealing their growing hostility and resentment Conor placed Fergus next to himself in the land. But all the time Fergus watched with great jealousy, for Conor was getting old and bitter and the knowledge that he sat in Fergus' rightful seat was with him always, and he knew that many of the older chiefs would like to see Fergus resume the throne even after all that time.

If he dared he would have shut Fergus up in his foulest dungeon or have had him killed outright, but he knew that this would be disastrous to himself for the men of Ulster would not have stood for it. And so, year by year, suspicion and hatred grew in Conor so that some men feared and dreaded him and few felt for him the affection and reverence that is due a true king.

Yet for the younger chiefs, who knew nothing of what had passed between Conor and Fergus years before, or who learned it only as history that happened before they were born, the reign of the gigantic Fergus and his mighty deeds were hearsay; old wives' tales told by toothless men and to be taken with a sceptical smile and a fistful of salt. And though they looked on the giant hero with interest and considerable awe, he seemed more like an ancient demigod than a human being like themselves, who had somehow lingered on from an historic past.

At this time Ulster was at peace and instead of the grim aura of war, days of laughter and sunshine filled the lives of the people; the corn ripened and was harvested; the cattle fattened; the gold and precious metals were worked and trade prospered. The young men contended on the playing field instead of among the carnage of the battlefield, and the young women grew up with the expectation of marriage before them. And it became the custom, as in earlier times, for each chief in his turn to provide a great banquet for the king and his followers and in due course it became the turn of Felim, chief of Conor's storytellers, to prepare such a feast.

For a year he had been in preparation. He had a great, immense hall built close to his own castle, big enough to accommodate the king's retinue and his own guests. Oak trees by the hundred had been felled and trimmed for the beams of the walls and the ceiling, which had been laced and latticed with wattle and then sealed with clay. Outside the doorways and the lintels were of marble stone, and the flags of black basalt. And all around the banqueting hall were also built sleeping quarters for those guests who could not be accommodated in the castle, kitchens and stables for the horses. From the surrounding countryside butter and cream, cheese and curds, cakes and bread; cattle, sheep and swine for the table were brought in in preparation, and fruit and vegetables from Ireland and across the seas were stored, together with great quantities of honey and ale, mead and the wine of Greece and Rome. Musicians, dancers, men and women; those who played the harp and the lute, from foreign lands with strange uncouth romances, and from Ireland with the stories of the ancients; all were there and in readiness for the great feast, about which, Felim swore, the men of Ireland would talk for many years to come. And about that he was right, but not for the reason which he anticipated.

On the day appointed Conor set out from Emhain Macha, which was his seat of state, with all the champions of the Red Branch Knights in attendance. It was a glorious day in which the sun wheeled overhead like a great chariot of fire in a blue plain, and below the splendour of the king all but matched its own. For as he left the great gate of Emhain Macha and turned his face eastward on the road to Felim's country, a great emblazoned banner spanned the highway like an arch. A hundred knights in scarlet cloaks embroidered in gold and riding black horses pranced at the head of the column; then a hundred more in emerald green on white horses; then yet another hundred in deep blue cloaks with silver fringes riding chestnut steeds, and then five hundred of the knights in saffron yellow cloaks, tall and proud, in chariots of beaten bronze drawn by well matched pairs and driven by charioteers in white tunics appeared, the scythes and armour of the chariots flashing in the sun. But the scythes were folded up from the axles of the war-chariots, and there was grandeur in the sight without an element of war or foreboding.

King Conor, in all his glory, came next. And from where he sat in the large open, four-wheeled chariot that carried him, with its canopy of purple, he could see the glitter and the twinkle of the sun on the helmets and spear points of the knights who rode before him. More knights followed, and then the remainder of his retinue which was upwards of a thousand people. But in spite of the sunshine and the glorious panoply, the mouth of the king rarely smiled and his watching eyes seldom stopped moving, as he himself seldom relaxed in comfort.

Slowly the cavalcade moved along the highway under the sun, but as the afternoon wore on some dark-centred clouds blew up from the east and more followed until, like a curtain drawn by a cord from the west, a grey cloud came between them and the sun; and before night fell a wind followed and raised high clouds of choking dust that hung around them and filled their eyes, their ears and their mouths with grime and settled on everything.

Then, just as they reached the castle of Felim, the storm broke with a huge crash of thunder and a flash of brilliant light that showed the place for a moment in a blue-white light, and then shut it out again as suddenly as the rain emptied from the sundered clouds above.

Felim stood at the door of the banqueting hall, framed by the light from inside, and his cloak billowed and flapped behind him in the wind as he went forward to welcome his royal guest.

'Welcome, Conor,' he cried, 'come in out of this terrible night and let's have music and a song – and a drink for Conor.'

But his excitement and goodwill were no use; indeed his evening looked like being completely spoiled, for the king sat there and glowered, scarcely bothering to speak to anyone, while the storm roared and thundered outside; such a storm as no one could remember before.

The king took this as an omen. 'This is no common storm,' he muttered, 'I have the feeling that some catastrophe will fall on us after this night.'

But Felim continued to try and cheer him up and make his banquet a success, though he was fighting a losing battle. However, after the guests had been washed and warmed and given drink, they sat at the enormous table groaning wiih the food, and the banquet began.

But the king had hardly raised the first bite to his mouth when a dreadful scream came from the palace.

'What is that?' asked the king, his face going pale.

And Felim, cursing the impulsive night three-quarters of a year ago, said: 'It is nothing, Conor; my wife, she is in labour.'

'That didn't sound like the scream of any woman to me,' said the king. 'Bring her here till we see for ourselves, if she is able.'

So messengers went and brought Felim's wife into the banqueting hall, and sure enough she confirmed that it was not she who had screamed, but the child itself who had screamed in the womb even before it was born. Then Catha, the king's druid, stood up and put his hand on her and said: 'Aye, indeed! It is a girl-child who is here, and her name will be Deirdre – which is alarm – and she will be well-named because she will bring evil and woe and war to Ulster with her.'

Then, when Catha had said this, the woman left again for her bed, and the entire company returned to the banquet, but without an appetite for it. The king was deep in thought, and no one had the courage to interrupt him.

Then, after a little while, a messenger came to say that Felim's wife had given birth, and it was indeed a girl who had been born.

'Let her be killed,' cried the knights, afraid of the prophecy.

'No,' said the king, in a perverse humour. 'We will not commit an evil deed to avoid the course of a prophecy.' Though, indeed, it was no fear of doing evil that prevented him, or had ever prevented him in the past. 'Let Catha go out,' he said, 'and consult the stars to discover her destiny. We owe our host no less than that, and may the future be good and prosperous for him and his family.'

So Catha went out into the night, where the storm had passed, leaving dark clouds behind racing across the face of the night to catch it up, and stood on the ramparts of the castle trying to read the stars. He studied the moon and from his robes took out his tablets and runes and studied them, and performed several other mystic rites which would help him. He did everything with great care, because he knew that what would be revealed was of the utmost importance to Ulster, and when he knew it all he was startled.

He was gone a long time and meanwhile those in the banqueting hall had been celebrating, following the king's lead, the birth of the child and all the earlier ominous atmosphere was gone. Now all were merry and the place rang with noise and laughter and Felim in particular was delighted at the turn things had taken, for the king was in great spirits. But when Catha stood in the doorway, silently looking at them with a strange look, silence ran down the length of the room like a wind rippling across a cornfield. The laughter stopped, and everyone turned to look at Catha. The king's eyes were fastened on him, almost hypnotically, for an instant and then, with a sudden movement, he laughed too loudly and said: 'Well, we hope the omens prophesy good luck, and no harm to her parents.' And he drank a toast to her with a flamboyant gesture. But even as the drink passed down his throat the laugh flew out of his mouth and fear gripped his chest, making it difficult for him to swallow. He nearly choked on the draught, but turned his eyes, expectantly and challengingly, on Catha.

Catha returned his look gravely. 'Not to her parents, but to the province and its king and chiefs will this child bring misfortune,' he said. 'She will be so beautiful that queens will be jealous of her and kings go to war for her. Beware, Conor, she is born for misfortune to Ulster and the downfall of the Red Branch Knights.'

Then, again, the knights and nobles sprang up and together shouted that if such evil were going to follow her, then it would be better to kill her while she was still an infant.

But Conor quietened them, out of perversity or what strange motive it is hard to say.

'Let us see this harbinger of bad luck,' he said. 'Bring in the child.'

So the tiny infant was brought in, straight from its birthplace, and when it felt the warmth and the lights and the sounds about her, she, marvellous to relate, puckered up her face and crowed and smiled up at the stern king.

At this he was moved to gentleness. He reached out and took the baby from the nurse's arms and stood with her for a moment. Then, loudly, he addressed the company: 'The prophecies and omens of the seers I believe and honour, but I do not believe that any good can come out of killing this child. Therefore I will make at least one part of his cold prophecy come true, for I will take her as my wife when she comes of marriageable age, and so she shall be a queen. I shall place her under my special protection now and make myself responsible for her. She shall be reared by me in a secret place and any who lifts his hand against her must reckon with the king himself. In that way I will be better able to guard against the prophecy.'

And the knights did not raise a protest, though they were not satisfied with the way things turned out. When they said nothing Catha said: 'Conor, you will live to regret this, but, since it is your will that she must live then she will be a child of sorrow, and Deirdre of the Sorrows will be her name.'

'It is a nice name,' said Conor, 'I like Deirdre. And when she is old enough to foster with a nurse, let her be brought to me.'

As soon as she was old enough Conor took the child away from her parents and had her brought up by a nurse called Leabharcam, a wise and skilful nurse, who reared her in one of Conor's hidden fortresses deep in a wood private to the king. The fortress had a lovely garden around it surrounded by a high wall where no man could see her, and outside the wall was a deep moat. Savage wolf hounds guarded the place at night, and Conor was satisfied that Deirdre was secure there; secure from the fate foretold by Catha, who was the only one allowed to visit her other than himself, and secure for himself when she matured in his old age.

And for years Deirdre grew there with Leabharcam her teacher and Catha and the king as her visitors, and they were the only men she knew. But she was not unhappy, for Leabharcam loved her very much and taught her all that she knew; the secrets of living things, birds that fly and beasts that run; she taught her about plants and roots and their names and uses, both of them and of their fruits. And Leabhharcam taught her the motion of the stars and the planets so that she understood time and the changes of the seasons. Deirdre grew tall and lissom and beautiful; more beautiful than any maiden of the world; beautiful of body and of mind. And as she grew older and more womanly beautiful, so did the ageing king's visits become more numerous.

Then, one winter's day when the snow lay over the garden in smooth layers and hung upon the dark branches of the bare trees like livid fruits, Deirdre was standing at a window looking out at where Catha had killed a calf so that she might have veal for her meal.

And suddenly she sighed. Now Leabharcam hearing the sigh, a thing she had never known Deirdre to do before, turned to her and said: 'What ails you, child?'

'I don't know, Leabhar,' said Deirdre, who used this affectionate name – which means book – because of her fondness for Leabharcam and because of her nurse's wisdom – 'I don't know,' she said, 'I feel sad.'

'Sad,' said Leabharcam, who had lived in fear that the day would come when Deirdre might say that, for she knew what it meant, 'for what?'

'And lonely,' said Deirdre.

And Leabharcam knew that this was worse.

'Lonely?' she said.

'Yes,' said Deirdre.

'But how could you be lonely, child dear, with me here and the king and Catha to visit you?'

'Oh Leabhar,' said Deirdre, 'I don't know. I mean I do know, but don't misunderstand me when I say it. I'm lonely for youth ... you – are all so old.'

'Hush, child,' said Leabharcam, 'you must not say that the king is old, and he's coming to visit you today.' And she looked around nervously in case he had already arrived, for he was a silent man.

'But he is old,' said Deirdre, 'and I would dearly love to meet someone who is not; a young man. A young man with those three colours,' she said, pointing to where a raven stood in the snow dipping its beak in the blood of the calf: 'hair as black as the raven; cheeks as red as blood and his body as white as snow.'

'Oh,' cried Leabharcam in terror, 'whisht child, and don't let the king hear you or he would kill him for sure.'

'Kill who?' asked Deirdre immediately.

'Never mind who,' snapped Leabharcam, angry at her mistake, 'there's only one who is the like of that.'

But Deirdre wasn't listening to her.

'Last night,' said Deirdre, 'I saw him in a dream ...'

'The gods between us and all harm,' said Leabharcam, 'you did not!'

'I did,' said Deirdre, 'and it is him I would marry and not the king. The king is old and grey and his face is ugly, and I think he is cruel too.'

'Hush child,' said Leabharcam, seriously worried, 'for if the king heard you talk like that Naisi's life wouldn't be worth that,' and she snapped her crooked fingers with a crack.

'Naisi,' said Deirdre, 'who's he?'

'The man you have just described to me,' said Leabharcam dryly, but with pity and understanding too, for she had been in love once herself, 'though how it is you could do it I don't pretend to know.'

'Naisi,' said Deirdre, 'Naisi?'

NOW NAISI AND HIS brothers Ainle and Ardan, the three sons of Usna, were the best loved of the Red Branch Knights; gracious and gentle in peace, skilful and swift-footed in the hunt, and brave and powerful in battle. And of the three Naisi was foremost of all Ulster's young chiefs. He was also an accomplished musician and he loved to wander abroad by himself with his small harp and sit somewhere and make music, to which he would put a song about what he saw, or what he thought or what he felt, or remembered.

One day he had gone out with his harp and was sitting under a beech tree on a hillock playing and singing just like this, his strong, aquiline face with the long dark hair thrown back, and the notes issuing from his white throat in competition with the birds.

It was springtime and the time for Deirdre's marriage with the king was approaching. And the closer it came the more restless and uneasy she had become until at last she was unable to stand being confined any longer and she persuaded Leabharcam to allow her to go for walks outside the limits of the fortress and the garden, where she could feel free, if only for a time. At first, from fear of what Conor might do if he found out, Leabharcam refused, but as Deirdre's distress increased, and she seemed to become really ill, Leabharcam at last agreed, and, secretly, Deirdre would go out in the morning or afternoon when the king wasn't expected and walk abroad in the world she knew little about.

And on one such day, when she had wandered to the edge of the wood where the sunlight on the grass was broken into brocaded strips by the leafy branches, she stopped when she heard music and the voice of a man making a song.

Now it is said that when Naisi made music the cows who heard it gave two-thirds more milk – and it may be true, for farmers today are milking to music for that very reason – and any man or woman who heard him sing forgot their troubles while they listened and were filled with joy. And it was just like that with Deirdre; she was filled with joy.

She walked towards the music and, as soon as she saw who it was who sang, she recognised Naisi, though she had never set eyes on him before. And she went, at once shyly and impelled beyond herself, to pass him, but with her eyes down. And as she went past him, Naisi, seeing her beauty, couldn't help but remark on it because he had never seen her before, in Emhain or anywhere else; and he knew very well that a girl as beautiful as this wouldn't stay away from Emhain for very long unless there was a reason for it.

'Oh,' he cried, 'how beautiful ...' and then, mischievously: 'How fair the doe that springs past me.'

But Deirdre answered him seriously: 'It is easy for does to be gentle and fair where there are no bucks.'

Then Naisi recognised her from the stories he had heard, and he was circumspect in his answer.

'You have your buck,' he said, 'the buck of the whole province of Ulster, King Conor himself.'

'But I don't love him,' she said, 'he's old and ugly, and if I were to choose, I would choose a young buck like yourself.' And she looked straight at him. Now this was not brazenness on her part, but she spoke with her heart and with truth.

'You are the king's,' said Naisi.

'You say that only to avoid me,' said Deirdre.

'No,' replied Naisi, 'but because of the prophecy of Catha.'

Then Deirdre pulled a briar of wild roses and flung it at his head, saying: 'You are disgraced now if you reject me.'

'Please,' said Naisi, 'Deirdre, I love you too, but ...'

She went up to him, half laughing, half crying; and in anger too and took both his ears in her hands.

'Two ears of mockery and shame you'll have,' she said, shaking his head, 'if you leave me.'

He grinned at her then.

'Let me go ... wife!' he said, and she let him go and they put their arms around one another.

Then Naisi said no more, but picked up his harp again and composed another song straight out of his heart and it was the sweetest, and the saddest; the most moving, the most joyous that he ever made. And Deirdre sat beside him until his brothers Ainle and Ardan came through the wood looking for Naisi.

They were horrified when they heard who Deirdre was and that Naisi intended to take her with him, and tried to dissuade him. But he was adamant, for he had given her all his love; all his stored knowledge and memories, all that he was and all that he knew. He told his brothers and, when they saw how it was between them, they said no more. Then Deirdre gave Naisi three kisses, and to his brothers each a kiss, and Naisi put her on his shoulder and together the four of them went through the wood.

They spent that night at Naisi's father's castle and, next day, with their entire following – a hundred and fifty men, a hundred and fifty women, and the same number of hounds and servants – they left Ulster, but not before Naisi and Deirdre were married.

For several months they went from place to place, serving with this king or that; in Assaroe, near Ballyshannon, to Ben Eadair near Howth; from north to south and from east to west, and all the time Conor sought revenge and tried to kill them, either by ambush or by war, and always they escaped.

Because, apart from the prophecy and the fact that she was under his protection which had been flouted, as Deirdre grew into a beautiful young woman and in spite of the fact that he was surrounded in his court with the choice women of the land, Conor had grown a passion for Deirdre who was lovelier than anything that he had seen or dreamed of; and he had nursed his passion jealously and kept it for his old age and his marriage with Deirdre which was to have taken place a few weeks after she ran away with Naisi.

And so he harassed and harried the sons of Usna; plotted and planned for their destruction with a bitterness and vengeance that consumed his life from the moment he learned that Deirdre was gone; consumed his life, and grew in him as it consumed it.

And so Naisi, when he found no resting place in Ireland where he was driven and always driven by the men of Ulster, determined to leave the country and to go to Alba, Scotland, where he landed with his followers, drove the wild inhabitants from the place, and carved out for himself a kingdom which had its seat in Glen Etive. And there he ruled with Deirdre and his brothers and became a powerful prince who loved his queen, Deirdre, with an immensity of love that grew and multiplied with the experience of each day.

They lived there in great happiness and contentment for many years. Sometimes Naisi and his followers warred with the native Picts, but more often they were at peace with their neighbours and with themselves.

But all the time King Conor's bitterness and lust for revenge grew, for old though he was, with sons in middle age, he burned for the lovely Deirdre; she had become an obsession with him and, at the moment when he was about to achieve it, she was whipped away from him. Now only one thought was in his mind: revenge. But try as he would he could think of no way of achieving it. There was no point in sending a man, or a group of men, to assassinate his enemies, even if he could find the knights willing to do it, for Naisi had a strong camp in Glen Etive, and short of a full-scale invasion there didn't seem a solution. An invasion Conor wasn't prepared for; his people would not stand for an undertaking of that magnitude for such a little cause and might – as he very well knew with his own example and that of Fergus before him – depose him for another if he pressed the point.

But, as these things so often happen, the answer came to him one evening at a mighty festival at Emhain Macha, when all the greatest lords and nobles in Ulster were assembled.

Conor sat at the head of the enormous principal table, with Fergus, old now but still vigorous, at his right hand; on the other side sat the mighty warrior Conall Cearnach and completing the awe-inspiring foursome at the top of the table was Cuchulain, still young, but of a terrible, fate-filled, brooding aspect:

Beside Conall as of old
Sat Cuchulain, sombre, cold.
For though his youth lay on his shoulder
His deep eye was cold, and older;
And in a red gloom round his head
A dark raven of the dead
Sang slowly songs of doom;
All who looked at him and saw
Felt their thoughts grow great with awe
For his tragedy loomed loudly by his head.
Like a god he sat before them
Never seeing those about him
And all men when they saw him went in dread.

Conor looked round the tremendous hall, whose farthest depths he could not distinguish from where he sat, though he knew that it was thronged with knights and retainers. Nearer, close to the seats of the three heroes and himself, there were three empty seats that he could see very well. They were the places of the three sons of Usna which had remained like that ever since they went. And none ever remarked on it for it was known that the king had commanded that no one should speak of the sons of Usna in his presence. And it was while he looked broodingly at these three empty places that the means of getting his revenge occurred to Conor.

Slowly he glanced up from beneath his brows, his hard eyes beginning to light with excitement that he made an effort to conceal.

Gradually the scowl vanished from his face and he began to be merry; he laughed and made jokes and pressed more food and drink on the knights and his guests, and when the banquet was at its height, he raised his kingly voice and cried: 'Well, oh nobles and chiefs of Ulster, and Knights of the Red Branch, I would have you tell me something ... in all your travels among the countries of the world have you ever seen a court more royal or a banquet more satisfying?'

'Never,' they roared.

'Is there anything lacking?' shouted Conor back at them.

'Nothing,' they roared again.

'But there is,' shouted Conor, silencing them. 'The Three Lights of Valour of the Gael, as we know them; the three sons of

Usna.'

For a moment there was a great silence. Then Conor continued: 'It is a pity that for the sake of a woman they are not here with us.'

Then there was a tumult.

'Had we dared to say that, Conor,' they cried, 'we would have had them home long ago. Had we the three sons of Usna back again, all Ireland would give way before Ulster, so great is their strength.'

'I didn't know,' said Conor, 'that you wanted them back, but if that is your wish, let us send a messenger to Glen Etive to bring them home.'

There was another silence then; for the nobles realised that there was hardly a man among them whose word the sons of Usna would trust after the way in which they had been hounded.

'And whose word would they trust?' asked a voice.

Conor smiled craftily to himself, but it did not show on his face.

'I understand,' he said, 'that of all my nobles there are only three whose word the sons of Usna would accept; and they are Fergus, or Conall Cearnach or Cuchulain himself.'

'Then let them go,' cried the knights, 'and bring us back the Three Lights of Valour of the Gael.'

This was according to Conor's plan. Later that evening, when the banqueting was nearly done, and stories and music and drinking were being followed in groups around the fires and in the corners of the hall, Conor took Conall Cearnach aside into an ante-room.

He had already prepared his speech. He ushered Conall to a seat beside him on a cushioned couch and, leaning forward in the gloom, for the ante-room was lit only with a rush-wick lamp, he said: 'Conall, you heard what happened at the banquet tonight. Much to my surprise, it seems the men of Ulster want the sons of Usna home again. I, of course, would like nothing better. And you know that you, or Fergus or Cuchulain must be the ones to bring them back. But a thought occurs to me. Suppose, by any chance that they did come back under your protection and safeguard, and that something should happen to them, they were killed, for example, through some mischance, then what would happen?'

Conall looked back at the king levelly, and said: 'If such a mischance,' and he stressed the word slightly, 'should happen while they were under my protection, not only him whose hand was stained, but every man in Ulster who had done them harm would feel my vengeance.'

Conor sighed and frowned. 'I was afraid you'd say that,' he replied. 'You are a man of great loyalty, Conall. But it is misguided. I had a good reason for asking you that question. To find if your loyalty was to me, or to anyone else.'

Conall Cearnach said nothing. He stood up, looked at Conor, bowed a little stiffly, and stalked out quivering with anger.

Conor next had Cuchulain summoned. But when he saw the young man with the countenance of a tormented god standing before him, even Conor's cruel purpose faltered.

He asked his question falteringly and without looking Cuchulain in the face.

Cuchulain remained standing while the king spoke. Then quietly and without expression; almost without inflexion, he said: 'Conor, if any harm came to the sons of Usna while they were under my protection, not all the riches of the eastern world would keep your head on your shoulders in lieu of theirs.' And without saying another word he turned and walked away, leaving Conor, shaken, behind him.

Then Conor sent for Fergus.

It was on Fergus that he knew he must rely, so, while he was waiting, he thought about what he would say to him. When Fergus came in Conor greeted him warmly and threw an arm around his shoulder, and said, as if he were speaking to a lifelong comrade and friend:

'Fergus, there's a problem about the sons of Usna that just occurred to me; supposing any harm did come to them while they're here, what then?'

'What do you mean?' asked Fergus.

'Well, what would you do, for example?' asked Conor. 'It's not unforeseeable, you know.'

Now Fergus didn't know how to reply. For one thing Conor's question had been so veiled that there was no indication of anything behind it; and even if there had been, Fergus' own position was such that he might not have seen it. For he had been set high in honour and position by Conor; to bring back the sons of Usna would raise his prestige even higher, particularly among the nobles and people of the province, and might mean the return of the throne, if not to him, at least to his children. And so, after a long silence in which he considered all these things, and while Conor watched him closely, he replied: 'If any Ulsterman harmed them, Conor, I'd avenge the hurt. But I don't anticipate that any hurt would come to them while they came under the protection of your sovereign word.'

'Nor,' said Conor opening his eyes and spreading his hands wide, 'do I. But it could happen. And if it did ...?'

'If it did,' said Fergus darkly, 'then I'd have revenge.'

'On whom?'

'On whoever did it, of course,' replied Fergus.

'And what about my position?'

'Your position?'

'Yes. Would you have revenge on me too?'

'Why should I,' replied Fergus, 'for I know well that you would not harm them when they come under the seal of your word.'

'Therefore you would not turn your sword against me; I knew I could trust you, Fergus, you are a loyal man, and a true king. Therefore tomorrow let you go and bring the king's message to the sons of Usna, and say that he longs to welcome them, and tell them eat no meat until they reach the feast I will have prepared for them here at Emhain.'

And so, on the following day, Fergus with his sons Illan the Fair and Buinne the Red, together with Fergus' shield bearer Caillan, sailed from Dun Borrach for Glen Etive.

But they had hardly sailed out of the harbour, where Conor had come to see them off with every appearance of goodwill, when he began to put his plan into effect. He turned and rode towards the fort of Borrach which dominated the harbour, Borrach, who was the local chief, by his side.

'I believe,' said Conor, 'that you are preparing a feast for me.'

'That is so, Conor,' replied Borrach, 'and right glad I am to be able to do it.'

'Well,' said Conor, 'it is a great hardship to me to think of disappointing you, but I shall reward you in other ways. Affairs of state confine me to Emhain at the moment, but Fergus Mac Rí stands beside me in power in Ulster and I would have you accept him in my place. When he returns from Alba invite him in my stead, and I will hold the honour paid to him as paid to me.'

'He will feast with me for three days,' said Borrach, 'for we are brothers of the Red Branch and he is under vow not to refuse the hospitality of any man when it is offered to him.'

Conor smiled again to himself when he heard this, which he already knew; for, in common with the other knights of the Red Branch, Fergus had made pledges which would bind him for life when he took his knighthood. These vows they made in the presence of kings and nobles and they dared not violate them, for whoever did so was utterly dishonoured; and one of Fergus' vows was that he would never refuse such an invitation.

Furthermore Conor knew that he would not refuse to accept the banquet at which he represented the king. But he had also laid it on Fergus to bring the sons of Usna to Emhain, knowing that they, too, were bound to come without delay when summoned by the king. And so he intended to separate the sons of Usna from their protector, and get them in his power.

Meanwhile Fergus' ship sailed north-east from Ireland, through the rough passage of the North channel between the two countries, and onward until he sighted the coast of Argyle and turned towards Loch Etive. As his ship sailed up the calm loch, bordered by the rounded shoulders of heather-covered hills, the rippling water brown near the boat but blue and silver where it reflected the sunlight and the sky, Fergus stood in the prow and raised a great hunting cry.

Deirdre and Naisi were sitting in the sun-garden of their castle in the glen just at this time. It was warm, and the sun played on them as they sat there with a chess board between them. All around them the peaceful activities of the castle were in progress, and they could see and hear their people contentedly at work in the township that had grown about the castle.

But Naisi was oppressed and frowning, for he was suffering from a severe bout of homesickness for Ulster. His thoughts were not on the game and Deirdre was winning, even though she did not want to and ached within to comfort him.

She smiled at him encouragingly, but the look he returned was bitter; not with the reproach she read in it, but bitter for all that. And as she was about to ask him what ailed him, they heard the shout from far down the loch.

Naisi looked up, like a stag suddenly alert.

'That's the cry of an Ulsterman,' he said, his head cocked and his ears straining.

Deirdre too had heard the cry and moreover had recognised the voice which brought fear to her heart.

Quickly she replied: 'Don't be thinking wishfully, my love. It is only some poor Scotch hunter coming home late. Your move ...'

And Naisi sank back in his seat and tried to play; but twice more Fergus hallooed, and each time nearer until at last Naisi sprang up and cried: 'It is an Ulsterman, and Fergus at that; Deirdre ...'

But she stood up too and came beside him and laid her hand on his arm.

'I know,' she said, 'I knew it all the time, but Naisi ...'

'But why didn't you say so?' he asked.

'Because,' she replied, 'last night I dreamt that three birds flew here to us from Emhain carrying a drop of honey each in their beaks which they left here with us; but when they flew away they took with them three drops of our blood.'

'And what do you think that means, my princess?' asked Naisi indulgently.

'That Fergus comes here with false messages of peace, sweet as honey; but he will take away with him three drops of blood, you and Ainle and Ardan to your deaths.'

'Oh, nonsense,' cried Naisi, his heart bursting to see Fergus and hear from Ireland, 'above all others, we can trust Fergus ... run down, Ardan, and show him the way here.'

And Ardan ran to the shore and the sight of Fergus and his two sons was to him like rain on the parched grass. He welcomed Fergus, and threw his arms around his neck and those of his sons and gave them three kisses and brought them to the castle.

There Naisi and Deirdre greeted them warmly and asked for news from home.

'The greatest news I have,' said Fergus, 'is that Conor has sent me to bring you back to Emhain and your place in the Red Branch and will restore your lands and property; I am myself a pledge for your safety.'

'There is no need for them to go,' said Deirdre, 'here they are as powerful as Conor is in Ulster.'

'To be in one's native land,' said Fergus, 'is better than power and prosperity elsewhere.'

'That is true,' said Naisi, 'for I would far rather be in Ireland, though I have more land and power here.'

But Deirdre was not so easily satisfied; the memory of her dream and her fear of the consequences made her argue against return to Ireland from Alba where they were peaceful and happy.

'You need not worry,' said Fergus, 'I myself am the pledge and guardian of your safety.'

But still Deirdre tried to stop them. 'Do not go, Naisi, do not go,' she cried, 'it is a trick. I know it, in my heart I know it.' And she began to lament and cry in great anguish so that it was hard for the four men to see it or to comfort her. Then Naisi said: 'Deirdre, my love, your fears are understandable, but ... that is all. You know as well as I do that we can accept Fergus' word, and that is good enough for me. We'll go tomorrow.'

THAT NIGHT THEY SPENT in reminiscing and learning all the news from home from Fergus, who was amazed and impressed in his turn with what they had accomplished in this wild and uncultivated land. Only Deirdre remained quiet and while the night was still young she crept away to bed on the plea of a headache; but it was heartache that sickened her as she lay alone staring though the window of her room at the moon drenched glen.

Next day they made their preparations early and before the sun was high were sailing down the still loch towards the ocean and Ulster. The men stood gaily about the deck, craning forward to see ahead, but Deirdre alone sat in the stern and looked back towards Scotland; at the round, blue hills and wooded slopes, and in her heart she made this song:

> Dear land of Alba, I would not go
> From your green slopes beside the sea;
> My heavy heart is dull and slow
> To be abandoning your peace with Naisi.

Dear glens I know and love so well
Where he and I made love together;
Hearing the cuckoo's summer spell
And the hush of the snow clad winter heather.

Dear to me your crystal water;
Dear to me your sunlit sea;
I'd never leave your welcome laughter
Only to be with my love, Naisi.

Next day they sailed into the harbour beneath the fort of Borrach who was at the quayside to greet them. He welcomed them all with warm kisses and then, turning to Fergus, said: 'And for you, comrade, I have prepared a banquet which will last three days, so stay with me. But Conor wishes the sons of Usna to speed to Emhain Macha that he may welcome them with a banquet of his own.'

When Fergus heard this he became crimson with anger, and said: 'You have done wrong, Borrach, to invite me to a banquet knowing I cannot refuse; and knowing too that I am under obligation to bring the sons of Usna to Emhain under my protection without delay.'

But Borrach, who was in the king's confidence, insisted: 'It is the king's command,' he said, 'that you represent him here.'

Then Fergus asked Naisi what he should do, but it was Deirdre who answered for her husband. 'The choice is yours, Fergus, between a feast and the lives of the sons of Usna. They seem a high price to pay for a dinner.'

'I will not forsake them,' said Fergus, 'nor will I break my vow. I will stay here and my two sons, Illan the Fair and Buinne the Red, will protect them and my honour.'

Then Naisi said, and he could not hide the contempt from his voice: 'We don't need your sons' protection, Fergus; our own arms have always been enough protection for us.'

And so saying he walked away from Fergus in terrible anger, followed by Ainle and Ardan and Deirdre and Fergus' two sons. But Deirdre called Naisi and tried to persuade him not to go to Emhain Macha that night.

'Let's go to Cuchulain at Dun Dealgan,' she said, 'we can stay with him until it is time for Fergus to come with us to Emhain Macha.'

But the others would not agree, saying that it would look like cowardice on their part if they did so. And the sons of Fergus said that they would protect them as if they had been Fergus himself.

They reached Slieve Fuad and rested there for a while, and as they were about to go on Naisi noticed that Deirdre was asleep. Gently he woke her, but when she saw him a look of terror crossed her face and she threw her arms around him and clung to him.

'What is it, my love,' he asked her, 'what is the matter?'

In grief and in fear she told him. 'I had a dream,' she said, 'I'm afraid.'

'Another one,' Naisi chided her gently, 'you are too apt to dream, love.'

But she clung to him while he tried to comfort her and said:

'I dreamt that I saw you and Ardan and Ainle and Illan the Fair headless and bloody, but there was Buinne the Red without a mark on his body.'

'Hush,' said Naisi, 'hush. It was only a dream.'

'Oh Naisi,' she cried, 'I'm frightened. Let's not go to Emhain.'

But Naisi thought, so terribly upset was Deirdre, that weariness and terror had made her distraught and only pressed on all the harder so that she might get rest, in spite of all her protests.

'Look,' she cried as they approached, 'even over the city there hangs a bloody cloud. Isn't that omen enough for you?'

But Naisi was too worried about her to listen to what she said, for he loved her greatly.

Then she said in a quieter voice: 'Naisi, there is one test by which you will know if Conor is planning harm to us or not. If he welcomes us into his palace, then everything is all right, for no king will harm a guest in his own house; but if he sends you elsewhere, then he means treachery.'

Well then, when they reached the city they were met at the gates by a messenger from Conor to light them through the streets, and who said to them: 'Conor bids you welcome, and for this night would ask you to share the hospitality of the House of the Red Branch where a banquet awaits you.'

And he began to lead them towards the House of the Red Branch. Deirdre said to Naisi: 'It is as I said, he is planning some treachery, let us go somewhere else.'

But Naisi said no, that there was nowhere more fitting for the champions of the Red Branch to spend the night than in the House of the Red Branch, and he said this to comfort her, for he was annoyed that the king did not take them to the palace, and Illan the Fair said: 'The sons of Fergus have never showed cowardliness or unmanliness, and we will not show it now.'

So they were taken to the House of the Red Branch where a banquet was spread for them. But neither Deirdre nor Naisi were interested in food; he because he was worried about her, and she because she feared Conor. So Naisi called for a chessboard, and said: 'You remember the last game we played in Scotland and you beat me? Well, now that we are home again, I'll beat you.' And he smiled lovingly at her.

But Deirdre did not smile back, for a great heaviness and terror for what might happen soon was weighing on her heart, and in her mind she felt that there was not long more for them to enjoy.

Meantime Conor sat in his palace brooding with impatience at the thought that Deirdre was so near and yet unattainable. So he called Leabharcam, who was still alive, and said to her: 'Go and see if Deirdre is still as lovely as when you reared her, for if so there is not on the ridge of the world a woman more beautiful.'

But Leabharcam still retained her great love for Deirdre and when she reached the House of the Red Branch they fell into each other's arms. She greeted Deirdre and Naisi with kisses and tears mixed; with laughter and with lamentation, and among her warm greetings she warned them of what Conor planned.

'Child,' she said to Deirdre, 'be careful; and you, Naisi, and your brothers and the sons of Fergus too, be careful. For this night there is evil planned in Emhain, and I know that the Three Torches of Valour of the Gael are to be assailed and attacked and killed. So guard well and fight well and defend well that ye may last until Fergus comes.'

Then she went back to the king, and Conor asked her for her news.

'I have good news,' she said, 'and bad news. And the good news is that the three sons of Usna, the three valiant champions of Ulster, are back among the Red Branch and at your side once more; and the bad news is that care and worry and suffering have changed Deirdre so that she has little of the bloom and beauty that were on her when she went away.'

When Conor heard this his jealousy went from him and satisfaction took its place, but, when he had drunk some more, the thought of Deirdre returned to him and he distrusted the word of Leabharcam. Then Conor called a man called Trendorn to him and said: 'Do you remember who killed your father, Trendorn?'

'I'm not likely to forget it,' said the glowering Trendorn, 'it was Naisi the son of Usna.'

'Very well,' said Conor, 'then go now and tell me what Deirdre is like.'

So Trendorn went down to the House of the Red Branch, but when he found the great doors and windows barred and bolted, he became afraid that the sons of Usna were waiting for him or one like him, so he climbed to a small window high in the wall and looked through.

Naisi and Deirdre were still playing chess, but as Trendorn looked in Deirdre happened to glance up and seeing the face at the window let out a gasp. Naisi following her eyes, flung the chessman he had in his hand at the window with all his force and struck Trendorn in the eye with it, so hard, that it blew the eyeball from its socket and Trendorn fell back to the ground.

Then Trendorn returned to Conor and told him what had happened. This suited Conor admirably for, in the appearance of great anger, he rushed into the palace hall where some of his nobles were and cried: 'The man who has maimed my servant would himself be king.'

He had already learned from Trendorn that Deirdre was as beautiful as ever and he let his jealousy work on his wrath until he roused his troops crying that the sons of Usna had tried to kill Trendorn.

He rushed out of his palace and ordered a battalion of mercenary troops that were standing by in the yard to attack the Red Branch House at once, capture the sons of Usna and bring them to him for punishment.

And the troops attacked the House and tried to set it on fire. But the great oaken doors withstood their siege. Then Buinne the Red stood up and said: 'It is my place to go out and fight, for it was on me that my father laid the charge of protecting you.' So the great doors were thrown open and, together with his men, Buinne ran out to do battle with the mercenaries of Conor.

Between them he and his men succeeded in putting out the fires that threatened the Red Branch House, and in slaughtering about a hundred and fifty of the attacking troops.

'Who is that man who is destroying my attack?' asked Conor.

'Buinne the Red, son of Fergus,' said someone.

'We bought his father to our side,' said Conor, 'and we must buy the son.'

And so saying he stepped forward with his arm raised and stopped the fighting. The terrible noise that is like no other noise died away the way thunder dies away across a hill, and the men stood back from each other warily and breathless. Conor looked closely at Buinne; the heavy face, the determined clenched hand on his sword, and called him over. Buinne came stalking over, his heavy sword still dripping blood held out before him as he came up to the king.

Without preliminary Conor said: 'Buinne, you do not know what you are about, fighting me. I have given your father ten thousand acres of land and ten cattle for each acre; you'll get the same if you'll fight with me against these traitors.'

Buinne merely shook his head and turned to go. But when he turned his back upon the king and faced again the black and armed hosts he fought, and every face a warrior's face, and every spear full ten feet long and every arm a strong arm and every sword gleaming dull and bright along its centre where no blood as yet had run along the ridged blade, he knew that he must die. He knew the sons of Usna, too, must die, and that they'd die in any case if he should die or not. So he spoke to the king and said: 'I will do that.'

And when Deirdre saw him join the throng she cried: 'Buinne has deserted you, Naisi; like father like son.'

'But he did good work before he left,' said Naisi. By now the king's mercenaries were thundering at the door again, and Illan the Fair said: 'If Fergus was a traitor, and Buinne was a traitor, then I will not be one as long as this straight sword is in my hand; I will not forsake the sons of Usna.'

Then the doors were thrown open and Illan the Fair and his men rushed out and made three swift onslaughts on the hosts of Conor round the House of the Red Branch, and slew and killed three hundred of his men and then rushed in again between the mighty doors held open for the purpose.

Inside Deirdre and her husband were still intent upon their game, for the champions and their wives would never show a sign of fear or of alarm; and calmed their hearts as if it was nothing but a wind that raged outside. Again the troops of Conor thronged about and tried to fire the ancient House and out upon them like a lion rushed Illan, destroying their work and them in one red rout. Then Conor, who had seen it all, enquired who this young hero was and when he heard, said: 'Fiachra, my son, both you and Illan were born on the same night. Take my shield, Ocean, Flight, my spear and Victory, my sword, and vanquish him before he does more harm.'

And Fiachra went and so they fought a fair and warlike, red and bloody, manly, bitter, savage, hot and vehement, terrible battle with each other between the silent hosts of men who, in the flickering torchlight and from the fires that glowed where battle had incendiarised the city streets, looked on. Till Illan in a sudden twist hurled Fiachra to the ground so that the royal king's son was forced to crouch beneath the shield, the Ocean. And it was also called the Moaner because in battle it was known that the king's shield moaned when he who wore it was in danger, no matter if it were the king himself or one of his own blood; and if he were in fear of death the moan was heard across the face of Ireland and was answered by the Three Great Moaning Waves of Erin; the Wave of Tuatha at the Bann, the Wave of Rory in the Bay of Dundrum and the Wave of Cliona in Glandore.

And so it moaned. And when from a distance Conall Cearnach heard the moan, he thought it was the king himself who lay in danger and rushed fiercely to the spot and, without pausing to see who it was, attacked the man beneath the shelter of the Moaner, struck him from behind.

'Ah,' cried Illan the Fair, 'who struck me from behind when he might have had fair battle had he sought it?'

'And who are you,' cried Conall, for he still didn't recognise him, 'to attack the king?'

'Illan the son of Fergus – and you are Conall Cearnach – and you have done wrong to kill me while I am defending the sons of Usna who are in the Red Branch House under my father's protection.'

'By God,' cried Conall, 'you will not go unavenged.' And lifting his sword he struck the head from Fiachra below his beard. Then he turned in grief and rage and stalked fierce and silent from the battlefield.

Illan, dying within the circle of his enemies, called to Naisi to defend himself bravely; and then, with his remaining strength, he flung his arms into the House of the Red Branch so that the victors would not have them, and the shadow of death fell on him and he died.

Now another great battalion of mercenaries attacked the House of the Red Branch and tried to fire it with burning faggots. And Ainle sallied forth and held them back a while, and then came Ardan to relieve him, and finally Naisi came himself and fought with them until the morning's dawn and so terrible was the slaughter that they made, the sons of Usna, on the hired hosts of Conor that he feared his army would be spoiled; for until the seashore sands and all the forest leaves; the gleaming dew-drops on the morning grass or the fiery stars of night are calculated, then it would not be possible to tabulate the heads and hands, the severed legs and sundered limbs that there lay red and bloody at the hands of Naisi and his brothers.

Finally the three heroes and their few followers made a phalanx with Deirdre in its centre and swept down upon the ranks of Conor. When the king saw what was happening he called Catha, the druid, and said: 'It would be better for us if these three heroes fought for us rather than against us. With their few followers they have near decimated my army, and I would willingly receive them back into my service. Go to them and bring them to me under my pledge that no harm will befall them.'

And Catha, by no means distrusting the king, for his face was earnest and in his deep brown eyes the sombreness of truth looked out at him intensely, went and raised a mighty wood before them, through which they thought no man could pass, so black and tangled were its limbs. But without pausing; without a halt to see the way, the sons of Usna strode through it. And then the druid rose and stood tall and white and straight against the pale light of the dawn and raised his arms before him. His face was lined with lines of concentration and the sweat rolled from his brow and suddenly a stormy sea rose up before them on the plain, roaring and boiling to prevent their progress. But on and through the waves they went without a backward glance, with Deirdre riding on Naisi's shoulder as when he carried her away.

'Your spell is good,' said Conor with a hidden curse, 'but not good enough. Try another.'

Then, willing up so great a force that all those people standing round could feel the power of it, the king himself no less, the druid threw the stored strength of all his mind about the sons of Usna.

He conjured up a great morass, a bog of green and brown that clung about their feet and dragged them down and clogged their limbs so that they could not move. Then to where they stood, held fast in the bog, the men of Ulster ran, for they were not affected by the spell, and bound them with chains. Then Catha raised the spell, and reminded the king of his promised word. But Conor laughed at him and told him he was an old man who didn't understand the art of diplomacy.

Then the king called loudly, a smile of triumph on his face, for one of his men to kill the sons of Usna. But no man came. He called again and still no one came to do it. And a third time he called and as he called his anger grew in him, because he knew why they would not come. Turning to where they stood, Deirdre standing beside Naisi, holding his hand bound as it was with iron, the king cursed and swore at them, but got no answer other than a steady look from each, more kingly than he ever owned himself.

But in the household of the king a son of Lochlann's king called Mainni Rough Hand lived, half savage and half wild and willing to do anything he was bidden. The king sent for him whose brothers Naisi had some years before killed in battle, and this man undertook to kill the sons of Usna.

Then, with a grin of pleasure on his face, this Mainni stooped to where the sword of Naisi – a heritage from Mananaan – lay fallen on the grass. He swung it so it sang above his head, then quicker than the eye might follow him he turned completely round and struck, with that one blow, the sons of Usna's heads from off their shoulders.

And, when they saw what happened, the men of Ulster sent forth three great cries of sorrow and lamentation. Then Deirdre fell down beside the bodies wailing and weeping in unsurpassable grief; she tore her hair and her garments and fondled the mutilated bodies and bitterly moaned over them.

Then the men of Ulster opened a grave for the sons of Usna, and Deirdre, when her calmness had returned, made this lament for them:

The lions of the hill are gone
And I am left to weep alone.
Without my love I can't abide,
So dig the grave both deep and wide.

The hawks of the mountain are flown
And I am left to weep alone.
My grief the turning world would cover
Until I lie with my true lover.

I am Deirdre the joyless
For a short time alive
Though to end life be evil
It is worse to survive.

Then Conor had her brought to Emhain Macha by force, and for a year she lived there, but no smile or laugh or any sign of living stirred in her for all that time. And finally, when he grew tired of her disdain and found that he did not, in truth, love her at all, Conor decided to taunt her and try to get some satisfaction that way, and provoke her anger by his cruelty.

So he said to her: 'What is it, Deirdre, that you hate above all things on this earth?'

And she replied: 'You yourself, and Eoghan of Durracht' – which was the name and title Conor had bestowed on Mainni for his job as executioner.

And Conor smiled and said, 'Well, in that case, since you have spent a year with me in Emhain, it is only right that you should spend another year with him in Durracht.'

Then, wasting no time, he ordered that his chariot should be harnessed to the swiftest horses in the yard. Now this cruelty of his was no accident, for Mainni, or Eoghan as he now preferred to be called, was standing near them all this time; and it was perhaps the remembrance of what had passed between the three of them a year before that moved Conor to this final act of perverted passion.

All this time while waiting for the horses Conor smiled, and Eoghan smiled; but Deirdre never smiled. And when it was ready the three of them with the driver mounted the great chariot and drove to Durracht, Deirdre sitting between Conor and the lasciviously smiling Eoghan. Across the hills of Emhain they charged at a gallop, the black clods of the earth flying like birds flocking behind them, thrown up by the stampeding feet of the horses.

Then Conor turned to Deirdre and she looked back at him, so that his eye dropped; but it passed on to Eoghan, and she followed his look. And from some great malice in him Conor spoke, just as they were passing the grave of the sons of Usna: 'Deirdre,' he said, 'the look you pass between Eoghan and myself is like the hot look of a ewe between two rams.'

Then, with a cry, Deirdre sprang up and leaped out of the chariot, smashing her head against the stone that rose above the grave of the Three Lights of Valour of the Gael, Naisi, Ainle and Ardan. And when they buried her, in the same grave which she had asked be dug for four and not for three, her arm fell round the neck of Naisi where he lay as fresh as on the day he died, and on his mouth her mouth rested, and so they were buried in the one tomb. All the men of Ulster who stood by wept aloud.

And from their grave there grew two straight and slender trees of yew, the branches and the leaves of which entwined and made an arch above.

This, then, is the story of Deirdre and the Sons of Usna. And when Fergus had freed himself from Borrach's banquet and found that the sons of Usna had been slain and himself dishonoured, he left the court of Conor in a mighty rage and with all his people went to Connacht.

There, mindful of his word at last, in a fire of immense rage, he gathered all the warlike hosts of Maeve and made war on Ulster. And Catha, who indeed was the grandfather of the sons of Usna, for they were his daughter's children, cursed King Conor that none of his breed might ever rule in Emhain Macha again. And so it was, for when the mightiest of the heroes Cuchulain died, strapped against a pillared rock having stood alone to face the warring hordes of Maeve, then Emhain fell, and overgrew with great and waving tufts of grass.

The Children of Lir

At the battle of Tailteann, fought so long ago that no one now could tell you very much about it save its name and location and even about that they might be doubtful, the Milesians, who brought with them the modern wonders of the eastern world, overcame the Tuatha de Danaan who clung to the older and more mystic ways and wrested from them the lordship over all of Ireland. And it is not known whether that battle at Tailteann, which was the place of hosting each year for the great games like those held across the ocean on the Corinthian Isthmus; it is not known whether that battle was one of blood and carnage and death and destruction on the jagged battlefield, or of honoured and symbolic victory on the sculptured field of sport. All that is known is that at Tailteann the Milesians were victorious over the De Danaan, but that they subsequently held them in high esteem for their knowledge, wisdom and command of mysteries, while they themselves took over the duties of administering the country.

As time passed the Milesians became more and more people of the world, active and vigorous, whose minds were turned towards the future and its development, and the Tuatha de Danaan receded more and more into a sphere of mystery and of imagination where they were their own lords and masters. And so each side conceded to the other what was of least significance to itself, and gained from the other what was of most importance to itself, which was a very sensible arrangement ... for it is unknown the number of wars and disputes; countless the amount of blood spilled and bodies mutilated, for want of a few people having the good sense to exchange something of little value to them, instead of holding fast to something that is of little value to them but of great value to another, merely because they happen to have it.

In any event, the De Danaan retreated from the world which the Milesians charged at so successfully, and cultivated their skills as magicians and spirit people and soon inhabited a region parallel to, but quite apart from, that inhabited by the Milesians. And for their great powers and because of their ability in these fields, which the Milesians respected greatly and stood in awe of, they were paid considerable honour and acknowledgement from the newcomers.

But, before all this happened the De Danaan from the five provinces of Ireland assembled together to choose a king to rule over them, for their leaders were of one mind that it was no longer to their advantage, but greatly to their disadvantage, to be divided and split up into separate communities each owing its allegiance to one lord or prince, so that there was no common purpose among them except when all were in peril – and even then it wasn't always too easy to put them of one mind about a thing.

So the chiefs and lords, of whom there were many, decided that they would have a single king above the others to rule over them and to provide a common leader, lawgiver and seat of justice for all and they went into conclave to elect such a one. Now of all the chiefs there were five from whom the king would be chosen. These were the greatest and most powerful chiefs among them; also the wisest and most respected, and they were the two sons of the Dagda, Eoai Ollamh, oracle and once great king of all the De Danaan for more than seventy years, but who had been wounded so severely at the second battle of Moytura with the Firbolgs and Formorians (wounded, indeed, by Caitlin, the buck-toothed wife of Balor of the Evil Eye himself) that he died shortly afterwards in his palace at the Boyne, Bruch na Boinne. His two sons were Aengus Óg, who himself lived now at Brugh na Boinne, and Bodbh Dearg, the great king of Connacht who had been attacked by the Fomorians and Firbolgs so that it sparked off that same battle of Moytura in which his father was fatally wounded, and to which Lugh Lamh Fada had come to help beat the Fomorians. But that story is told elsewhere. Aengus had no wish to be king preferring to stay at Brugh na Boinne where he could pursue his interests in the wisdom and learning of the race, in which he was the most skilled of all. Also candidates for the high office were Illbrec of Assaroe, of whom little is known at all, Midhir the Proud of Bri-Leith, part of whose tale is told elsewhere, and Lir of Sidhe Fionna, and it is with Lir and what happened after the conclave that our story proper begins.

The chiefs, all except the five named above, went into solemn session and debated who would be king above them all. The decision they arrived at, at long last, was that the most proper and fitting person for the high place was the Bodbh Dearg of Connacht, son of the great Dagda. And when the result of their deliberations became known all the candidates were pleased and overjoyed that the Bodbh Dearg was elected – all, that is, but one; and that one was Lir of Sidhe Fionna who took the election of another as a personal affront. He was filled with anger and envy, so certain was he that none but himself would have been considered, and when the truth became known he rose up in a white blaze of anger and straightaway left the assembly, not speaking a word to a man, or showing any mark of respect or homage to the new king.

His ill-mannered behaviour angered the other chiefs who would have sent troops against his fortress at Sidhe Fionna, which was in the County Monaghan near Newtown Hamilton, to burn it and destroy it and kill Lir himself for his ignorant and ill-bred ways, and because he had not submitted to their king elected freely by their council and with his own agreement as well as theirs.

But Bodbh Dearg prevented them. 'Lir,' he said, 'is a powerful man and now an embittered one too. If we attempt to reduce him by force he will defend his territory and many will be killed; but the result will not make me any more your king than I am now, even though he has not submitted to me.'

The lords and chiefs of the De Danaan were impressed with the wisdom and justice of what he said and matters were allowed to rest thus for some time. The Bodbh Dearg ruled over the De Danaan from his palace at Killaloe and Lir lived with his people in isolation and bitterness at Sidhe Fionna. But, in the midst of his loneliness, for it was a lonely stand he had taken where none of the De Danaan other than his own people would associate with him, a new misfortune struck him. His wife died suddenly after an illness that lasted only three days. She was a young and beautiful woman much respected throughout the whole country and the event caused a considerable stir among the De Danaan when they heard of it. When the news reached Killaloe, indeed, where the great Bodbh Dearg was sitting in court with his nobles, the king was moved to compassion at the misfortune of Lir.

'It is at a time such as this,' he told the assembled company, 'that a man stands most in need of friendship, and for Lir, where he is in Sidhe Fionna, separated from his peers, the warm hand of friendship has long been a stranger. Now that his wife is dead my friendship would be of service to him, if he would accept it. As you know,' he went on, 'I am foster-father to the three beautiful daughters of Aillil, king of the Islands of Aran, who are with us here in Killaloe, Niamh, Aoife and Albha, the most accomplished as well as among the most beautiful women in Erin, and Lir would be foolish if he spurned my offer of friendship now.'

The De Danaan again agreed that the king's wisdom was great and his nobility warm and messengers were accordingly sent to Lir at Sidhe Fionna. They took with them the following message: 'Lir, Lord of Sidhe Fionna, Chief of the De Danaan of Frewen, greetings; If you will submit to the king, the Bodbh Dearg, he will give you for a wife one of his three foster-children, the daughters of Aillil of Aran, and his friendship forever.'

When Lir received this message he was pleased. He was bored with lack of congenial companionship and had had time to get over his annoyance at not being elected to the kingship; furthermore alliance with the king, as he considered it, both in friendship and by ties of marriage, was not to be lightly considered. He therefore set out for Killaloe on the following day with a retinue of fifty chariots and they never stopped nor turned aside on their journey from Sidhe Fionna until they reached the palace of the Bodbh Dearg. They were greeted with great enthusiasm by the king and his chiefs, for they were all happy to see the breach in the ranks of the De Danaan healed and though Lir had not at first submitted to the king, he was a good, if proud, man, held in high esteem by his fellows and by the king himself ... therefore he was welcomed with due ceremony, he made his acknowledgements to the king, and that night they were entertained at a banquet given by the people of the Tuatha, the De and the Dan – the entire company of the Tuatha de Danaan, who were at Killaloe.

And it might well be a good thing to explain here that there are many notions of how the Tuatha de Danaan achieved their name. Some say that they brought it with them from the eastern world where they had their origin, some say that they are named after the three sons of Danaan, Brian and Iuchair and Iucharbha and so called because they were skilled in wisdom and magic, and so were known as Tuatha or sorcerers. But it is hard to believe, for they brought with them to Ireland their sorcery from the east. Others say that they were so-called because they were three distinct tribes, but that is a fanciful notion; while the truth, so far as we know it at all, is that they were one people of three parts, or three estates, it might be held today – such as we all are, indeed, for man has not changed very much for all the time he's been here to think – and the first estate was that of the leaders and nobility, for Tuath is the name of a lord; and the second estate were the De, or gods; the druids and magicians, and the third estate were the Dan, the artificers and craftsmen. And it was the representatives of the three estates that gave to the lord Lir a noble banquet when he arrived at Killaloe to make submission to the king of the Tuatha de Danaan.

Next day Lir went to the great hall where the Bodbh Dearg sat on his throne with his queen beside him; and beside them both were their three foster-daughters, Niamh, Aoife and Arbha. And the Bodbh Dearg said to Lir: 'These are my foster-daughters, the most beautiful and most accomplished among all the women of Ireland. Take your choice among them and whichever you choose, she will be your wife.'

Lir looked at them with wonder. For they were all beautiful, and none more beautiful than another. Niamh, the eldest, had the beauty of the winter about her, for her hair was as dark as the trees of the forest against the deep snow lying about their feet, and her skin was as white as that snow that stretches, smooth and gentle, above the bones of the earth. Her eyes were dark and sparkling like the frosted night, and her body was as beautiful, slender and well-shaped as a doe in November.

Aoife, the second daughter of the king of Aran, was like the beauty of the autumn; her hair was dark russet with the glint of gold in it and her skin was the colour of cream from a richly fed cow; her eyes were hazel with green flecks in them and her form was soft and voluptuous with the ripeness of youth, while the third daughter, Albha had the beauty of spring, so young and fresh and fair was she, but she has no part in this story, so it is sufficient to say that she was as beautiful as her sisters, and leave it at that. With their beauty the three maidens combined intelligence, charm and wit and Lir found it impossible to choose one of them for her own sake. Therefore he said: 'They are all beautiful, but to choose one of them is beyond me for I cannot say which of the three is best.' (And in this he showed a wisdom, perhaps, derived from one of his Hellenic forebears called Paris who, when he found himself in a somewhat similar situation, displayed the bad judgement of making a distinction.)

'Therefore,' went on Lir, 'I will take the eldest, for she must be the most fitting to be wife to a chief of the De Danaan.'

The king agreed and with tremendous pomp and ceremony the wedding was arranged and celebrated. The newly married couple remained at Killaloe for a month and then left for Sidhe Fionna and Lir's castle, where the marriage was celebrated all over again with a great wedding feast at which the nobles and kings of Ireland were made welcome.

Lir and Niamh were happy at Sidhe Fionna where they lived in comfort and in friendliness with everyone now that Lir and the Bodbh Dearg were reunited. In the course of time Niamh bore children to Lir, twins, and they were called Finola and Aedh; and they were fine, healthy children who grew fat and pink in the grianan of Sidhe Fionna until they were a year old, when their mother again gave birth to twins, two boys this time, called Fiachra and Conn; but unhappiness and tragedy arrived with the birth of these two sons, for Niamh died in giving them birth, and for a second time Lir was left without a wife to love and to love him. So great was his anguish and despair that he nearly died of the vast grief that consumed him and only his great love for his children turned his mind from the sorrow that lived within him.

When the news of this new tragedy reached Killaloe the grief of the Bodbh Dearg was scarcely less than that of Lir himself, and the people of his household raised a great wail of sorrow and loss for Niamh which lasted for a fortnight. When their period of mourning was over, the king assembled them in the great hall and said: 'We have been afflicted with a terrible sorrow and loss in the death of Niamh, and we grieve for her both on our own account and for the sake of the noble to whom we gave her, for we acknowledge his alliance and friendship. But it is in our heart, and in our power, to alleviate his sorrow and in so doing to soften our own and cement the ties between us with an even stronger bond, for I will give him her sister for a wife, my second foster-child Aoife.'

Messengers were again sent to Sidhe Fionna tc tell Lir of the king's decision. Lir received them and their message with affection and with sadness in equal parts; affection because of the king's nobility of mind, and sadness because he had loved Niamh so well and felt her loss so deeply. Nevertheless after a period of mourning he went to Killaloe to the king's palace where he and Aoife were married and united, and after the wedding he brought her home with him to Sidhe Fionna.

Now Aoife did not have the blessing of children of her own as her years with Lir accumulated and grew, but that did not unduly trouble her, for she loved her husband greatly, and gave to his children the love which she would have given to children of her own. She cared for them with great tenderness and, indeed, her love for them increased every day that the sun rose upon the world. In fact, the whole race of the De Danaan loved these lovely children, who were their joy and their delight, for those who saw them were captured by their beauty and their gentleness – which is a thing rare enough in many children nowadays, thanks to the fact that it is even rarer in their elders – and could not help loving them with their whole hearts. The king himself loved them with the love of a grandfather and went frequently to Sidhe Fionna to visit them; and when he was not thinking of going to Lir's castle to see them and bring them gifts, he was thinking of bringing them to Killaloe and assembling gifts there for them, where he kept them for as long as possible and was a sadder and an older man each time they had to leave to go home again.

Now, at this time the Tuatha de Danaan celebrated the Feast of Gabhann which was a notable occasion dedicated to their power over sickness, decay and old age and instituted by Mananaan MacLir. Now Mananaan was not the son of our Lir, but of a much older origin, and had at this time assumed the stature of a god among the people of the Tuatha de Danaan. The Feast of Gabhann was a ceremony which ensured that the people of the Tuatha de Danaan would join the Marcra Sidhe, or Mystic Cavalcade in the Tír Tairrngire, or Land of Promise, called Tír na nÓg or Land of Youth by those who don't know any better. And the Feast was celebrated at the houses of different chiefs in turn. It was when it was celebrated in the castle of Lir that the hosts of the De Danaan came to know and love the children of Lir. And as they did so, the pride and love of their father in them grew as well, and it was a delight to see how it showed in him. The four little children slept close by him; and he would often rise from his bed at the dawn of the day and go to them to talk with them and to play with them before the work of the day began. But it was this very delight in and love for his children that brought great sorrow in its train.

Aoife, perhaps feeling the years of her youth flying from her – but why she should feel thus is a mystery, since the Feast of Gabhann was as beneficent to the women of the De Danaan as to the men – or perhaps feeling the deep ache in her rich body that is the ache of a yearning but infecund woman, when she saw those children receiving such attention from their father and from all the others who came to the castle, began to fancy that she was neglected on their account. The barb of unreason, jealousy, lodged in her heart, and she began to seek for reasons on which it might take hold; suspicion provides its own reasons and envy its own logic, and it did not take long for the love that she had felt and lavished upon them to turn to hatred which fed upon their happiness.

AOIFE'S JEALOUSY BECAME SUCH an obsession with her that she became ill, not only sick her mind, but in her body too as the torment of the one was transferred to the other. For a year she lay in bed, full of bitterness and brooding evil, and her speech and appearance were attributed to her sickness of body for which there appeared to be no remedy. Her sickness worried Lir, who had already lost two wives, a great deal and he paid her much attention, but even this did not offset Aoife's jealousy, but rather fed it, as she considered he turned to her only out of pity. However, at the end of a year, she had reached a decision and made it known that she was well and arose from her sickbed.

She called the children to her and told them that to celebrate her recovery she was going to take them on a visit to their foster-grandfather, the king Bodbh Dearg at Killaloe. They were delighted, of course – all except Finola, who had dreamed on the previous night a dark dream of foreboding in which Aoife had perpetrated some dreadful deed on herself and her brothers.

Finola was afraid that their step-mother intended some harm to them, even though it was only a dream she had, and did not want to go. Nevertheless she was persuaded, since she was ashamed to speak her fears in case she would be laughed at and thought ungrateful.

Aoife ordered her carriages and chariots to be harnessed and, with her personal servants as guards, she set out from Sidhe Fionna for Killaloe with the children. They had not gone very far when she called aside one of her most trusted retainers, and said to him: 'You love me well, Conan, or is it just that you are my servant?'

'You know me better than that,' he replied indignantly, 'didn't I come from Aran with you when you were only a small child and haven't I watched over every hair of your head since then in case any harm would befall you?'

'Then you do love me?' she asked.

'There isn't a thing in the world I wouldn't do for you,' he said.

'Good,' replied Aoife, 'and if I was in any danger, or suffering from a great loss what would you do about it?'

'Remove the one and restore the other if I had to face the battlefields of the world to do it,' he answered, and that satisfied her.

'Well then,' she said, 'listen to me. I am losing the love of my husband.'

'Glory be to God,' he replied, 'is that a fact? Is it another woman or what? Tell me her name and it's the end of her.'

''Tis no woman has me neglected in his eyes and forsaken in his house,' she said, 'but those children you see there before you. They have me destroyed and ruined and my life blighted and if you were to remove them and kill them out of my sight, I will reward you with what wealth your heart may desire.'

But Conan looked at her in horror as she spoke, and rage welled up in her at his look, for she could not understand the cause of it, so blinded was she with her hate and jealousy thinking that she could not be wrong and that therefore all things she would do were justifiable; she raged at his stupidity, but could do nothing about it. Conan in his horror backed away from her silently and no more was said between them about it.

And it was the same with those others of her retainers that

she approached. One and all they refused with contempt and horror on their faces and lips, warning her that evil would certainly follow her for the thing she contemplated.

Then, in her rage, she took a sword in her hand and determined to kill them herself, but her deep womanly instincts came between her and her hatred, and prevented her. So they set out once again and continued their journey until they came to the shores of Lough Derravarragh in Westmeath where they made a camp and sat about while a meal was being prepared.

With a smile of false friendship on her face Aoife led the children to the lakeside and suggested that they have a bathe while they waited for the meal; delighted they threw off their costly clothing and ran into the water with childish shouts of joy, but one by one as they passed her, Aoife struck them with a golden druidical wand and transformed them into four beautiful, snow white swans. Then she spoke to them these words:

> Fly to your homes on Derravarragh's shore
> And with its clamouring birds protest your fate;
> Your friends may seek to find you evermore
> In vain, now I have satisfied my burning hate.

The four bewildered and frightened children fluttered this way and that way in the shallows of the lake in frantic efforts to shake off their carapace of snow-white feathers, soft as a whispered word on a pillow on the outside, but, for them who were captured within, as hard as the forged and ringing iron bars of a prison cell.

Finally they quietened down and added to that solemn dignity of all swans the immeasurable sadness that now descended on them as they realised the full extent of their plight.

Finola who, like the other children, still possessed the power of speech, like them turned her face towards their stepmother, and spoke for all of them: 'Oh, Aoife,' she said, 'why did you do this terrible thing to us? Your friendship for us has turned out to be the friendship of a traitor and you have destroyed us without a cause that we can see. But what you've done will cry out for vengeance for as many years as vengeance takes to reach you; your power is not greater than the power of the Tuatha de Danaan and their punishment, Aoife, you may be sure, will be that much greater than ours as yours now is greater than what we were.'

And having said this the children together made this song:

You, who loved us in the days that fled
Down the vortex of sweet things, now dead;
Who summoned up those old and horrid words
In newborn hate, that wrought us into birds,
Have cast aside that fostered love you bore
And hurled us forth, from storm to stormy shore.

Finola, when they had finished this song, turned again to Aoife and said: 'Tell us one thing at least, how long shall we be in the shape of swans, so that we may know when our misery will end?'

Aoife smiled grimly at her: 'You'd have been wiser not to have asked that question,' she said, 'but since you have asked it then I'll tell you the truth, and may it be a solace or an anger to you as you wish; three hundred years you'll spend, on lake Derravarragh; three hundred more on the Sea of Moyle between Ireland and Scotland; three hundred years in Erris and Inis Glora on the Western Sea ... as many years you will spend until the union of Lairgnean, the prince of the north, with Deichthe, the princess of the south; until the Taillceann comes to Ireland from abroad, bringing with him a new belief in the word of God come to earth ... and neither by your own power, or by my power or the power of your friends can you be freed until the time comes.'

But now that she had spoken the words, the venom and the bitterness that was in her heart flew with them out of her mouth and she repented what she had done; it was as if the release of the words themselves released also the jealous hate in her, and she said: 'Since I cannot give you anything else, I'll grant you the power to keep your human speech; and your voices will be so sweet that you will sing music sweeter than any music heard in the world before and which will lull into sleep all who listen to it. Moreover you will keep your human intelligence and will not be sad any longer for being in the shape of swans.'

Fly from me you gentle swans
And make your home on the restless waves,
Build your nest on the ocean's breast
Drape yourself in its snowy white crest,

Find shelter in deep-bitten caves.

Fly from me you drifting swans
And fill with music and ancient songs
Derravarragh's wind-swept shore,
The coasts where endless oceans roar,
A thousand years will not seem long.

Unhappy Lir, in grief and pain
Your names may call across the world.
His sundered heart will halt and fail –
His empty hearth repeat the wail –
On me his vengeance shall be hurled.

Across the margins of an age
Your agony no hand may cease
Until across the narrowing sea
Will come the Word of Him who'll be
For all the succour and release.

Then Aoife, her face hardened again with her own determination and the knowledge that she was committed to an unalterable course, turned away from the lakeside and ordered her horses to be yoked to her chariot again. She left the four swans together on the lonely lake behind her, swimming aimlessly close to the shore. Their own sorrow was enormous, for they were still children thrown athwart the world for a bitter age. But they made this song, thinking of the sorrow of their father:

Our hearts break for our sad father
Searching the world with sick eyes,
Leaping at shadows in lands and skies
Seeking his children, wrenched from his home.
Four swans adrift on the voiceless foam,
Treading the water for evermore,
Flying from the storms to a cold shore.

When Aoife reached Killaloe and the palace of the Bodbh Dearg, she was given a tremendous welcome, for the news of her sickness had gone before her, but not that of her recovery, and her foster-father received her with great joy. After he had welcomed her, he asked her why she hadn't brought the children of Lir with her this time.

Now Aoife knew that he would ask her this, and she had prepared her answer on the way – even though she knew it would be found to be untrue in time. But in the manner of all those who have committed an evil, she had no choice but to lie unless she made the truth known, even though she piled another wrong on what she had already done and knew that this would count against her eventually. Still she bought a little time for herself. And so she said: 'I did not bring them because Lir is no longer your friend and ally. He has turned against you, as he has turned against me, and will not trust his children to you in case you would do them harm.'

The Bodbh Dearg was, naturally, astonished at this, for he was aware that Lir knew he loved the children as if they were really his grandchildren, and not just the children of his own foster-child. 'How could that be,' he asked her, 'I love those children as I love my own.'

Now he was no fool. He questioned Aoife further, but the vagueness and discrepancies of her answers only made him all the more uneasy. He suspected that something was wrong from her attitude, but had no idea what it might be. Secretly, therefore he sent messengers northwards to Sidhe Fionna to enquire for the children and to ask that they might come on a visit to him with their foster-mother.

When the messengers arrived and told this to Lir he, in his turn, was astonished and upset.

'But didn't they reach Killaloe with Aoife,' he asked, 'they certainly left here with her for the Bodbh Dearg's palace.'

The messengers answered: 'Aoife arrived alone, and she told the king that you refused to allow the children to come.'

Lir didn't know what to make of this. With his mind in a turmoil he first of all raged at the messengers that they were fools and liars, but they eventually convinced him of the truth of what they said. This only made him worse, for he could not understand why Aoife should say this to the king. He loved her and trusted her and she had never lied to him so far as he knew. Then he thought of her illness, which was inexplicable, and the thought struck him with terror that her mind had become deranged and that she had murdered the children while in that condition. In terror and distraction he ordered his chariots to be yoked and, with whatever men he could lay his hands on, set out immediately for Killaloe covering every inch of the ground they passed on the way. Slowly, for the mind of Lir was burdened as it had never been before, they came towards Lough Derravarragh.

The four swans who had been left there by Aoife were swimming silently a little way from the shore, just outside a sprouting bank of reeds, when the cavalcade topped the hill above the lake. Finola was the first to see it, and she sang, with all the power of music and song that Aoife had left them:

Over the hilltop and down to the lake
Slowly and sadly the warriors make
A path through the heather and by the wild shore,
Tardy the wheels now for chariots that sped
And heavy the feet of the soldiers who bore
Our parents past here when first they were wed.

Their hearts are dull, dull too their shields;
Dull their eyes that reap shorn fields,
The royal hosts of De Danaan
Under skies of changing hues
Seeking us from dawn to dawn,
Who've found us here, and lost us too.

When Lir and his men came to the shore and heard the swans speaking in human voices, they wondered greatly at this miracle and stopped. Lir walked to the water's edge, his heart thumping within him, for he knew that this strangeness was no small thing and sensed that it would mean much to him. He spoke to the swans and asked them how it was they had human voices.

'Oh dear father,' cried Finola, 'you do not know us. I am Finola, and these your other children, changed to swans and ruined by the hatred and witchcraft of Aoife, our own mother's sister, and your wife.'

When Lir heard this he gave three great cries of grief and lamentation and looked as if he would lose his reason altogether in his sorrow. After a while he recovered sufficiently to ask them: 'How can I restore you to your proper form? What must I do?'

'Nothing,' replied Finola, 'no one has the power to release us for more than a thousand years. Until Lairgnean the prince from the north and Deichthe the princess from the south are united.'

When they heard this Lir and all his people again raised three shouts of lamentation. Their grief was lifted by the wind and carried across the face of Ireland until the trees bent beneath it, and the waves beating her shores receded from it. When they had become silent again, and their silence was like the dropping of snow after the thunder of their grief, Lir said: 'You still have your speech and your reason, so let you come to land and you can live with us at Sidhe Fionna, talking and behaving as if you still had your proper shapes.'

'That is not possible either,' cried Finola, 'we are condemned to inhabit the waters of the lake and cannot live with human people any more. Aoife has only allowed us to keep our minds and our speech, and we have the power to make music so sweet that those who hear it will never desire any other happiness.'

Lir and his people stayed by the lakeside that night and the four children of Lir sang and made music for them so that they were lulled into a calm, gentle sleep as they listened and their cares and worries fell from them. But as dawn broke over the low hills to the east, Lir stood up, and slowly walked again to the water's edge to say goodbye to his children while he went to search for Aoife:

Broken the heart in my bonded breast
That I must leave you children here
Far from where your heads sought rest;
Far from the empty halls of Lir.

I curse the day that first I saw
Aoife's smiling face that screened
A cruelty no love might thaw
Like poison in a cup concealed.

I know no rest, I know no sleep
For through the never ending night
I glimpse the children I would keep
Forever in my fading sight.

Finola, daughter of my heart,
Proud Aedh than whom was none more bold,
Fiachra, gentler than the hart,
And little Conn – more dear than gold –

Oh, here on Derravarragh's shore
Trapped by Aoife's evil power ...
Oh God! My children! Never more
Will Lir enjoy a tranquil hour.

When Lir left he travelled directly to Killaloe, where he was welcomed. He said nothing of what he knew, but greeted the king and Aoife without showing his feelings. The Bodbh Dearg then began to reproach him for not bringing the children with him, and all the while Aoife was standing beside him.

Then Lir turned and looked directly at his wife. She looked back at his expressionless face for a moment, and then dropped her gaze. Lir turned back again to the king.

'It was not I who prevented my children from coming to stay with you, Bodbh Dearg,' he said, 'but Aoife, your own foster-child and sister of their mother. She has turned on them and treacherously turned them into four swans, now trapped on Lough Derravarragh.'

At first the Bodbh Dearg didn't believe Lir. He could not understand how one of his own foster-children, on whom he had lavished love and attention, could do such a thing. He turned to her, wordlessly, for a denial, but when he saw the expression on her face, he realised that what Lir had said was the truth.

'Aoife ...' was all he could say, and it was as much an appeal to prove Lir wrong, as a shocked reaction to what he said. But there was no movement from Aoife, who looked stonily before her, knowing that the vengeance she had tried to avoid had come upon her all the quicker.

The Bodbh Dearg drew himself up and terrible he looked in his tormented anger.

When he spoke his voice was low and fierce: 'What you have done,' he said, 'will be worse for you than for the children you have harmed, for their suffering will come to an end and they will find happiness at last.'

Then for a while he stayed looking at her with a frown of awful anger and justice on his face. When he spoke his voice was even fiercer than it had been before. 'Of all that is on the earth, or above it, or beneath it; of all that flies or creeps or burrows, seen or unseen, horrible in itself or in its nature, what do you most abhor?'

Now it was incumbent on Aoife that certain questions put to her must be answered truthfully, for she was under an obligation older than the Tuatha de Danaan itself to do so and if she did not the fate that would befall her would be worse and more lasting than any fate that mere man might devise for her, and so she was forced to answer truthfully. And she said: 'Of all that you have said, the things most loathsome to me are the Morrigu – the demons of the air.'

'That, then, is what you will be,' said the Bodbh Dearg, and as he spoke he struck her with a druidical golden wand, such as the one she had herself used on the children of Lir, and transformed her into one of the dreaded Morrigu, which can take many shapes, and relishes in battle and spilling the blood of men, but is most often seen in the black and dreaded shape of a croaking raven.

Immediately Aoife was turned into something so horrible and revolting to behold that all those in the great hall of the palace of Killaloe turned away or hid their faces in their cloaks, save only Lir and the Bodbh Dearg alone who stood and looked at the transformation with imperturbable countenances.

The thing that was now Aoife crouched low on the floor for a moment, flapping its ugly, leathery wings. Then, with a scream from its gaping mouth, it spread them wide and flew upwards, over the heads of those below who cringed away as it passed above and out through the great door until it disappeared among the clouds in the distance. She had become a demon of the air, a Morrigu; and a demon of the air she remains and will remain until the end of time.

Then the Bodbh Dearg and all his court, and the Tuatha de Danaan from the four corners of Ireland, assembled on the shores of Lough Derravarragh and camped there, that they might remain with the white swans and listen to their music. And there too came the hosts of the Milesians from Tara and their kingly courts and made another camp to listen to the music of the swans. For it is said and written that no music was heard in the world before that, or since, to compare with the music of the swans.

And round the lake there lived and grew a great community of people bonded together by their love of the swans and the music made by them. During the day the swans would talk with their friends and at night they sang their incomparable music so that all those who heard it, no matter what their grief, or sickness; sorrow or pain, forgot what it was that troubled them and drifted into a gentle sleep from which they woke calm and refreshed. This, then, was how they lived for three hundred years; the De Danaans and the Milesians in their own, vast communities by the lakeside, and the three swans in the shallow water near the lake's edge. At the end of that time Finola said to her brothers: 'The time we were to spend on Lough Derravarragh has come to an end and we have only one more night left to us here, for tomorrow we must leave our friends and our own people and fly from here to the cold sea of Moyle.'

When the three sons of Lir heard this they were disheartened for they were as happy, almost, on the lake and with their own people as if they had lived in Sidhe Fionna where they had been born. Now they were doomed to the dark waves of the Sea of Moyle, threshing its passage between Ireland and Scotland, far from human companionship.

Early the following morning, therefore, in sadness and sorrow, they approached the shore to speak to their father for the last time and to bid their friends farewell. And this is the lament that they sang before they left:

Tears are swelling in our hearts
As the lake must swell and weep
When time lays down a hand athwart
Its water, calm and deep,
And sunders it and blows black storms
Across its tranquil path;
For we must leave your courts and warmth
And seek the endless wrath
Of Moyle's wild sea; three hundred years
There to linger in our fears.

Far down the twisted roads of time
Our paths ahead are mapped;
Though men may with the fates combine
Our destinies are trapped;
No dreams we dream, no hopes may raise,
No laughter in tomorrow;
Till comes that holy voice of praise

Our lives are doomed to sorrow.
But though we go our hearts remain
To ease your grief and mortal pain.

Then, as the last notes of their lament died away across the surface of the lake, the four birds, all together, began to skim over the lake, their wings and their feet combining to lift them from the water and their long necks outstretched before them. They lifted gently until their feet were barely running on the surface and then, with powerful sweeps of their broad wings, they abandoned the lake which had been their home for so long and rose upwards into the air. Higher they climbed and higher, making great circles as they rose, the sound of their beating wings coming down clearly to the many thousands of people below. And when the swans had reached a great height, where they could look down and see not only Derravarragh and the camp of the men of Ireland beside it, but much of the country around as well, they paused in their flight for a moment, and then flew northwards, straight and true, until they saw the bitter foam and white savagery of the Sea of Moyle, scouring the ocean bed between Ireland and Scotland, rising ahead. Lower they sank and lower until they touched the first cold wave to reach up for them. Then they landed, awkwardly, on the cruel sea that was to be their new home.

The people of Ireland were so saddened and upset at their departure that they made a law forbidding anyone to kill a swan in Ireland from that time on.

THE FRAMING OF THIS legislation and its passing was done in a fervour of activity and energy; the enthusiasm of those who became caught up in it and who supported it was sincere and infectious and carried the wholehearted support of the entire people with it until it became law. But when it was passed, and had become a law of the land, there was no more to be done; gradually it was realised that this made not the slightest difference to the plight of the children of Lir, wild and hot though the enthusiasm had been for the passing of the law. Nor was there anything further that could be done to help them. And so sadder, wiser perhaps, proud of their unimportant piece of legislation, the people forgot about the Children of Lir, for there was nothing else left for them to do.

All, that is, except Lir himself, the Bodbh Dearg and a few more who had known all along that all the laws in the world won't redress a wrong if equity and justice are not possible, and who loved the children of Lir for their own sakes and not because they represented anything.

Meanwhile the Children of Lir themselves were adrift on the jagged face of Moyle, tossed from wave to wave by the growling sea. Their hearts were full of sorrow and sadness for their father and their friends even in their own terrible plight; and when they looked about them, at the dark-green-bellied, wild sea, and the steep, rocky, far-stretching coasts, they were overcome with fear and despair. Cold and hunger struck at them too, for it was not like the warm, inland, well-stocked waters of pleasant Derravarragh; here the wind swept bitingly down from the north, with sleet and snow in its teeth; the sea harboured little of food in that wild place, and Derravarragh appeared like nothing compared to what they now suffered.

This was how they lived for some time, thinking their lives and misery could never be greater than it was, until one evening when – wintry though it was, with pale, milky clouds stretched coldly across the sky, and the sea heaving restively beneath them – the sky suddenly became darker and seemed to close in about them. They realised a storm was on the way, and Finola said: 'Brothers, this storm has taken us by surprise and we are unprepared for it. It is certain that we will be separated in it so it would be as well if we fixed a meeting place afterwards, otherwise we might never see each other again.'

And Fiachra said: 'That is sensible, so let's meet at Carricknarone, for that is a place we all know well.'

And for a few hours, they stayed together, huddled in a group on top of the bellowing sea. With midnight came the storm. A wild wind swept across the black sea, roughening the billows, and lightning flashes threw themselves forth from the clouds so that it seemed as if the ocean was under attack from the sky and was rousing itself mightily to fight back, for the sea rose as if from its bed and clawed at the sky with angry fingers of lashing spume. And as the storm grew worse the swans were separated and scattered across the surface of the fighting sea so that not one of them knew in what direction the others had been driven. All through the night they were tossed and hurled, whipped and blown, sometimes in the sea and sometimes in the air and sometimes in a raging mixture of the two, from one place to another place, but never knowing what place they were in. Only with great courage and willpower did they manage to survive at all, and even then they were more dead than alive when the dawn began to lighten the east. With the dawn the storm abated, and by full light the sea was again calm and smooth, but with the troubled look, restless underneath, that it always has after a storm. When she was rested a bit, Finola made her way to Carricknarone. But there was no sign of any of her brothers either on the sullen waves beating about the rock, or on the craggy corners of the rock itself. She climbed to the top of it and looked around over the desolate wastes, but there was still no sign of them. Cold and terrified, she believed them dead, and began to lament them:

> There is no shelter, there is no rest,
> My heart is broken in my breast;
> Gone, my three loves in the bitter night;
> Gone, all but the deep, cold fright
> Of despair, and life without light.
>
> My brothers are lost in the wild sea
> Where death itself would be a mercy;
> Oh, is there no pity in this place?
> Will I never see again each face
> Dearer now to me than the human race?
>
> There is no shelter, there is no rest,
> My heart is broken in my breast;
> Was not the agony we bore enough?
> Was not the cruelty, the deep trough
> Of long anguish sufficient pain to suffer?

Then she sank down on the rock and buried her head under her wing. Her spirits sank lower and lower, for she believed herself to be alone of the four children of Lir, and wished to die. Finally, when she had made up her mind to accept death, she raised her head to take a last look at the bleak world that she was about to leave. She looked out over the pale sea, almost one colour with the inhospitable sky and there, in the distance, she saw a small speck of bedraggled white being tossed this way and that way by the careless sea, but making its way towards the rock slowly with feeble motions; it was Conn that she saw, and when she recognised him she forgot her terror and despair and plunged into the moving water to help him towards Carricknarone – which is properly called the rock of the seals, for it is there that the seal people congregate when the weather is welcoming. But, needless to remark, there was no sign of life about the rock at this time save for themselves, and the few ravaging sea birds that circled above in search of prey. She helped Conn to the rock and there they rested. Shortly afterwards they saw Fiachra limping through the water, and it took both of them a mighty effort to bring him to safety for he was closer to death than he was to life and when they spoke to him he could not summon up a word or any acknowledgement whatsoever in return, and so Finola and Conn placed him under the warmth of their wings to bring back the heat of life to his perished body, and Conn said: 'If only Aedh were here now, all would be happy with us.'

And after some time, indeed, they did see Aedh coming towards them and his condition very different from that of the other two for he swam proudly on the lip of the ocean, his head erect and his feathers dry and radiant. He was welcomed by the others and told them that he had succeeded in finding shelter in a Scottish cave from the fury of the storm. Finola placed him before her breast while the other two sheltered under her wings, and she said to them: 'Oh, it is wonderful to be together again. But we must be prepared for many more nights like this so let us not be either too disheartened or too optimistic.'

And so they lived for many lonely years on the Sea of Moyle. They suffered and they endured and they were bound together by their hardships and their love for one another until one night of great wind and snow, storm and frost, so severe that nothing they had undergone before that or nothing they were to undergo after it could surpass it. The cold that was in that night might have come from the uttermost region of the infinite sky, and the wind from the bowels of the turning earth; the frost fell and enveloped them like a covering of fire and the storm broke the sea asunder where they struggled to survive.

As the nights of that storm passed from one torment into another the very waters of the heaving sea became frozen into torn and ragged walls, grotesque and ugly all around them. They had reached Carricknarone in safety, but their feet and wings were frozen solid with the high flung spray and manacled with ice to the torn floor that was the sea, so that the skin was ripped from their feet as they moved and the quills from their wings and the protecting feathers from their battered breasts.

When the salt of the sea reached their cuts and wounds their torture was doubled, and yet they could not leave the blasted Sea of Moyle for a safer retreat. They were forced to swim out into the channel where the water had not frozen and, wounded and torn as they were, had no choice but to remain there in the sharp and bitter stream. They stayed as close to the coast as possible until the fearful cold passed and their feathers grew again on their breasts and wings.

Nothing again ever compared to that time, and for many years afterwards they lived close to the coast, now of Ireland and now of Scotland, but always they remained on the Sea of Moyle.

Then one day they were swimming by the mouth of the River Bann in the northern part of Ireland when looking towards the land they saw a great cavalcade of chiefs and lords riding from the south. They were mounted on white horses and as they approached the splendour of their cloaks blazed across the fields and their weapons glinted in the sunlight like the gathered stars glinting in the night.

'Who are these warriors?' asked Finola.

'I've no idea,' replied Fiachra, 'unless they are a party of Milesians, for they would hardly be our own people riding abroad in the land.'

'Let us swim closer to the shore and find out,' suggested Conn, and with that they swam together towards the river mouth where the horsemen were heading. They, in their turn, when they saw the swans coming towards them, changed course so as to meet them. They were indeed a party of the De Danaan led by the two sons of the Bodbh Dearg, Aedh and Fergus. They had been searching for the Children of Lir for many years before they found them, although they had traversed the coast of the Sea of Moyle backwards and forwards for so long that they knew every blade of grass on its margins and every pebble that lay on its beaches.

Now that they had found them they exchanged the warmest greetings of friendship and love and the Children of Lir at once asked about their father and the Bodbh Dearg and the others of the De Danaan whom they had known at Derravarragh and before that at Killaloe and at Sidhe Fionna.

'They are all well,' said Aedh and Fergus, 'and they and the hosts of the De Danaan are again celebrating the Feast of Gabhann with your father at Sidhe Fionna. Their happiness would be complete if only you were there with them to share in the festivities, for they have no idea what happened to you since you were forced to leave Derravarragh and come to the Sea of Moyle because of Aoife's evil.'

The four swans looked at each other and their eyes clouded with the memory of what they had been through.

'No tongue can tell you the suffering and torment we have gone through here,' they said, 'it is too much to remember. But perhaps you will carry this song home with you when you go?'

And, so that Lir and the Bodbh Dearg might know that they were still alive in spite of everything, they made this song to be carried back to the Feast of Gabhann:

Gladness and laughter and great rejoicing
Fill eyes and hearts of our people at home –
Checked by their inner thoughts still voicing
Grief for us on the slow sea's loam.

Bleak and cold the home we know.
Our sodden down is thin and light,
Yet we wore once – oh, long ago –
Clothes that glittered in the night.

Once, too, our lives were filled with laughter,
As our brimming cups of gold,
Now pain and sickness follow after;
Lost, forgotten, in the cold.

Our beds are rocks in wave-torn caves
Our lullaby the washing sea;
No voice to hear but the tongueless waves;
No sound but the dirge of the pitiless sea.

After this the De Danaan and the Children of Lir said farewell to each other, for the four swans had to return to the flow of the

Sea of Moyle. Sadly they drifted away from its shore, their graceful necks and heads turned back so that they could look to where their friends waved to them as they floated away. When they were out of sight the De Danaan returned to Sidhe Fionna where they told the chiefs what had happened and how the Children of Lir were. The Bodbh Dearg, having listened to what they said, answered them; for Lir was so moved that speech was beyond him.

'It is not in our power to help them,' said the Bodbh Dearg. 'But we are glad to know that they are still alive, and we know that in the end the enchantment will be broken and they will be free of their sufferings.'

Now the children of Lir, after they left the host of the Tuatha de Danaan, returned to the Sea of Moyle where they remained for many years more. Countless were the nights and the days that passed them by; the months and the seasons as the years of their imprisonment accumulated. But at last it came to a close, and they fulfilled their period of three hundred years on the Sea of Moyle.

And when the time was up, Finola looked at her brothers and said: 'We must leave this place, and go to the west.' Again they were being hurled by the power of Aoife's long-lived magic into the unknown, and together they made this song before they left Moyle:

Three hundred years we've spent
Suffering here without rest;
Now we may leave this torn and rent
Sea, and fly to the west.

Out from the cold sea of the east,
To the far storms we fly,
Battering the west like a wild beast,
To live in the tempest's eye.

Then, when their farewell to Moyle was sung, the swans lifted themselves from its cold billows and turned westwards across the face of Ireland. High they flew, not seeing what happened beneath them and not looking for fear that the longing it might bring would break their hearts, until they saw the western sea beneath them, peopled and dotted with many islands near the shore of Ireland. They came down on the sea at Iris Domnann near Glora, and were little better off there than they were in the Sea of Moyle; it was not so cold, but the storms were greater, so that their hardship was not the same, but was of equal intensity.

Now it happened that there was a young man called Aebhric living close to the shore in this place, who had a great tract of land running down to the sea. Here he would hunt and spend his time and cultivate certain crops – for the land in that part of the world is not rich and game is scarce, so that crops must be tended even by people of noble families if they are to find a living. While he was here one day he saw the birds and overheard them singing their wonderful songs and making that music which Aoife had bestowed on them the ability to make when she placed her curse upon them. Like everyone else who heard their music he came under its spell and was entranced by it so that he wanted no other joy or pleasure in the world other than to listen to it, and so he came there every day for that purpose.

Gradually he made himself known to the swans and they to him and it came as no small surprise to him when he found that they could talk and converse as well as sing. In time he came to love them very much and they him, and they told him their whole story from beginning to end. And it is true, though it may not be an easy thing to believe, that it is to Aebhric and him alone that we owe thanks for knowing the story at all. For he it was who told his neighbours about the speaking swans and they told more, and many people would come from near and far to hear Aebhric telling the story; but he would not allow the people to meet the swans themselves for fear that some harm might befall them, in spite of the law that had been passed by the Bodbh Dearg six hundred years or so before. He it was who arranged their story as it is here and who told it abroad, so that it was passed on from one generation to the next and so on through the passageway of the centuries until it reached us.

But that is enough about Aebhric. The swans, meanwhile, found their hardships renewed to such an extent that to describe their hardships on the western sea would be only to repeat again the story of what they endured on the Sea of Moyle. There was, however, one night of difference. On this particular night black frost so severe and so prolonged lacerated the face of the land and of the sea that the whole of it was frozen, as it were, into one mass of coldness, and the sea from Iris Domnann to Achill was frozen into a floor of ice and the snow came thick and solid in a blinding, masking blizzard from the north-west. No other night of their centuries of torment was so desolate; never was their pain so great, never such an accumulation of suffering so that the three brothers were unable to stand the immensity of it any longer and made loud and bitter and pitiful complaints. Finola tried to console them, but she could not for her own condition was no better than theirs and, indeed, it seemed as if the end for them all was not very far away in the white, terrible storm of the night, and she herself began to lament with the others.

But then a strange, and awe-filled thing took place; in the depths of her misery and lamentation, Finola felt a spirit mingling with her own that was strange and terrifying, but comforting and consoling too; greater than anything she had ever experienced of destitution or of happiness, it was indescribable, intangible, mighty, and yet inexplicable, and full of wonder she stopped her wailing and listened to herself or more properly, to what was at once within her and without.

Then, when she was sure of what it was she wanted to say, she spoke to her brothers and asked them to stop their complaining for a moment until they heard her, and when they did so she said this to them. 'Brothers, there is Something here with us that I do not understand, for it is past my understanding and past yours and past the understanding of any mere man, but It is so great and awe-inspiring, so manifest of Love and of Goodness; of things so far beyond my comprehension, and yet for which my whole being strives, that I must believe in It for It is Truth. It is the Truth that has made the world, the earth with its fruits and the sea with its wonders; the heavens with their infinity. Put your trust in that Truth, brothers, and It will save us.'

'We will,' they said, 'and we do; for we feel It too.'

And that is how it happened, that at that hour when they were beyond any hope from within themselves or from without, they believed and the Lord of heaven who had not yet made Himself known to the people of Ireland, sent them help and protection; so that neither cold nor storm, hunger or want of any kind troubled them from that time on while they remained on the western sea. And so they remained there until they had fulfilled their appointed time.

THEN FINOLA GATHERED HER brothers around her and said: 'My beloved brothers, our time on the western sea has come to an end and we can leave without let or hindrance; let us go now and pay our respects to our father at Sidhe Fionna and the people of the De Danaan.'

Of course her brothers agreed gladly and, lightly, they rose up from the surface of the sea, casting round once above the bay they were leaving without regrets, and turned eastwards with happiness in their hearts, flying swiftly until they reached Sidhe Fionna.

But when they got there nothing but sadness and desolation was before them. The great castle that had once dominated the surrounding plain, where they had spent their joyful youth, was broken and tumbled. The windows gaped emptily, and the mortar had fallen from between the buckling stones that had themselves fallen in pyramidical piles from the once proud walls. Nothing stirred save the wind. The halls were empty and ruined and overgrown with rank grass and weeds; the villages and houses that had flourished about the castle were gone completely with nothing left to show that they had ever been there. Nothing remained but the falling castle.

In horror and pity the four swans clustered together and gave three great cries of mourning and sorrow, and sang this lament in the place where they had been born:

Gone are the noble and stately halls,
Crumbled the pillars and tumbled the walls;
Weeds and nettles, bent and blown,
Grow where our pride was overthrown.
Gone: All is gone!

Silence fills this empty place
But for the winds that round us trace
Faint whispers of forgotten shades
Bright with rich, gay cavalcades.
Gone: All is gone!

No warriors here, no men at arms,
No tales of victory and alarms;

Heroes, chieftains, great and brave
Are still and mouldered in the grave.
Gone: All is gone!

The Children of Lir stayed that night in the ruins of their father's castle, and several times during the night they stirred and felt uneasy as old memories came out of the crumbling corridors to trouble them; and when this happened they made their sad, sweet music as an offering and a tribute to the past.

Early next morning they left the site of Sidhe Fionna behind them and flew back again to the only home they had left, the western sea, where they circled over Inis Gloire and settled on a small lake on the island. There they sang so sweetly that all the birds of the island, and of the mainland, and of any place that was known to birds, came and settled there beside the lakeside to hear them sing and make music so that from that day to this, and until the memory of it has faded from the mind of man, the little lake became known as the lake of the birds, so thickly were they crowded about it and on it and near it.

During the day the swans flew from one place to another, gratified in their freedom; now they would go to Iniskea – where the lonely crane has lived in isolation since the beginning of the world and will live there until the day of judgement – and now they would go to the island of Achill or elsewhere along the shores of the western sea, north or south as they fancied, but always they returned to the lake to spend the night.

And so they lived their lives until Saint Patrick came to Ireland bringing with him the knowledge of the true faith; and until one of his disciples in Ireland, Saint Caemhoch, came to Inis Gloire. That night the swans heard a strange sound coming across the island and reverberating over the waters around it, one that they had never heard before. They were frightened at its strange, repetitive sound, and filled with terror began to run wildly about thinking that it meant something dreadful for them. In fact it was only Caemhoch ringing his bell for matins. The three brothers were more afraid of the sound than Finola, who had always shown herself to be the wisest and most sensible of the four Children of Lir, and, having listened to it for a while she said: 'Don't you know what that sound is?'

And they said: 'No. We hear it, and are afraid of it, for we don't know what it is or what it might mean.'

Then Finola said: 'That is the sound that we have been waiting for, and the end of our suffering is near; that is the voice of the bell which is the sign that soon we will be free of Aoife's curse.' And together they made this song:

Hear the reverberant boom of the bell
Throbbing down the aisles of Time;
The metal voice we've waited to tell
The end is near of Aoife's crime.

Listen, oh swans, to the throbbing bell
Ringing across the shaded night,
Rung by the priest in his lonely cell,
Yet, for us, the voice of light.

That is the bell of the Lord of all
Repeating His faith across the world;
Be joyful, brothers, and hear the call,
For soon in His arms we'll be safely curled.

When their song was over the four Children of Lir stayed in silence and listened to the tolling notes of the bell in the evening until it faded away altogether on a last lingering note. Then, as the sun faded too across the lake and silence came with the approaching night, they began to make the most beautiful music they had ever made in their long lives in praise of and in thanksgiving to the Almighty Creator of heaven and earth whose instrument was at hand for their deliverance.

Caemhoch heard their music from where he was and he listened in great wonder, for he had never heard anything on this earth so magnificent as the music coming out of the night in that lonely place. Gently he made his way towards the source of the music, but could see nothing for night had passed his own hurrying feet, and it was dark. Nevertheless he stayed close by listening to the music and giving thanks, for he realised that it was the Children of Lir, whom he had come to find, who were singing.

When morning dawned he saw the four white swans lingering in the water close to the shore, and he spoke to them and asked them if they were the Children of Lir.

They told him they were, and Caemhoch replied: 'Praise be to God that I have found you, for that is why I came here, having searched the coast from south to north and back again until now, always looking for you. Come ashore now and trust me, for I will end your enchantment.'

And the Children of Lir were filled with immense and profound joy when they heard what Caemhoch said, and they walked ashore and placed themselves under his care. He told them that it would take time and preparation and that they must put themselves entirely in his charge before what they wanted could come about, but they trusted the gentle priest – for indeed, they could do nothing else, but even if they could they would have trusted him anyway, such was his kindness and understanding. He brought them to his little house and, sending for skilled workmen, had two chains of silver made, one of which he put between Finola and Aedh and the other between Fiachra and Conn. And so they lived with him for some time, listening to what he told them day by day and telling him of all that had happened and of all that they knew to have happened, during the past thousand years and before. He taught them and instructed them in his beliefs and they were his delight and his joy and he loved them with a great love and tenderness; and the swans on their part were so happy with Caemhoch that the memory of their long years of misery and suffering became dim and caused them no distress.

Now the king who ruled Connacht at this time – which was about fifteen hundred years ago as anyone can establish if he takes the trouble to enquire – was Lairgnean MacColman and his queen was Deichthe the daughter of Finin of Munster – the same king and queen mentioned by Aoife when she put her spell on the Children of Lir so long before.

Now Deichthe was a proud and vain woman and, like many another in an exalted position, was gracious and kindly towards the rest of the world – so long as she was satisfied that she had and possessed all that was best in it for herself. But she could not abide to think that there might be a thing or an attribute with another that she did not have or possess herself; and if it was with or belonged to someone she considered beneath her station – as she considered most people to be – then her torment was all the greater.

It so happened that the story of the four wonderful singing and talking swans reached the court of Connacht and so the ears of Deichthe. She heard their whole history not once but many times and was consumed with desire to own the swans for herself as a great and unique wonder. So she went to the king and asked him to get them from Caemhoch for her. But the king was reluctant to do anything of the kind, knowing that the Children of Lir were not birds or beasts to be bought or sold for the vainglory of any man or woman. But, of course, he didn't put his objections to his wife like that, he just said that he could not. But she was adamant, for now her pride was hurt as well as her vanity since Lairgnean had never refused her anything she asked before, and she told him that she would not stay another night in his palace unless he did what she wanted. She being a high-spirited and selfish kind of a woman who had often made similar threats before, the king paid little attention to her this time, but she left that very hour and fled southwards towards her father's palace in Munster.

When Lairgnean discovered this he was very upset, for in spite of her faults he loved her greatly, and sent messengers after her to tell her that he would do as she wished; but they did not overtake her until she was at Killaloe, as it happened. However, she returned with the messengers to Lairgnean's palace and as soon as she arrived he made promises to her that he would send to Caemhoch for the swans. Straightaway he sent messengers to Caemhoch asking that he would send the swans to the queen, but, of course, Caemhoch refused to give them.

Lairgnean became very angry at this, for now his own pride was involved and he badly needed someone anyway on whom he could vent his anger, since he was extremely put out by Deichthe's behaviour, and of course it was not possible for him to be angry with her the way things were. Some say, as a matter of fact, that Deichthe was with child and that was the reason for her behaviour, but be that as it may, when Lairgnean got Caemhoch's answer he went off in a rage himself for the priest's house. When he arrived there he asked Caemhoch whether it was true that he had refused to give the swans to the queen.

'Indeed and I did,' said Caemhoch, 'for I have no power to give them any more than you have power to take them.'

When Lairgnean heard this he became even angrier than before and, going up to the swans, grabbed hold of the two silver chains. 'No power,' he shouted, 'I'll show you whether I have power or not, priest, for they are coming with me this minute. If I have no power in my own kingdom, then who has?'

And with that he took the chains, one in each hand, and began to pull the birds after him from the house, while Caemhoch followed in case they might be hurt by the king in his anger.

And it was this time that a strange and wonderful thing happened. The king had gone only a very little distance to where his horse was being held by one of his attendants when, suddenly, the white feathery covering of the four swans began to fade and their shapes to alter before the eyes of all who were present and in the broad light of the summer's day. Slowly the four Children of Lir began to reassume human shape, but with what a difference. For, instead of the four, golden, bright, happy, delightful children who had been the pride and the great love of the Tuatha de Danaan so long ago, they carried with them the accumulation of their years. Finola was transformed into a bent, old and extremely wrinkled woman whose flesh was shrivelled on her bones so that she seemed to be but bones itself covered with an ancient skin. Only the eyes sunken deep in her head bore the brightness of youth about them still; and her three brothers were equally old, white-haired and wrinkled. When the king saw what had happened he was transfixed with terror and fright; and then, instantly and without speaking a word, he turned and left, while Caemhoch reproached and denounced him bitterly. Meanwhile the Children of Lir, unable to stand for they were so feeble, called to Caemhoch, and said: 'Oh friend and priest, help us and baptise us now for there is not much time. You will be sorry, perhaps, when we die, but no more sorry than we will be to leave you; all we ask is that you bury us here, together, standing facing one another with our arms about each other as we have often stood when we were in the world.'

And if it seems a strange request to us today that they should be buried standing, remember that such was the old custom among the Gaelic and Celtic peoples of long ago. When they made this request, they sang this last song – and it is a strange thing that the beautiful music they had made when they were swans left them, and they sang with old, cracked voices; but their words were beautiful and made in unison:

Come, oh priest, and stretch your hand
Forth, over us here;
Our long pain is over and
Death is near.

Dig a grave, oh dig it well,
Deep and wide;
Where we can hear the tolling bell
Asleep inside.

Lay us as we often lay,
Four together;
Held upright in the cold clay,
Four together.

Lay little Aedh before my face
Those at hand;
And about each place
A loving hand.

And so we'll sleep for evermore,
Children of Lir.
Come, priest, and shed your power,
Death is here.

This song took all but the last remnant of their strength and Caemhoch hurried to baptise them before they died; and even as he did they died under his hand. When they died Caemhoch was moved to look up and, strange and yet perhaps not so strange in this story, above him he saw a vision of four lovely children whose faces were radiant with immense joy. They gazed at him for a moment with great love and affection, and then, perhaps because his own eyes filled with tears as he looked, they faded from his sight and were gone when he wiped the tears from his face. But he was filled with gladness because of what he had seen, knowing that the children who had suffered so greatly on earth would suffer no more but live in infinite happiness; yet, even so, when he looked down at the poor, crumpled bodies at his feet, he was overcome with sadness, and wept.

Then Caemhoch had a deep, wide grave dug near his little church and in it the Children of Lir were buried as Finola had requested with Conn at her right hand and Fiachra at her left and Aedh standing before her face.

When this was done Caemhoch raised a burial mound above them and a tombstone with their names engraved upon it and performed their funeral rites and made a lament, of which this story is part.

And that is the story of the Fate of the Children of Lir.

Diarmuid and Grainne

Grainne speaking of Diarmuid:
There is one
For sight of whom I'd gladly spare
All! All the shining, golden world
Though such a bargain be unfair.

Cormac MacArt was king of Ireland. That was about a hundred and fifty years before St Patrick brought the light of Chrisianity to Ireland, which makes it a considerable time ago, but not a long time according to the way the world is judged. For Cormac was a good deal nearer to our own time than he was to, let's say, that of the Dagda or even of his son, the Bodbh Dearg; but that is a point that need not concern us greatly now as it has nothing much to do with the story except to give you some idea of when it happened. Cormac was not only king, he was a particularly good and enlightened king at a time when there was no great incentive for kings to be either. He was the son of Art the Lonely, and the grandson of Conn of the Hundred Battles and he was known particularly for his learning and wisdom which have come down to us in the form of a book – which if it had been better studied by those for whom it was intended might have averted much mischief in the world – a book called *Teagusc-Rí,* or *Instructions for Kings.* Indeed it might be profitably studied today by kings, and those who have replaced them, for it is available enough and no less applicable now than it was when it was written. Besides this book which was his own, Cormac filled the court with scribes and philosophers, lawgivers and lawmakers and had the records and laws of his kingdom collected and written down in a great work which he called the *Psalter of Tara,* where he had his magnificent court. And at Tara he established three schools; one for history and philosophy, one for law and one for military science, and it is with the third, or more properly with the reason for it, that our story begins.

In the time of Conn of the Hundred Battles, and even before him, there had been recruited and maintained by the king a regular standing army in Ireland called the Fianna. Each province supplied contingents, but the whole army was under the command of one general who had his permanent headquarters on the Hill of Allen close to Naas, where he kept seven battalions of the Fianna in constant readiness. At the time of Cormac MacArt's kingship Fionn MacCumhal was general of the Fianna, as his father had been before him ... but it is not necessary to go into that or how Cumhal met his death at the Battle of Castleknock and at the hands of Gall MacMorna, because it is a long, involved and, sometimes, puzzling story without much satisfaction in it and without any place at all in the story of Diarmuid and Grainne.

Now Fionn was a man of mature years at the time of this story with a son, Oisin, and a grandson, Oscar, both of whom were already full members of the Fianna, having passed through the military college at Tara described above; for that was the purpose of Cormac's academy, to instruct young men and boys in the art and science of war in preparation for service as officers in the Fianna.

Fionn was a strong, powerful man, as indeed he needed to be to command the respect and leadership of the Fianna; to his friends he was open-hearted and generous, to his enemies implacable. Now, when he was a boy a strange thing happened to Fionn. A wonderful fish, the Salmon of Knowledge, was believed to inhabit the pool of Linn Fiach in the Boyne, and it was further believed that whoever first tasted this salmon would acquire the gifts of knowledge and divination; and, indeed, it was prophesied that a person named Fionn would be the first one to taste the salmon.

Now there was a certain old man, a poet and bard of no great merit and a bit loose in the head, by all accounts, called Fionn, who had his heart set on being the first one to taste the Salmon of Knowledge – and God knows he could have done with the bit of strengthening it would do his wits, I suppose.

At all events he settled down for himself on the banks of the pool of Linn Fiach and spent his days, and a large part of his nights too, fishing in the pool in the hope of catching the Salmon of Knowledge. Now at this time Fionn MacCumhal was only a boy, but he was a boy whose life was in continual danger and he was on the run from his enemies, the Clann Morna, whose chief, Gall MacMorna, had killed his father at the Battle of Castleknock. Consequently the young Fionn didn't care to use his own name overmuch as he wandered from place to place as to do so might relieve him of his head, to which he was attached, so to speak. So, in disguise and giving the name of Domhnach, he arrived one day at the camping place of Fionn the Poet who took him on as servant to tidy the place up and so on while he was fishing for the Salmon of Knowledge ... and lo and behold if one day he didn't catch the self-same salmon after all. With less wisdom than he might have shown if he had tasted the salmon first, he gave the fish to 'Domhnach' to cook for him, warning him impressively on no account to taste it whatsoever. Cheerfully 'Domhnach' proceeded to cook the fish and soon it was doing to his satisfaction; a pleasant smell rose up from it, and together with the smell, a great blister on its side. Now 'Domhnach', who was a reasonably good cook, knew that the blister didn't mean a thing, but absentmindedly – for he was thinking about where he might go next once he got away from this silly old poet who spent his time fishing – he pressed his thumb against it and got burned. Promptly and with a yelp he stuck his thumb in his mouth and sucked it.

When the fish was cooked he brought it to Fionn the Poet on a platter and the old man sat down before it, clasped his hands and closed his eyes with a look of fatuous ecstasy on his face. Soon his patience would be rewarded. Gently he opened his eyes; reverently he picked up the fish in his hands – which he had even taken the trouble to wash beforehand – and bit into the flank of the salmon. He swallowed expectantly; and then waited a moment. But nothing happened. He blinked. Still nothing happened. He was just as stupid as before. Slowly he turned to 'Domnach'. 'Did you,' he asked, 'taste the fish?'

'No,' replied the lad, 'but I burnt my finger on it and sucked it.'

'Ah,' said the old poet sadly, 'then you are no Domhnach. Your name is Fionn and in you the prophecy has been fulfilled.'

This is the story of how Fionn obtained his wisdom and power of divination, which were both great and accurate; but it is likely that it is no more than a story built up to account for the general's extraordinary perspicacity which, of course, is one of the reasons why he was a general.

In the course and fullness of time Fionn became the general over all the Fianna, even over the Clann Morna who were his enemies, and lived in his castle on the Hill of Allen. Now, although it was where his castle was, Fionn was under *geasa*, the most solemn vow which could not be broken without loss of all honour and reputation forever, which forbade him from sleeping there for more than nine nights in succession. One day he was sitting with the chief men of the seven battalions when one of them, Bran Beag Ó Buachan, reminded him that this was the tenth day with the tenth night already beginning to encroach on it. Fionn looked up, startled.

'Indeed,' he said, 'I had forgotten. But where will I go tonight?'

He wasn't very worried as any of a hundred great houses in the vicinity would gladly have welcomed him, but he had accepted hospitality from all of them and he did not want to abuse it.

The restriction applied to no one but Fionn and most of the others moved off when they saw Fionn thinking, for they didn't particularly relish the idea of accompanying him to some strange house or other when they had the night in Allen well planned before them. Only a few stayed behind, and among them was Donn MacDuibhne, and it was he who answered Fionn's question.

'Well,' said Donn, 'maybe we can have pleasure and entertainment for both of us tonight where you've never received it before.'

Fionn looked at him, because there weren't many houses he hadn't visited in the length and breadth of Ireland, but he said nothing and Donn went on.

'My son, Diarmuid, is fostered with Aengus Óg of the Tuatha de Danaan, at his palace at Brugh na Boinne. And because of who I am' – said Donn, swelling his chest a little for he was a vain enough man, though it was his only foolishness – 'Aengus' steward's son was fostered with him to be a playmate and companion, and the steward, being only a common man, agreed to send each day to the Brugh food and drink for nine men as the price for having his son fostered with mine. And so I am free to visit the palace of Aengus when I please, together with eight companions, and claim the food sent by the steward – otherwise Aengus' people get it. Furthermore,' he said, 'I haven't seen Diarmuid for more than a year and we are sure to get a welcome.'

The idea appealed to Fionn, who wasn't too familiar with

the homes of the great De Danaan, and together with seven companions and their hounds they drove to Brugh na Boinne in their chariots. Aengus welcomed them and had a banquet for them and brought in harpers and minstrels to pass the time while the food was being prepared. Diarmuid and the steward's son were there, two lovely children, darting about the place with laughter on their faces. Donn was as delighted to see his son as Diarmuid was to see his father and the great Fionn of whom he had only heard and with whom he someday hoped to serve. But the visitors noticed that while Aengus loved Diarmuid very clearly, equally clearly the people of his house favoured the steward's son. Donn disliked this, for his pride was offended that a steward's son should be favoured by anyone above his own, and he brooded on it until the hurt to his vanity brought a cloud on his mind. He sat silent and glowering throughout the banquet, but no one seemed to notice except Fionn who knew him very well. But he kept his counsel to himself and didn't ask Donn what troubled him for, being Fionn, he had noticed how things were too.

That night, after the banquet which was held in the great hall, the hounds began to fight over some scraps of meat that had been thrown to them, and there was great snarling and snapping and threshing of great bodies about the hall so that the women drew back in panic, and the servants fled. The two children didn't know whether to fly like the women and servants, or to stay and enjoy it like the men; and their hearts sprang into their great eyes as they looked at the fighting dogs which no one could, or would, separate. Whenever a dog came too near they would back away hurriedly, falling over some piece of furniture as they did so, while the dogs ravaged each other about the hall.

The eyes of all the men present were fastened on the fight, consequently they did not notice the son of the steward run between Donn's knees in the dimly lit hall. Remembering the favouritism the people of the house showed him above Diarmuid, Donn gave the lad a sudden squeeze and killed him on the spot. Then, in the confusion and without being seen by anyone, he threw the body under the feet of the hounds.

When, at last, the hounds were quietened, the little body was found and the steward nearly lost his reason at the sight. Everyone there tried to comfort him, but it was almost impossible. At last he turned to Fionn and said: 'Fionn, of all the men in this house tonight, I am the most harmed. The boy was my only child, and now he is killed by your hounds and I demand a suitable eric fine for him.'

Fionn said nothing for a moment. He was compassionate towards the man, but also anxious that justice be done, so he said: 'Examine the body of your son and if you find on it the mark of tooth or nail, then I will give you the eric you demand.'

So the body was examined, but no hurt, either bite or scratch, was found on it. The steward looked up wildly from where he crouched above the body of his son and his eyes glared at the assembled company. Then he turned on Fionn and cried: 'You, Fionn, have the power to uncover the hand that did this; yours is the wisdom and the divination of the Salmon of Knowledge and I put this *geasa,* this solemn vow, on you to identify the murderer of my son.'

Fionn had been afraid that something like this would happen. Whether the steward called on the so-called power he had from the Salmon of Knowledge, or whether he appealed to Fionn in his capacity as a wise and skilful man difficult to deceive, is of no importance. What is important is that Fionn accepted the *geasa* -- indeed he had little choice, and brought to bear on the problem what he knew and what he divined in whatever manner. The conclusion he reached, of course, was the correct one, that Donn, in a fit of jealousy, had killed the steward's son. Not wishing to make this known, Fionn offered to pay any eric fine the man demanded, but he refused, saying that it was his right to know who killed his son. And so Fionn was forced to tell him. Then the steward said: 'It is easier for Donn to pay my eric than for any other man in this house, and the eric I demand is that his son, Diarmuid, will be placed between my knees; if he gets off safe, then I will forget the whole matter.'

When Aengus heard this he rose up in anger and would have arrested the steward there and then; but Donn was even quicker and, drawing his sword, would have struck the head from the steward's shoulders if Fionn had not come between them and saved the steward. They stood like that for a moment, their hate electrifying the air between them, and then the steward turned and walked away. Coming back, silently, a moment later, he struck the body of his son with a golden druidical wand and transformed the dead boy into the semblance of a great, bristling, wild boar having neither ears nor tail.

Then, standing above the boar, with the wand in his hand, he made incantation: 'For this boar and your son Diarmuid, I decree the same lifespan; and when it is fulfilled, then they will kill each other. Then shall my son be avenged.'

And the moment he had said this the boar rushed out through the door and vanished into the night. The steward followed and neither of them were seen at Brugh na Boinne from that time onward. When he heard the terrible curse of the steward Aengus, in his turn, placed a *geasa* on Diarmuid, who was still and silent at his foster-father's feet, and it was that during his entire lifetime he could hunt anything that he desired, save only a wild boar.

Now all this happened long before the story of Diarmuid – and it is the same Diarmuid – and Grainne began, but it has an important part to play in it.

One morning, many years later, Fionn rose early and went out onto the slopes of the Hill of Allen before his castle. It was very still and quiet and the dawn was just a hint of light behind the horizon in the east. A blackbird sang somewhere alone – for blackbirds are always the first to sing in the morning – and Fionn looked about him as things began to distinguish themselves from the dark cloak of the night.

Two officers of the Fianna, Oisin his son, and Diorraing, son of Dobhar Ó Baiscne, came round the hill towards him. They were on duty that night and were surprised to see Fionn abroad so early. 'What brings you out of your bed at this time of the morning?' asked Oisin.

Fionn looked at him sideways to see if they were baiting him, but they were not. 'Well, to tell you the truth,' he said, 'tis no pleasure to a man to spend the long morning in bed by himself.'

Oisin laughed. ''Tis little you have to trouble you,' he said, 'why don't you sleep while you can?'

'Who can sleep easy,' growled Fionn, 'when his life is lonely and he has no wife to comfort him?'

The others saw that he was serious, and grunted their agreement, whether they meant it or not.

'That's the way I've been this long time, unable to sleep or to rest since Maignes, daughter of Garad, died on me.'

'Well, of all the men in Ireland,' said Oisin, 'you have smallest cause to complain. There isn't a woman in the country would not give all she has, and more, to share your bed with you; and anyway there isn't a female, virgin or woman, in the green girdled island that we wouldn't bring you once your eye lit on her.'

'If it comes to that,' said Diorraing, 'I know a girl above all others in the country fitting to be your wife, this minute.'

'Who?' asked Fionn.

'Grainne, daughter of Cormac, king of Ireland and son of Art, son of Conn Cead Cath. Of all the females I know, woman or girl, she's the most beautiful, most intelligent, most wonderful of the lot.'

And they knew that Diorraing didn't speak lightly when he said that, for he was the kind of man who would know about these things.

Fionn looked at him thoughtfully for a moment. He was impressed by what he heard – for he had not seen Grainne himself since she was a small baby for reasons that will be clear in a minute – and the lonesomeness of his nights and private hours weighed on him heavily. Although he was a great commander and a great companion, he was also the kind of man to whom the love and attention of a woman was necessary; a woman with whom he could share the secret and gentler side of his nature that he sometimes thought of as the weaker side. It was a great hunger in him which he would have to satisfy one way or another, and it occurred to him that if it was going to be satisfied at all then the finest available was worth seeking.

'There is a problem,' he said. 'King Cormac and myself have not been on the best of terms for some time, and there is a little distance between us; if he were to refuse me in this there would be the width of the Shannon between us over it and that wouldn't do. Let you two go to Tara and ask for me; if Cormac refuses, well and good, no one need hear another word about it; but it would be better if he refused you than me.'

'Good enough,' said Oisin, 'but say nothing yourself about why or where we are gone unless we get a favourable answer.'

So, after they had eaten they prepared themselves for a visit to the king, had their chariots made ready and set off. When they arrived at Tara, Cormac, as it happened, was in council. Even so he welcomed the two officers of the Fianna and adjourned the meeting, for he was certain that two of Fionn's officers had come to see him on important matters. When they were alone Oisin and Diorraing told the king what their errand was. Then, in his turn, Cormac looked at them speculatively before replying.

'There is hardly,' he said, 'in all Ireland a prince or young noble who hasn't sought Grainne's hand, and they have all been refused. But not by me. Yet each and every one of them holds me responsible for it, for she has always made me answer for her. This time, however, she must answer for herself, since I do not want the differences between Fionn MacCumhal and myself to widen as might happen were the refusal to come from me.'

Oisin and Diorraing were pleased to find that the king felt about the situation precisely as Fionn himself did, so when Cormac suggested that they ask Grainne herself they agreed instantly. So Cormac brought them to the women's quarters in his palace, and into Grainne's bower with its window of blue glass, and he introduced Oisin and Diorraing and asked her to fetch them bread and meat and wine so that they might relax while they talked. And Oisin and Diorraing were very impressed at this treatment by the king, for they were, after all, merely officers in his army. But Grainne said nothing but instructed one of her maidens in waiting to provide the food and drink. Then Cormac sat on the couch beside her and said: 'These two young officers are here on the instructions of Fionn MacCumhal to ask your hand on his behalf. What answer do you want to give, daughter?'

Now Grainne, who was indeed a most beautiful woman, but perhaps a trifle spoiled and wayward, hardly looked at the two young men; and her answer was as languid and as evasive as her looks. 'I have no idea if he is a fitting son-in-law for the king of Ireland,' she said, 'but if he is, then why would he not be a fitting husband for the king of Ireland's daughter?'

This reply did not please Cormac, who was a man of straightforwardness and righteousness. Angrily he said: 'There are no ifs about it so far as I am concerned.' And he looked sternly at his daughter for a reply, but she did not answer.

The two emissaries said nothing to this, but secretly studied the princess, who, slightly flushed, looked through her window away from them, as she was somewhat put out by her father's rebuke. Diorraing noticed that she was wearing a coronet of gold about her head and an amber jewel about her neck, and – for he was a romantic young man – said to himself that, like the amber and the gold, Grainne was a fine and rare woman, but unpredictable; while Oisin, the poet, was more practical and observant in his assessment of her. He noted what he could about her so that he could give Fionn an accurate account of her when he went back to Allen Castle. She was young, he thought, to be in the place of his own mother; indeed, she was younger than either of the two wives Fionn had had even when they were their youngest. On the other hand, she was lovely and she was accomplished. Her hands were long and well-shaped, and her finger-nails well kept and reddened; she was long legged, from ankle to knee and from knee to thigh. Her hips were full and round, her waist slim and her stomach flat with beautiful, well shaped breasts filling two halves of her garment above. Her lips were red and not too full; her eyes were bright, but not sunken. Just as he was considering her eyes she turned and looked at him steadily, but like one who keeps her thoughts to herself.

'She would,' he thought, 'make a good wife for Fionn, for she is attractive, intelligent and displays the dignity of a princess.'

Cormac then suggested that Fionn himself should come to Tara in the following month when he would have prepared a banquet to welcome him and at which it could be announced that Grainne and Fionn would be married, and her hand publicly be placed in his.

Then, for the first time for a while, Grainne spoke.

'I have never seen Fionn,' she said, 'what does he look like? Is he like either of you?'

'Indeed,' said Oisin smiling, 'if he is like either of us he should be like me, for I am his son.'

Grainne looked at him with her steady gaze again, and Oisin felt suddenly embarrassed.

'Ah yes,' she said, 'Fionn would have a son who has reached an age when he is as famous as you are, Oisin.'

And Oisin, unaccountably, blushed again.

However, Oisin and Diorraing returned to Castle Allen in Leinster – for it should be noted that Ireland, at that time, was divided into five provinces, not four, and the fifth was that of

Meath where Royal Tara lay. They reported to Fionn everything that had happened, how they had been well received by the king, how Grainne looked and how the king had appointed a day for Fionn to come to Tara. And when the Fianna heard the news they gave three great shouts of joy that their general was to be married to the king's daughter.

And, as all things wear away, so the time between then and the coming of Fionn to Tara for his bride wore away and, with the officers of the seven battalions of the Fianna as a guard of honour, Fionn set off from Allen.

Cormac received them with great honour and ceremony in the great hall of Midcuartha where he sat on his throne on the raised, crescent-shaped platform in the centre of the hall where he could be seen by everyone who was there, and that was a great number. He placed Fionn to his right, while on his left sat his queen, Eitche, and on her left Grainne and all the others were seated for the banquet that followed according to their rank and station.

As the banquet progressed the talk became centred in little groups here and there and Fionn's bard and druid, Duanach MacMorna, who was sitting near Grainne, sang and recited to her in a low voice many of the songs and poems and stories of her ancestors and their original kingdom, Cruachan, from where they had come to be the kings of Ireland at Tara.

After listening to him for a while, Grainne asked: 'What brings Fionn to Tara tonight, Duanach?'

Startled, he answered: 'If you don't know, then it is hard for me to know.'

She was silent for a moment at this. And, perhaps, it should be pointed out here that there was nothing strange or odd in Duanach's sitting beside Grainne, for the Irish people of that time, in their great wisdom, ranked bards and lawmakers as equal with kings and nobles and treated them accordingly.

After a moment Grainne spoke again. 'I'd like you to tell me what brought him,' she said.

'It's strange that you of all people should ask that,' said Duanach, 'for surely you know that he has come to ask for you as his wife?'

Grainne was silent again. Then she said: 'If he had come to ask me for Oisin, his son, or Oscar itself, his grandson, then I could understand it and there would be nothing to wonder at. It would be more fitting for me to go to one of them than to a man who is older than my own father.'

Wisely Duanach said nothing. Grainne was quiet again with her own thoughts for a while. Then she said: 'That is a great company of men who came with Fionn, but I don't know one among them except Oisin. Tell me, who is that warrior to his right?'

'That,' said Duanach, 'is Gall MacMorna, the terrible in battle.'

'And the young man beside him?'

'Oscar, Oisin's son,' said Duanach.

'And who is that graceful man beside him?'

'That's Caoilte MacRonan, the swiftest runner in all Ireland.'

'And next to him, the proud and haughty looking one, who is he?'

'That,' said Duanach, 'is Fionn's nephew, MacLughaid.'

'And beside him, the one with the gentle, handsome face, and dark curls; he's speaking now, with a soft voice – who's he?'

'That,' said Duanach, 'is Diarmuid Ó Duibhne, beloved of all the Fianna for his nobleness, his bravery and his generosity – and not only by the Fianna,' he added with a smile, 'but by every maiden who ever saw him as well. The foster-son of Aengus Óg.'

'Indeed?' said Grainne, 'that sets him apart from the rest of you, then, for it isn't every one is fostered by one of the Tuatha de Danaan. Who is that beside him?'

But Duanach had been asked a question by the king and was busy answering it. Grainne looked around until she caught the eye of one of her ladies-in-waiting. She beckoned to her.

'Get me my golden goblet – the jewelled one my father gave me on my birthday,' she said. 'It is in my jewel box.'

When the goblet was brought, Grainne filled it to the brim – and that was no small measure, for it was a great, two-handled, jewel encrusted goblet, that no one man could empty at a sitting – and said: 'Take it now to Fionn from me, and say that I would like him to drink to me from my own goblet.'

When the lady-in-waiting gave Fionn the goblet he was pleased that Grainne sent it to him first and, standing up, he raised the goblet and took a draught from it before passing it on to King Cormac. Cormac gave it to his wife, the queen, who in turn passed it on and so it went about the lords and nobles sitting at the high table.

But Grainne had put a powerful drug in the goblet and soon its effects were noticed for those at the table became drowsy and soon they had all fallen into a deep sleep; Fionn the king and all those who had supped from it. Then Grainne stood up from her place and went to where Diarmuid was sitting. With her heart beating in her breast and her eyes lowered, she spoke to him in a low voice.

'Diarmuid,' she said, her voice trembling, 'I love you.'

His head jerked as if he had been struck, and he looked wide-eyed up into the earnest, shy, but determined face of the beautiful girl. Then his wonder changed to amazement and alarm as he thought of Fionn, his commander, and his duty. And although he had been filled with joy when he realised what she said, he answered her sternly.

'You are to marry Fionn,' he said, 'I cannot love you and even if I could I would not.'

'I am not yet married to him, Diarmuid,' she replied, 'will you return the love I give you?'

Even though they were speaking in low voices, the tension between them was electric and had communicated itself to those others in the great hall who had fallen silent now and were watching them. But they were unaware of it at the time.

'I cannot, Grainne. You do not know me to begin with ...'

'That is not so,' said Grainne. 'I know you well. Do you remember a hurling match that was played between the men of Tara and the Fianna in which you saved the match for the Fianna by scoring two goals against my brother, Cairbre?'

'I do,' said Diarmuid.

'I watched it,' said Grainne, 'not from the field, but from the window of my room. And I saw how you, when one of the Fianna was hurt, leaped from the sideline and picked up his hurl all in one movement, and never stopped in your flight until you scored against the men of Tara, and repeated it again a moment later. In that moment, too, my heart went out to you and I gave you my love, Diarmuid, and I will never give it to anyone else no matter what comes or goes.'

Diarmuid remained silent, looking at her mutely; for he was torn between his duty and the love that rose in him for the princess beside him. But he could not speak of one or of the other.

'I know well,' said Grainne, 'that it is not right for me to speak so boldly; but you know my position. Would you have me married to an old man – a man older than my father – when I love you? Please, save me from this, Diarmuid.'

Then, with a frown on his face, and deeply troubled, Diarmuid answered: 'It is a wonder you wouldn't love Fionn who, more than any man alive, deserves the love of women and the respect of men ... and why should you single me out more than any other of the Fianna or the nobles of Tara, for of them all I am the least worthy of your love. But even if you were to love me, and I love you –' and he faltered, for he did and he knew it – 'and we were to be married, there is not a wilderness or a fortress in the whole of Ireland that would protect us from Fionn's anger and revenge.'

Grainne looked at him for a moment without replying, and when she did answer him there was a smile playing about her lips. 'Oh Diarmuid,' she said, 'I know that you are speaking from your sense of duty and not from your heart, for my love for you is so great and so understanding that I already know of your love for me even though you will not admit it. But now I am putting you under the obligations of *geasa,* and bind you under the laws of our ancient religion to take me from this palace tonight and make me your wife before Fionn and the others waken.'

Diarmuid was in a torment of love and despair, but he made a last effort to retrieve the situation.

'Even if I agreed to your *geasa,* Grainne,' he said, 'how could we get away, for you know as well as I do that when Fionn sleeps at Tara he alone has the privilege of guarding the keys of the great gates to the fort, and without them we cannot leave.'

But she said: 'There is a wicket-gate leading from my apartments that we can use.'

'No,' replied Diarmuid, 'for it is another *geasa* on me that I may never enter or leave a king's palace except by the main gateway.'

'Then,' said Grainne angrily, 'come or stay as you please, but I am going in any event with or without you.' And, paying no attention to the hundreds of pairs of eyes that followed her, she turned and swept angrily out of the hall.

Then Diarmuid turned back to his companions and, with a sudden feeling of guilt, understood that they had seen and overheard the whole conversation, for they had that silent and embarrassed pre-occupation with silence that people acquire in such circumstances.

Being the straightforward and honourable man that he was he decided to take the direct course so, turning to his close friend, Oisin who was also Fionn's son, he said: 'What should I do, Oisin, for Grainne has laid heavy obligations on me?'

'What can you do,' replied Oisin, 'you are blameless in this matter, but you must keep your obligations or lose your honour, and no man of us here will hold you to blame for that. Go with Grainne, but guard yourselves well against the vengeance of Fionn.'

Then Diarmuid asked Oscar, Oisin's son, who said: 'It is no man who does not honour his obigations; go with her.'

'And you, Caoilte,' asked Diarmuid, 'what do you say?'

'I have a wife of my own,' said Caoilte, 'yet I would gladly give the world's wealth if it was me the princess had offered her love to.'

Last of all Diarmuid asked Diorraing, who said: 'Even though it would mean the end of you and I were to cry over your grave, go with Grainne.'

And Diarmuid, still in doubt himself, said: 'And do you all feel the same way?' And all together they answered 'Yes.'

Then Diarmuid stood up and stretched his hands out to his friends with tears in his eyes and took farewell of them, for he knew that the end of his days with the Fianna had come, and that when he met them again it would mean trouble and war for them all. Then, without saying a word, he put on his armour and his helmet, took his shield, his sword and his spears and strode out of the hall.

He climbed the ramparts and looked out across the plain beyond. There below him in the moonlight stood Grainne, waiting. When she saw him she called up to him: 'Are you coming, Diarmuid?'

'Oh Grainne,' he said, 'I don't know what to do. The life facing us is not fitting for a king's daughter, and I don't know where we will be safe from Fionn.'

Then Grainne, sad and gentle but as determined as ever, said: 'It makes no difference to me, Diarmuid. I will go alone if I have to, but I am not going back to marry that old man.'

'Then you will not go on alone,' said Diarmuid and, taking his spears in his hands, he put the butts on the ground and, grasping them near the heads, vaulted across the ramparts and landed lightly besider her.

As he regained his balance she moved towards him and put her arms around him. Without a word he folded her within his cloak and made no further effort to deny the love he felt for her. The harshness and coldness of his voice was gone, and he spoke gently and lovingly to her.

'I love you, Grainne,' he said, 'more than it is possible for me to say. You are all that I ever thought of or dreamed of, and there is nothing that I ever thought of or dreamed of that isn't you or in you. May I be worthy of your love ...' and then he stopped because he knew the words were pointless and heavy; too heavy to express what he felt, so he folded his cloak around her again and gave his spirit up to hers for a long moment. Then he said: 'Let us go, Grainne, for the further we are from here when Fionn wakes in the morning the better.'

They hadn't gone very far when Grainne stumbled and cried out that she couldn't keep up the pace that Diarmuid was setting.

'Diarmuid,' she cried, 'I can't go on like this.'

He stopped, a worried frown on his face. Death lay behind them in the night, he knew, and was closing in with every passing minute.

'Go back,' said Grainne, 'to the stables and get a pair of horses and a good chariot. I'll wait here for you.'

And back he went to the stables, which lay outside the palace, and yoked a pair of strong horses to a speedy chariot; then he turned the other horses loose and drove back to where Grainne was waiting for him. He lifted her into the chariot and they drove through the darkness, facing towards the west. The sun rose behind them, and Diarmuid drove the horses faster, and it was full and broad daylight when they reached the wide Shannon. There Diarmuid broke up the chariot and threw the pieces into deep water. He led one of the horses across the broad reaching river, and left the other to stray along the eastern bank. When he had that done, he turned to Grainne and said: 'It will be easy for Fionn to follow us this far, for our tracks are plain enough. But from here on we must vanish if we are to be safe, therefore it is better to abandon the chariot.'

Then he lifted Grainne onto his shoulder and carried her across the ford so carefully and gently that not so much as the sole of her foot or the hem of her dress became wet. Then they went on into the fastnesses of Connacht where there are many places, unknown and hidden, in which to seek refuge.

For a long time they went from place to place, always pursued by the trackers of Fionn, until at last they found themselves in a forest where Diarmuid built a small cabin of clay and wattles, and there they lived off the land for a while.

Meanwhile Fionn's rage when he awoke the following morning and discovered what had happened was terrible. Indeed his jealousy and rage were so great that for a while he was incapable of either speech or action. But when his brain and his consuming passion cooled, leaving behind an anger perhaps more deadly than either, he sent for men of the Clan Nephin, the most famous trackers in Ireland, and therefore in the world, and set them after Diarmuid and Grainne.

Their task was simple until they reached the ford across the Shannon but, as Diarmuid had travelled both up and down the far bank and laid several false trails, they were unable to pick up the true one. When they reported back to Fionn he looked at them coldly and said: 'Pick up that trail again, and stick to it, or I will hang every man of you on both sides of the ford to mark the spot where you failed.'

There was no course open to them but to follow and re-follow every mark, every trail, no matter how fresh or how old it was. Finally, with many of the Fianna following, they hit on the correct trail and followed it towards the south-west.

'Good,' said Fionn, 'I know now where they are heading.'

Now, as it happened, Oisin and some of Diarmuid's other friends were with Fionn when the men of Clan Nephin reported that they had picked up Diarmuid's trail again, and they were worried.

They discussed the position among themselves and Oisin, who knew how much Bran – one of Fionn's great hounds –

loved Diarmuid as well, took the hound and set him on the trail ahead of the trackers. Without once losing the trail he followed it night and day until he eventually reached the place where Diarmuid and Grainne were hidden in the depths of the forest. Silently he crept into the little cabin and placed his muzzle on the bed where they lay. Diarmuid started up, reaching for his sword, but Bran whined with pleasure and Diarmuid recognised him immediately. He also realised that he had come alone, for the first thing he did was to leap from the cabin and search outside, but there was neither sight nor sound of the Fianna to disturb the sleeping forest.

Grainne was sitting up in alarm when he returned, afraid as much of the great hound that stood near her as of what Diarmuid might find outside. But when he came back he reassured her.

'It is nothing,' he said, 'only Fionn's hound which has been sent to warn us that he is close behind.'

'Then we must fly,' she said.

But Diarmuid would not leave. When Oscar and Oisin and Diarmuid's other friends came closer to the heart of the wood with the men of the Fianna, they found Bran returning, but with a drooping eye and dragging tail, and Oisin was immediately alarmed. He suspected that Diarmuid had not taken the warning he had sent. So he spoke to Caoilte MacRonan who had a man called Fergor with the greatest shout of any man in the land.

'Tell Fergor to give a bellow out of him,' said Oisin to Caoilte, 'that Diarmuid might know how close we are.'

So with that Caoilte spoke to Fergor who drew enough air for six men into his lungs and let go a shout that rose the birds from the treetops, and the little animals from their nests in a pandemonium of fright, and which could be heard across half of the whole of Connacht.

And Diarmuid heard that shout. So did Grainne – for she couldn't help it – and she said: 'What was that dreadful shout?'

'That,' said Diarmuid, 'is the shout of Fergor, one of Caoilte Mac Ronan's men, and well I know it for I often heard it before and I think that they have him shouting now to warn us that he is near, and if he is near Caoilte and Oisin are near, for they are with him, and if they are near then Fionn and the Fianna are near for they are with the Fianna.'

'Then in God's name,' she said, 'let us go.'

But Diarmuid was very stubborn and very proud too when something like his honour was involved, but eventually Grainne persuaded him to run with her from the pursuit of Fionn and he led her in safety through the forest.

When Fionn and the Fianna reached the place where they had been and found them gone his rage was terrible, and he let all who would see it; but he calmed himself in time, and finally decided to return to his castle at Allen and wait; for he felt that if he waited long enough they would fall into his hands at last. But nevertheless he made use of every opportunity to trap them.

He proclaimed Diarmuid an outlaw and put penalties on anyone who gave him any help or kindness. And so it was that, although Fionn had called off the Fianna, Diarmuid and Grainne still travelled through the land as a hunted and wanted couple, living by the strength of Diarmuid's hand and the temper of his sword on the flesh of the wild deer and the crystal waters of the springs. As for Fionn MacCumhal, he had only one person in whom he confided, and she was his woman-spy and agent Deirdru, who went up and down the face of Ireland as this kind of a woman or that, seeking information about Diarmuid and Grainne, where they sheltered, who were their friends and who were not; for it was – and still is very often – easier for an intelligent woman to glean this kind of information than it is for a man, as long as she's not too particular about how she does it.

Then one day as he was sitting playing chess with one of the chieftains of the Fianna in the sun-garden behind the castle, Deirdru slipped in through a wicket-gate that only she – beside himself – had a key to. She signalled to him from behind a shrub and he abruptly excused himself from the game and strolled away towards the end of the garden; he was by nature a secretive man who didn't like to let his left hand know what his right hand was doing, as the saying is, and even though his battalion commander knew Deirdru quite well and the work she did, Fionn was more satisfied when he knew least, particularly when he knew less than himself. In a bushy arbour at the end of the garden he met Deirdru who was in the garb of a wandering druidess.

'Well,' he said.

'I have them located,' she said. 'They have fled to the fort of the ancients in the far west, the one known as Da Both. They are there now. I have asked Clann Morna to maintain a constant watch on them and track them if they leave ... in your name,' she added hurriedly as he looked at her without change of expression.

And his expression did not change as his excitement mounted at her news. What he felt inside was not for her, or anyone, to share. But deep inside him, mounting his blood to his brain like the excitement of any passion flooding men from time immemorial, he felt the tide of anticipation rising in him hungrily. He knew the fort of which she spoke, it was one of the ancient, circular stone forts that had been dotted around the coastline for longer than the memories of man reached backwards into time. Built of high, loosely piled slabs of stone, the walls were anything from ten to twenty feet thick, often with conical apartments contained within them, with access from the circular enclosure. Along the top of the wall there was usually a rampart with a small wall facing outwards, and, for a considerable distance around the entire fort there was a formidable barricade of closely packed, upright boulders about three feet long, through which passage was slow and difficult. Only at the gateways to the fort was there a free passage. And it was here, in the stone huts and gloomy passages of the past, that Diarmuid and Grainne had taken refuge. Fionn smiled to himself.

Then, taking with him several battalions of the Fianna, Fionn made a forced march across country, the infantry running beside the chariots and cavalry, until they reached Da Both, and as they went the foot soldiers hung to the chariots or saddles with one hand carrying their weapons in the other that they might travel more quickly.

When they reached the outskirt of the fort guarded by the Clann Morna, Fionn sent one of his trackers from the Clann Nephin to scout the position inside the fort and tell him who was there and how disposed. After some time the scout emerged from the night silently: 'Diarmuid is there,' he said, 'and a lady.'

'Is it Grainne?' asked Fionn.

'I do not know,' replied the scout, 'for I never saw the lady Grainne, but there is a lady within anyway.'

And then in a spasm of sudden rage Fionn swore at Diarmuid: 'Curse him,' he said, 'and bad luck to him and all his friends with him; he's here now but he won't leave here alive.'

Then he stood up in a rage facing the fort and shouted: 'Do you hear me, Ó Duibhne; you won't leave this rat-hole of yours alive, do you hear?'

But there was no reply, nor any sound, from the great, silent, stone fort darker than the darkness ahead of them.

Then Oisin said, and his voice carried through the stillness of the silent army: 'It is your jealousy, Fionn, has you blinded. Do you think Diarmuid would wait here for you to kill him?'

But Fionn turned on him: 'No thanks to you, my son,' he said bitterly, 'if he did, for this time you have no hound to send ahead and no gillie to shout and warn him. He won't leave here until he's dead, I promise you.'

Then Oscar, Fionn's grandson, said: 'But Fionn, knowing Diarmuid as you do, what makes you think he would be here waiting for you to kill him?'

To that Fionn smiled a cold smile. 'Knowing Diarmuid as I do,' he said, 'we shall see.' Then raising his voice he shouted: 'Tell me now, Diarmuid, who speaks the truth; Oisin and Oscar who say you have run, or I who say you are inside?'

There was a pause. Then back from the solitary fort came the clear, proud answer: 'Your judgement was never faulty, Fionn; Grainne and myself are here; but no one will enter without my permission.'

And the battalions of the Fianna, Fionn standing among them on a hillock, saw against the night Diarmuid standing on the ramparts of the fort. They saw him raise Grainne beside him and they saw him give her three kisses on the mouth while Fionn stood there staring at them. When Fionn saw that the fire of his jealousy blossomed bigger than ever and roared in his heart and he cried: 'For that insult alone I'll have his head.'

He placed the men of the Fianna round the gateways of the fort, a company to each and there were seven gateways, and warned them: 'If Diarmuid tries to escape by this gate, capture him and hold him here for me. But do not harm the girl.'

Now while all this was taking place outside, an even stranger thing was happening inside the fort. For, as Diarmuid strode vigilantly from corner to corner of the position he had chosen to defend while Grainne crouched below above a cooking fire, Aengus Óg – Diarmuid's foster-father – suddenly walked into the firelight. Whether he had come through the ring of armed men, or through the fence of standing stones, or through some mystic power of the De Danaan Diarmuid neither knew nor cared, but he was glad to see him.

Aengus looked at him and said: 'What is it you have done, Diarmuid, that Fionn's anger is turned on you?'

Then Diarmuid told him from the beginning, how he was under *geasa* obligation of the gravest sort from Grainne, and in peril of his life from Fionn. Aengus stood looking at both of them for a long time. Then he said: 'I have the power to come in here, and I have the power to go also so that those outside will not see – or will not have any knowledge of – my coming and my going. Come now and I will take you with me, one on each side.'

But Diarmuid said: 'No. Take Grainne. I will stay here for it would not be honourable to do otherwise and I am tired of forever running. However, I will leave this place, and if I am alive I will follow you to Brugh na Boinne. If I am killed send the princess to her father, and ask him to treat her neither better nor worse than before for having taken me as her husband.'

Then, in spite of her protests and tears, Diarmuid kissed Grainne and told her to go with Aengus Óg. But she cried and lamented so much that he feared the men outside would hear her and guess what was happening. Then Aengus said: 'Leave her to me, Diarmuid.' He caught Grainne from behind by the shoulders and tried to turn her round, but she would not turn, crying and fastening herself on Diarmuid's breast. Then Aengus Óg stood back and spoke sharply and penetratingly: 'Grainne!' She looked up. He repeated her name, and again repeated it. Gradually her wailing ceased, though the tears still ran down her face, and her head lifted. She turned to look at him.

'Now listen to me, Grainne,' he said, 'and to nothing else. You are to be quiet. You are sleepy and you will rest and you will hear nothing but my voice ...'

And so it was, for presently she stood there, very still and docile, the expression of sleep on her face but with her eyes open. Diarmuid remained silent and awed at this exhibition of the De Danaan power. Urgently Aengus Óg whispered to him:

'Diarmuid. Listen to me carefully. Say goodbye to her now, kiss her, she is all right. But I must hurry. She will do whatever I tell her to. But we have little time. I must go as I came, for the guards may soon wake from the slumber I put them under. I will expect you at the Brugh.'

And with that he folded his cloak about Grainne and seemed to vanish like a wraith in the one movement. But looking over the wall Diarmuid could, to his surprise, see him walking unmolested past the rows of motionless guards at one of the gates; guards who, apparently, did not even see him.

Now, when Grainne and Aengus Óg left him, Diarmuid checked his armour completely, went up to one of the seven gates around the fort and stood, tall and straight like a pillar, deep in thought for a while. Then he lifted his great spear, the Gae Dearg, and hammered on the door with the haft.

'Who's out there?' he called.

'Oisin,' came the whisper, 'and Oscar and the Clann Baiscne. Come out to us and you will come to no harm.'

'I will not go out,' replied Diarmuid, 'until I find the gate that Fionn himself guards.'

And so it was at every gate – save two. At the second gate were Caoilte MacRonan and the Clann Ronan who swore to fight to the death for Diarmuid, but he would not go for fear of bringing Fionn's wrath on them. At the third door it was Conan Maol and the Clann Morna who also offered him safety, but Diarmuid would not go; next Cuan and the men of Munster offered him his freedom, but Diarmuid would not endanger them, and it was the same at the next gate which was guarded by the Ulstermen. At the sixth gate Diarmuid called again to know who was guarding the other side.

'Clann Nephin,' came the reply, 'no friends of yours, Diarmuid; come out this door, Ó Duibhne, and you will be the mark for all our swords and spears.'

And Diarmuid replied: 'Dogs and sons of dogs. Your only ability is to smell a track like the rest of your kind. I will not go out to you for I would not dirty my weapons with your disgusting blood.'

And he went on to the seventh and last gate. 'Who guards this gate,' he cried as he hammered on it.

'Fionn MacCumhal,' came the answer, 'and members of his

Clann and with them the Leinster Fianna. Come out to me, Diarmuid, till I carve your flesh from your bones.'

'Through this door I will come surely, Fionn,' said Diarmuid.

Then Fionn brought his men close to the gate and spread them along the great wall on either side, for fear that Diarmuid would slip across if he brought all his men to the one spot; for Diarmuid was too good a soldier and Fionn too old a one not to know a trick to draw the enemy off to one spot and penetrate at another.

But Diarmuid's trick was not the trick that Fionn expected. When Fionn had posted his men along the wall from the gate they guarded, Diarmuid climbed to the parapet directly above the gate and, using his great spears, vaulted forth, out beyond the men below, and was already running before they had time to turn around. To those figures that rose up in his path he gave short shrift and no mercy, he cut them down as he ran without stopping, and left a trail of dead and dying strewn behind him on the path as he vanished into the night.

He did not stop running throughout the night until long after the sounds of pursuit had faded away. Then, during the day, he hid himself carefully, and so, after several days of cautious journeying, he eventually reached Brugh na Boinne and his foster-father.

When he stumbled in through the great gates of Aengus' palace he made his way directly to the sun-garden where he knew he would find Grainne; she looked up as he came through the wicket-gate into the garden and the very spark of life itself all but fled through her mouth with joy when she saw him come towards her.

And that night they stayed there with Aengus, but next day they knew they had to be on their way again. Before they went Aengus, tall and wise and majestic, changeless and long lived, said to them: 'My counsel is that you fly from this place and from every place in which you are known, and in your going here and going there never go into a tree that has but the one trunk, nor a cave with but the one opening; never stay on an island that has only one landing place. Do not eat where you have cooked; do not sleep where you have eaten; where you have slept do not eat in the morning.'

And with this advice Aengus said goodbye to them, and

they walked out of his palace into the hunting world.

HAVING LEFT AENGUS ÓG Diarmuid and Grainne travelled west and south until they came to the River Laune near Killarney – then, as now, a good river for salmon, but known as the Rough Stream of the Champions – and they stayed beside it for a little while, and then went on to the plain beyond, between it and the Caragh River, called the Grey Bog of Findliath. One morning, while they were still journeying westwards, they met a stranger coming towards them. He was a man of enormous size, even in a land where big men were common, with a fine noble bearing about him and a long stride beneath him; but the arms and armour he carried, while complete, were ill-cared for and unused.

Diarmuid greeted him and asked him who he was.

'My name is Muadhan,' replied the other, 'and it would suit me well to be your servant.'

'If I took you on,' asked Diarmuid, 'what could you do for me that I could not do for myself?'

'I will serve you by day,' said Muadhan, 'and watch for you by night,' which was a good answer since Diarmuid was for a long time feeling the ill-effects of too little sleep and too much concern.

So they made an agreement between them and Muadhan went westward with his new master and mistress. They reached the Caragh River and Muadhan proved his worth by carrying Diarmuid and Grainne across it without bothering with a ford; once across they travelled on until they came to the River Behy and there they found a small cave on the side of a hill called Currach-Cinn-Adhmaid and above the sea where the Tonn Torna roars in wintertime with the forecast of rain.

Muadhan made the cave comfortable with rushes and birch tops for Diarmuid and Grainne, and when he had that done he went out and cut, with a great, rusty knife that he wore in his belt, a long, straight branch from a mountain ash or rowan tree. Then he produced a line of hair from his pouch and a hook of bone, and fitting one of the red rowan berries to the hook he made three casts with the rod across the stream and with each cast hooked a salmon. Then he put by the rod until the following day. He cooked the fish, giving the largest one to Diarmuid and another to Grainne, keeping the smallest one for himself, and then settled himself at the mouth of the cave to keep watch while Diarmuid and Grainne slept within.

Next morning as dawn came rising above the three humps of Currach-Cinn-Adhmaid, Diarmuid strode out upon the biggest of them, telling Grainne to keep watch while Muadhan slept. From the top of the hill he began to survey the surrounding countryside and the sea to the west of him and it wasn't very long before he saw a small fleet of black ships making their way up the bay beneath. At the very foot of the hill where Diarmuid stood the ships turned for shore and more than eighty warriors disembarked from them. Diarmuid watched them for a little while, and then, with great leaps and bounds on his heels, he hurtled down the hillside towards them.

When he reached them he greeted them and they, who had seen him coming and had stopped whatever they were doing until he reached them, returned his greeting. They were wild, hard-looking, ruthless sea pirates and Diarmuid didn't care for them at all.

'We are the three chiefs of the Ictian Sea,' they said, 'Dubhcos, Fionncos, and Trencos. Who are you?'

Diarmuid looked at them for a moment. He had heard of these three, Blackfoot, Whitefoot and Strongfoot, and what he had heard didn't make him any happier to see them there.

'A man of the locality,' he said. 'What brings ye here?'

They looked sharply at him with their hard eyes. But he did not move. 'We're here,' said one of them at length, 'at the request of Fionn MacCumhal who can't keep strange cocks out of his own nest,' and they all laughed coarsely.

Diarmuid smiled politely. 'So they tell me,' he said. 'What does he want you to do?'

'To pluck a cockerel for him.' They laughed again at this sally from Trencos. 'This Diarmuid Ó Duibhne is loose hereabouts it seems and Fionn, for all his Fianna, hasn't been able to get his hands on him ... but what can you expect from a crowd like that anyway, soldiers ...' and he grunted in contempt.

At this insult to the Fianna Diarmuid was tempted to draw his sword there and then and teach the foreigners just what the Fianna could do, but instead he smiled politely again, and said nothing.

'Fionn is paying us well to watch the coast while he combs the land behind so that we'll catch this outlaw between us,' said Dubhcos.

'And will you be able for him?' asked Diarmuid innocently.

'There isn't a man alive we're not able for,' said Dubhcos, looking as black as the foot he was named after.

'And anyway,' said Fionncos, looking just as black in spite of his name, 'we have three man-killing hounds from Gaul that will track him down and kill him. Now, tell us, have you heard anything of him?'

'Aren't ye the lucky men ye met me,' said Diarmuid still playing the simple innocent, 'indeed I did see him and only yesterday. And it would be as well for you to pay attention to what I say and go after him with caution for 'tis no common man ye have to deal with when ye're dealing with Diarmuid.'

After some more of this 'innocent' talk, when, despite their bluster, he could see that he had them uneasy if not worried, he asked them if they had any wine on board as he was thirsty. Confident that they had found a mine of information, and since Fionn was paying them well with a bonus guaranteed if they took Diarmuid, the pirates said that they had and produced a barrel.

They all drank until the barrel was empty, and then Diarmuid said: 'Now I'll show you a feat that Diarmuid taught me so that you may know the kind of man you'll have to meet if you have the bad luck to catch up with him; and I'll challenge anyone of ye to perform it after me.'

Now Diarmuid wasn't as foolish in this as it might seem for, while his companions had dipped liberally into the barrel of wine and transferred its contents from there to their stomachs with great enthusiasm, he had disposed of most of the wine given to him in quite another way; he had spilled it behind him, or beside him, or before him or wherever happened to be handiest, but very little of it had gone inside him. So that he was now as sober as he ever was, while they were boastful and unsteady on their feet.

Diarmuid picked up the barrel and ran with it to the edge of a high cliff overlooking the bay. At the top the cliff was very high and it plunged down to the sea and the rocks below, but it tapered down towards the beach in a gentle slope, becoming less and less, so that if you walked along the top of it you would eventually reach the beach. Diarmuid placed the barrel at the highest part with half of it hanging over the cliff and then leaped up on it. It started to roll towards the beach with Diarmuid balanced on it hanging over the precipice, but he brought it safely down to the beach. Three times he did this with the pirates looking at him.

'You call that a feat,' they cried derisively, 'surely you never saw a real feat in your life.'

Then one of them laughing picked up the barrel and ran with it to the top of the cliff intending to repeat Diarmuid's trick. He put it on the edge of the cliff and leaped on it. As he did so Diarmuid gave it a push with his foot to set it going and the man immediately lost his balance and, with a terrible scream, fell over the cliff and was dashed to pieces on the sharp edges and points of the rocks below.

Then another one of them tried, and he too was killed in the same manner, and then another tried and then another and the upshot of it was that ten or eleven of them were killed before they would acknowledge themselves beaten and then it was only because Dubhcos ordered them to stop. So the others went back on board their ship, gloomy and muttering to themselves, very sober again.

Cheerfully Diarmuid left them and returned to the cave, and Grainne was overjoyed to see him. Muadhan went then with his rod and putting another rowan berry on the hook, caught three more salmon as he had done on the previous night. He cooked them and shared them as he had done before, and then kept watch throughout the night while Diarmuid and Grainne slept until the dawn flooded the mountainside again.

Then Diarmuid left the cave again telling Grainne to keep watch while Muadhan slept, and he went back to the camp of the pirates where he found the three chiefs and their men on the shore before him. He greeted them and asked them if they would like to see any more feats of Diarmuid's: 'We'd much prefer to get some information about him,' they said surlily.

'Information is it?' asked Diarmuid innocently and wide eyed. 'Well aren't ye the lucky men ye met me, and sure isn't that why I came here this morning, to tell ye the information I have?' He paused, and dropped his voice. 'I met a man who saw him this very morning, eating a fish by the side of a stream above ...' and he waved his hand generously in the direction of the mountain. The three men made a start as if to set out after him there and then, but Diarmuid went on ... 'Of course that's several hours ago and he'd be long gone since, but maybe 'tis no harm, for if ye met him when ye were unprepared it might go hard with ye. I'll show ye another feat of his now that he taught me that ye might know what to expect from him.'

And so saying Diarmuid took off his helmet and his armour; his cloak and his tunic until only his shirt remained across his broad shoulders. Then taking the Gae Buidhe, his smaller spear, the one that had been Mananaan MacLir's, who had lived in Scotland and in Amhain Abhlach, he fixed it firmly in the ground with the point upwards. Then, walking backwards a little, he ran towards it and with a leap, landed softly on the point, before leaping safely to the ground without wound or hurt of any kind. The onlookers were amazed that he had not been pierced and believed it to be a trick – which it was; and that he wore some protection in his shoe – which he did not. The matter lay in the head of the spear which could be adjusted by one who knew how. But the pirates did not know how.

One of them a dark faced surly fellow, stood up and said: 'If you call that a feat it is plain you have never seen one in your life.' And running towards the spear he made a great leap in the air and came down on the spear and was impaled through his leg as far as his heart so that they had a terrible job to retrieve the spear from inside him. Diarmuid repeated the feat; and then Diarmuid repeated the feat again. Several more men of the pirates attempted it, and all were killed, but they did not give up trying it until ten or twelve of them lay bloody and dead about the place and Fionncos ordered them to stop. After that they returned to their ships and Diarmuid, in great good humour, returned to the cave where Grainne greeted him and Muadhan caught the salmon as before. After their meal Diarmuid and Grainne lay down to sleep and Muadhan spent the night on watch.

Next morning Diarmuid went out on the mountain and cut two, strong forked poles which he took with him to the beach where the pirates were as before.

Diarmuid greeted them and after some exchange of conversation they asked him what the poles were for.

'I brought these,' said Diarmuid, 'to show you one of the feats of this Ó Duibhne that ye hunt.'

He then fixed the poles firmly in the earth and taking his sword, the Moralltach or Great Fury, that he had received from Aengus Óg himself, he laid it between the two forks with the edge uppermost and bound it in position with strong thongs. Then, with a light jump, he landed on the edge and walked gently three times from one end to another along the blade and then leaped to the ground without any sign of injury. He challenged the strangers to do the same thing.

Then one of them rose up with a black look and, not saying anything, leaped upwards onto the blade. But he fell heavily on it so that it cut him in two. Another tried the same and was killed also and they did not cease until as many were killed as had been killed on the previous two days.

They stopped at length only when Trencos ordered them to do so and were about to return to their ships when they asked Diarmuid if he had any news of himself.

'I saw him today,' he replied, 'and I'll tell you what I'll do. I'll go and see if I can find him and bring him to you in the morning.'

They were pleased enough at that, for they had begun to be suspicious of him – and not before their time, I suppose – and Diarmuid returned to the cave on the hill where the night was spent as before.

Next morning Diarmuid went out on the mountain and this time prepared himself for battle. He put on his great armour, which was of the strongest sort so that it was all but impossible to wound him anywhere. He hung the Moralltach at his left hip and took his two spears, the Gae Buidhe, or small spear of Mananaan, and the Gae Dearg or Great Red Spear, from whose wounds no one ever recovered.

Then he woke Grainne and told her to keep watch until nightfall while Muadhan slept. When she saw him prepare for battle she was frightened and asked him what he intended to do.

'Have Fionn's soldiers found us?' she cried in alarm.

But he calmed her and told her: 'It is better to be prepared in case the enemy does come my way, but there is no danger.'

His calm words reassured her and he went down the hill to meet the foreigners as before. They greeted him and asked him if he had seen himself, and Diarmuid replied: 'He is not very far away, for I have seen him just now.'

At this they became very excited and demanded that he lead them to his hiding place. But he retreated a few steps from them and held up his hand as they rushed about to arm themselves, and they stopped what they were doing in their surprise.

'That,' he said, 'would be a poor way of repaying a friendship, and Diarmuid Ó Dubhne is my friend if he is anybody's and is now under the protection of my arms and armour, so you may be certain I will do him no treachery.'

When they heard this their rage was enormous and they cursed and swore at him. One of them said: 'Then if you are his friend you are Fionn's enemy and ours too; and now we'll have your head to bring him as well as that of Diarmuid.'

'Indeed,' said Diarmuid, 'that is a thing you might do if you had me tied hand and foot, perhaps; but since I'm not I'll make it hard for you.'

And so saying he drew the Moralltach from its scabbard and, as they drew forward to close with him, he sprang at them and clove the body of the foremost in two with one blow. Then he rushed through them and round them, seemingly above them and below them, like a wolf among sheep or a hawk among sparrows, cleaving them and slaughtering them until only a few were left who were hardly able to reach their ships and safety from his terrible fury.

After this Diarmuid returned to the cave and he and Grainne ate and slept as before while Muadhan kept watch until the morning. Then, arming himself fully again, and taking his great shield with him, he went and stood on the hillside and struck his shield with his spear as a challenge until the sound of it echoed and re-echoed across the bay and back from the surrounding hills. When he heard it Dubhcos immediately armed himself and sprang ashore to meet the challenger before the sound of the challenge had died away.

Now Diarmuid, after the insults and belittling of Dubhcos, had no wish to kill him quickly, and had a worse punishment in mind for him. So, casting aside his weapons, he closed with his foe and they struggled and fought until their muscles and sinews, their bones and veins strained and cracked with the agony; the earth seemed to tremble under their raging feet as they stamped and the very rocks threw back the noise of the combat. And so it went until Diarmuid, with one immense heave, threw Dubhcos helpless to the ground and instantly leaped on him and bound him with chain-bound thongs. After Dubhcos came Fionncos and then Trencos and Diarmuid defeated each of them and tied him up in the same manner.

Now this is the way in which he tied them. He tied their feet together and he tied their hands behind their backs. Then he made a noose in the thongs and put it around their necks and he tied the running end of this about their feet which he doubled up into the small of their backs. Then, if they did not stretch their legs they became cramped and died of contortion, and if they stretched their legs they choked themselves to death. Leaving them writhing in pain on the ground, he said: 'I would strike off your heads, but that I wish you to die slowly and in torment; and die you will, for none can release you from these bonds until you die.'

Then Diarmuid went back to the cave and told Grainne all that had happened and how he had caused nearly forty of the pirates to be killed in his feats and had killed many more of them in battle so that they were reduced to less than half their number. He told her that he had beaten and tied the three leaders and left them on the hill to die: 'Because,' he said, 'I want their torment to be long and not short. There are only four men in Ireland who can loosen them, Oisin, Oscar, MacLugha and Conan Maol, and I doubt if any of them will do it. Fionn will hear what happened to them and the news will sting him. But he will know we are here, so we must leave. Also the remainder of the pirates will set their man-hunting dogs after us, so we had better leave quickly.'

So they left the cave and travelled eastwards until they came to the Grey Bog of Findliath and whenever Grainne was tired or they had to cross water or rough places Muadhan picked her up and tenderly carried her without sign of tiredness himself.

Meanwhile those of the pirates who were left alive had come to where their three chiefs lay bound and tried to release them, but the more they tried to undo the Persian knots that Diarmuid had put on them, the tighter they became. While they were doing this they saw Deirdru, Fionn's secret agent, coming towards them across the mountainside. When she saw the numerous bodies around she asked who it was had made the fearful slaughter.

'Tell us first,' they replied angrily, 'who you are for we trust no one after what happened here.' And they put the point of a sword to her throat and would have run her through there and then if she had not said: 'I am Deirdru of the Black Mountain, the agent of Fionn MacCumhal who sent me here to look for you.'

They relaxed then and told her what had happened. 'We do not know his name,' they said, 'but we can describe him. He was tall and with a strong face and jet-black curly hair beneath his helmet. He has been three days fighting and killing us, but what is worse is the condition in which he has left our three chiefs who will die unless we can untie them, and so far we have been unable.'

Then Deirdru looked pitingly at them. 'You poor fools,' she said, 'you have begun your quest badly for that was Diarmuid himself that was here.'

And they swore and cursed in their rage at the way they had been tricked and immediately brought out the three man-hunting dogs to track him and tear him down. Dierdru in the meantime said that she would return and tell Fionn all that had happened.

The three dogs picked up Diarmuid's scent immediately and led the blood-seeking pirates to the cave where they found the rushy bed that Diarmuid and Grainne had slept in. From there they went eastwards on the track of Diarmuid and Grainne and Muadhan until they came to the slopes of Slieve Loughter near Castle-island, where they had taken refuge.

As Diarmuid sat by a stream on the mountainside he heard the baying of the dogs and the shouts of the pirates coming towards him in the distance. He stood up and looked back and saw them making their way upwards and in front were three men in green cloaks with the slavering dogs held on chains. And when Diarmuid saw this he was filled with hatred and loathing and a terrible rage.

Muadhan lifted Grainne and walked with Diarmuid a mile or so along the stream, but they were seen from behind and one of the green-cloaked warriors loosed the dog he held which came bounding towards them. When Grainne heard his awful baying behind her she was terrified, but Muadhan bade her not to be frightened for he would deal with the hound. He drew from his belt a small sgian, or knife, and when the great hound, sleek and black with red eyes and venomous jaws, came leaping at them, he threw the knife down the dog's throat and it fell at their feet dead and bleeding. Then Muadhan extracted his knife and put it back in his belt again and they went forward once more.

Then the second hound was released from behind and they could hear it covering the distance between them and the pirates with great raging leaps, and Diarmuid said: 'I will try the Gae Dearg on this hound, for nothing can withstand it.'

And he turned while Muadhan and Grainne went forward again. Diarmuid waited until the hound leaped onto a bank above him and then, putting his finger into the corded loop of the spear, he cast it with all his force at the beast, driving the spearhead down his throat so that his entrails were scattered about the mountainside. Then, leaping forward, he withdrew the spear and followed Muadhan and Grainne.

Soon after they heard the third hound close behind them and Grainne looking back gave a cry of fright for this was the largest and fiercest of the three and he was closer than either of the others and had come on them unprepared, for he had travelled silently.

'Diarmuid,' she screamed, 'Diarmuid!'

Even as she screamed the hound sprang, at a place known as Dubhan's Pillar. But Diarmuid, sweeping Grainne aside with one hand, ducked beneath the hound as he sprang to seize her, and grasped him by the two hind legs as he passed. He swung the brute around under its own momentum and flung it against the pillar, dashing out its brains.

Then, fitting his finger again in the silken loop of the Gae Dearg which he had rewound, he threw the spear at the foremost of the greenclad pirates, and slew him. He threw the Gae Buidhe at the second one, and killed him also and then, drawing the Moralltach, he sprang at the third and swept off his head. When the foreigners saw their leaders killed they turned and fled in complete disorder, while Diarmuid flung himself at them from behind killing and slaughtering them as they fled in panic so that there seemed no escape from him unless, indeed, they could fly above the trees like the wildfowl of the air, or hide themselves in the ground like the badgers and wolves or dive beneath the water if there had been any to dive beneath.

Meanwhile Deirdru had told Fionn that the pirates were on Diarmuid's track and, with the battalions of the Fianna, he set out at once for the hill where the three chiefs were lying. When he reached it they were nearly gone, crippled with the pain of their position, and he was angry and upset to see them like this. He knew that only Oscar or Oisin, MacLugha or Conan Maol could undo the fetters that Diarmuid had bound these men with, so he asked Oisin to loosen them.

'That I cannot do,' said Oisin, 'for Diarmuid put me under *geasa* never to untie an enemy that he bound.'

Next Fionn asked Oscar, but Oscar also refused saying that he would never undo an enemy of Diarmuid's; and when he asked MacLugha and Conan Maol they said the same thing.

At that moment the remnants of those pirates who had followed Diarmuid came running back from the field of battle, and there were few indeed of them, and they told what had happened there. And when the three chiefs heard this, being worn out with torment and suffering, they died of grief that their entire company save for these few were lost. Then Fionn buried them in a wide grave, placed a monument with their names engraved on it above them, and full of grief and bitterness, marched back to Allen with his battalions.

AFTER ALL THIS DIARMUID and Grainne travelled eastwards and northwards until they reached Limerick, and here Muadhan bade them farewell and left them, and they were sad when he had gone for he was very gentle and had served them faithfully, but he had to go his own way, and they understood that. So, on the same day that he left, they too left and turned their steps northwards again and didn't rest until they reached Tireragh in Sligo, which was at that time guarded by one Searbhan, a great Fomorian, who had been put there by the Tuatha de Danaan for a purpose. And the purpose was this.

Many years before a game of hurling had taken place between the men of Ireland and the Tuatha de Danaan on the plain beside Loch Lein in Killarney. They played for three days and for three nights without either side being able to win a single goal from the other during the whole of that time. And when the De Danaan found that they could not beat the men of Ireland, they were very put out and suddenly decided to withdraw from the game altogether – which wasn't very sporting of them – and they left the lakeside and journeyed northwards in a body.

Now the De Danaan are not like ordinary mortals as everybody knows, and they had brought for their food during the game, and for the journey to and from Killarney, crimson nuts and arbutus apples and the scarlet berries of the rowan tree, which they had brought with them from Tír Tairrngire, the Land of Promise which, as has been said before, those who don't know any better call Tír na nÓg. And, since these fruits and nuts had many secret virtues, the De Danaan were particularly careful that none of them should fall into the hands of the men of Ireland, or onto the soil of the land where they might grow. But as they passed through Tireragh one of the scarlet rowan berries dropped on the earth as they passed and they never noticed it falling.

From this berry a rowan tree grew and it had all the virtues of the trees that grow in Tír Tairrngire. Its berries had the taste of honey and gave anyone who tasted them a feeling of immense well-being, and if he was even a hundred years old, a man would return to the age of thirty when he had eaten three of them.

Now when the De Danaan learned what had happened they were alarmed in case anyone who wasn't one of themselves would eat the berries, and they sent a great Fomorian, this Searbhan, to guard the tree so that no one would approach it. He was a giant, as they say, of the race of Cain, huge and strong, and he carried an iron club tied by a chain to a massive belt that he wore around his waist, and there was no way of killing him except by giving him three blows of his own club. By day he sat at the foot of the tree watching for anyone who might come near, and by night he slept in a hut he had made for himself high in its branches.

Diarmuid knew all about Searbhan and calculated that he would be safe from Fionn and the Fianna in Tireragh, because Searbhan would not allow them to hunt there. Neither they, nor indeed anyone else, would go within a dozen miles of the wood where the rowan tree stood for fear of the gigantic Fomorian, so that the land for miles around was a wilderness and a sanctuary for all sorts of game.

Leaving Grainne safely in a dry cave, Diarmuid went forward boldly to where the huge Searbhan sat glowering at the foot of his tree, and told him that he wanted to live in the district and hunt the game and fish the streams there for food.

The great, surly, skin-clad guard turned his shaggy head and looked at Diarmuid out of the single, baleful, red-tinged eye he possessed; for he had lost the other one in some careless way or another in a fight in his youth. By God, thought Diarmuid, thanks be that he's not grown older than thirty from eating the rowan berries, for if he's that ugly at thirty, what unapproachable kind of an ugliness would he have at forty or fifty or more?

While Diarmuid was thinking this, the big man was studying him silently; then, in the few words of a man unused to much talk – easy to see he's a foreigner, thought Diarmuid – and in a voice as ugly as his appearance, Searbhan told Diarmuid that he could live where he pleased and hunt what he liked as long as he didn't try to steal any of the rowan berries, because if he made the attempt, it would be the last he would ever make.

And having said that much he said no more but glared unblinkingly at Diarmuid without moving his head or anything else until the latter went away out of sight altogether. Then the giant went back to his dozing again.

So Diarmuid built a substantial hut near a spring and put a strong fence all round it with only one doorway through it, and he and Grainne lived in peace for a while.

Meanwhile Fionn had returned to Allen and to his castle and the Fianna to its normal duties and everyone thought that the fire of Fionn's anger against Diarmuid and Grainne had died down; but this was not so. For, though he appeared to have mellowed in many ways on the surface, inside he was still a turmoil of bitter jealousy waiting its revenge. And one day an opportunity presented itself to him which he could not let pass.

While he was with some of the garrison troops on the great green before the castle, they saw a body of about fifty horsemen approaching from the west led by two who were taller and prouder looking than the others. They rode up at a fast trot and dismounted in front of Fionn, whom they saluted. He asked them who they were and where they were from, and was surprised and thoughtful at their reply, which was: 'We are your enemies, Fionn,' they said, 'but we are anxious to make peace between us. We are Aengus and Aedh, the sons of the MacMorna who fought against your father at the battle of Castleknock, when your father was slain, and for which you afterwards slew our father and outlawed us even though we were not born until after the death of your father. But now we seek peace and the place in the Fianna our father had before us.'

Fionn looked at them a long time. He very well knew that these young men were seeking a golden opportunity which they might not get again; they knew how unpleasant, how unsatisfactory and how lonely was the life of an outlaw, especially when it wasn't of their own choosing. They also knew, however, that all Fionn's vindictiveness was now directed away from themselves and their kind and towards the one who had done him the greatest injury of all, that to his pride – and in public. Fionn knew why Oscar and Oisin, his own son and grandson, and their friends still felt friendly towards Diarmuid; quite apart from the obligations put on him by Grainne, Fionn understood their unspoken sympathy for a young man in love with a young woman, and their resentment at an old man who coveted her; but their resentment was nothing compared to his own, first because they thought him old, and second because the insult had been public and was tacitly condoned in public.

Fionn realised that these young men now before him would not have thought this out in such minute detail, but he guessed, and rightly, that they had a pretty good idea of the situation, born of their burning desire to be outlaws no longer. They were here, he thought, to seize an opportunity, or to make one.

'I will grant your request,' he said at last, 'provided you pay me compensation for the death of my father.'

'We have no gold or silver or herds of cattle to give you, Fionn,' they said.

'What more compensation do you want from them, Fionn,' asked Oisin, 'surely the death of their father is compensation enough?'

'It seems to me,' said Fionn drily, 'that if anyone killed me it would be easy enough to satisfy my son in the matter of compensation. But, as for me, none of those who fought at Castleknock, or their sons, will join the Fianna without paying whatever compensation I demand.'

'What compensation do you require, Fionn?' asked Aedh.

'The head of a warrior,' said Fionn, 'or a fistful of rowan berries.'

'Take my advice,' said Oisin to the men, 'and go back where you came from. The head he asks you for is that of Diarmuid Ó Duibhne, the most dangerous of all the Fianna, and the rowan berries are from the rowan tree guarded by Searbhan the giant Fomorian, and which is the more dangerous task of the two I could not tell you.'

But the two proud young chiefs would not listen to Oisin's advice, saying that they would rather die in the attempt to fulfil Fionn's eric than go back to the outlaw life they had been living since childhood. So leaving their followers in the care of Oisin they set out on their quest and travelled north and west for several days until they picked up the track of Diarmuid and followed it to the hut he had built with the stout fence around it in Tireragh. Diarmuid, who by now had become accustomed to alertness even when he slept, and in spite of the fact that the two young men were outlaws skilled in moving silently and unseen in bare and noisy places, heard them approach and snatching up his weapons he went out to confront them and ask them who they were.

Proudly they told him who they were and added: 'We have come here from Allen to get either the head of Diarmuid Ó Duibhne or a handful of berries from the rowan tree guarded by Searbhan as an eric to Fionn for our father having killed his father.'

Diarmuid looked at them in surprise for a moment at their candour, and then threw back his head and laughed.

'This is unpleasant news indeed,' he laughed, 'for me to hear, for I am Diarmuid Ó Duibhne and much as I admire you, friends, I am most unwilling to give you my head and you will find it no easy matter to take it. As for the berries, they are just as hard to get, for Searbhan is a formidable man who can only be killed with his own club.'

He looked at them then for a moment and went on seriously, 'You are foolish men if you believe that Fionn will give you what you seek even if you are successful. He is making use of you for his own purpose and when that usefulness is over you'll find yourselves back where you were before, outlaws. Because that you will always be to Fionn. Now, which do you want to strive for first, me or the berries?'

'We will battle with you first,' they said. So Diarmuid opened the gate in the fence and made ready to fight them.

However, the two young men, who were extremely serious about their quest, proposed that they should discard their weapons and fight barehanded; if they were able to overcome Diarmuid, then they should take his head back with them to Fionn; if, on the other hand, Diarmuid defeated them, then their heads were his to dispose of as he saw fit. And seriously they began to circle the hero seeking the means of bringing him down. However, the fight was a short one. Diarmuid was not known as the most dangerous man in the Fianna without reason, nor had he taken part in many campaigns without learning much, and had they been ten times as many as they were, or twice that number, his task would have been little more difficult. Expertly and effortlessly he disposed of one and then the other. He did not kill them, for he had no bitterness towards them, but he knocked them senseless with subtle and calculated blows so that when they recovered consciousness they were bound hand and foot and Diarmuid was sitting on the ground in front of them, his legs crossed at the ankles, his back against a tree, his wife bending over a skillet in the background, gnawing on the leg of a pheasant and contemplating them.

'Well,' said Diarmuid, 'so you are awake at last. Did you sleep well?' he asked politely.

But they only glowered at him.

However, since they thought that he had only waited for them to recover so that he could take their heads from them, this was understandable. But this was not Diarmuid's intention at all, even though he hadn't much of an idea what to do with them.

'I suppose you're hungry,' he said.

'What difference does that make,' said they, 'can't you take our heads and be done with it and stop playing with us.'

'Indeed, my friends,' said Diarmuid, 'and what would I do that for? Your heads are much more use to you than they could ever be to me.'

'You mean you'll let us live,' they said.

'I do,' said Fionn.

'Well,' they said, 'aren't you the great man. Perhaps it's just as well we didn't go after the rowan berries first.'

And that's where something altogether unexpected and strange happened, for as they said this Grainne, who was just coming up with something for them to eat, said: 'What rowan berries?'

Now Diarmuid knew his wife very well. He knew her proud, sometimes wilful, nature; the fact that she could be generous over big things – for she had never complained once about the life they were forced to lead – but sometimes rather selfish about small ones. In fact, she was a very womanly kind of woman. And because of this he had decided not to tell her about the rowan tree knowing that, whatever she might say, no woman could possibly resist the temptation held forth by a trio of berries which would prevent her from growing old; and how right he was! But witholding the information, instead of doing good, now turned out to be infinitely worse. When Grainne heard the story of the rowan berries from Aedh and Aengus she turned to Diarmuid and said: 'And you knew about them all the time and never told me ... oh!'

But her anger was over as quickly as it had come, and when the danger was pointed out to her it seemed to disappear altogether. But in its place grew and grew a tremendous desire to taste the rowan berries.

At first she tried to hide it, but, as it grew in her day by day Diarmuid realised what was wrong and became very troubled as, knowing his wife's mind when it was fixed on something, he feared that some harm might come to her if she could not get them.

Now the sons of MacMorna had remained with them for all this time, bound lightly by the hands; for they were in no hurry to leave, and there was still hope that they could get the rowan berries, while, in addition, they were men of honour who owed their persons and their lives now to Diarmuid in any event.

So when they saw Diarmuid worried and troubled they asked him what was wrong and he told them about Grainne's fixation with the rowan berries. 'Well,' they said, 'let us loose and we'll go with you to fight this Searbhan.'

Diarmuid laughed. 'I'm afraid the help I'd get from you two would be small enough once you saw him,' he said, 'but in any event, if I'm to fight him at all, I'd prefer to go alone.'

'No matter,' they said, 'our lives are forfeit to you now, so let us go with you before we die, even if it is only to see you fight him.'

So Diarmuid agreed and untied them, and the three of them went straightaway to the rowan tree. There they found the giant Fomorian, ugly as ever, asleep in the sun beneath the tree. Diarmuid gave him a heavy blow to wake him up. The Fomorian opened his bleary, red rimmed eye and looked balefully up at Diarmuid.

'What ails you?' he said, 'There's been peace between us up to now, why do you come looking for trouble?'

'I'm not looking for any trouble,' said Diarmuid. 'But the Princess Grainne, my wife, the daughter of King Cormac MacArt, longs to taste one of these rowan berries and I am afraid that if she does not do so she will die. That is why I have come, and I beg you now to give me a few of the berries for her.'

But the ugly Fomorian, drawing himself up onto his feet so that he stood feet and inches above Diarmuid, looked down at him and said: 'I swear that if she, and all her line, were on the point of death this minute and one of my berries would save her, I wouldn't give it to her.'

Then Diarmuid replied, but there was a harder note in his voice this time: 'I don't want to take advantage of you and that's why I woke you up. I made my request openly wishing for peace between us. But now I want you to understand this, whether you agree or not, I will have some of those berries before I leave here.'

When the Fomorian heard Diarmuid say this, he lifted his great iron club and made three swings at Diarmuid which the latter had great difficulty in avoiding; indeed he didn't ward off the last of them which struck his shield and even though his shield was tough and his arm strong, it was numbed from wrist to shoulder. Then, watching the other closely and seeing that he expected to be attacked with sword and spear, Diarmuid suddenly sprang forward, letting his weapons drop at the same instant, and grabbed the huge man round the waist, taking him by surprise. With a quick twist, and a wrestling trick, he hurled the Fomorian over his shoulder so that he struck the earth with a mighty shock and then, picking up the great club, he gave him three blows, dashing out his brains with the last one.

Diarmuid sat down beside the fallen Fomorian panting for breath, holding the bloody club in his hand. He dropped his head between his knees and only looked up when he heard the two young men who had watched the combat falling over each other beside him in praise of his achievement. With some annoyance he told them to keep quiet and if they wanted to be useful to take the body into the wood and bury it before Grainne saw it and died of fright.

When they had done this Diarmuid asked them, for he was still tired after his battle with the Fomorian, to bring Grainne to the tree and when they had done so he said: 'Now love, there are the rowan berries. Take what you want of them.'

But Grainne was in that kind of mood that afflicts many women from time to time, and which had afflicted them and I suppose will always afflict them until the end of time; and the misfortune of it is this, that they have outrageous notions of what is an appropriate token of affection and esteem, perhaps, and set more store by that or some other triviality than they do by a thing that might rock the world. They will, for example, forgive a man easily for doing the wrong thing, but they will make a great noise about it if he does the right thing at what they would consider to be the wrong time. In these matters they are very particular. And so it was with Grainne now. She was put out because Diarmuid didn't come running to her with his fists full of berries, and more put out when he just looked at her and said as if it was of no importance: 'Take what you want.'

So she looked anywhere but at him, and said: 'I will eat no berries except those that are plucked by my husband's hand.'

So Diarmuid, who was a very understanding man if he was anything, stood up and plucked the berries for her and she ate until she was satisfied. Then he gave some to the two young men and said: 'Take these berries and go back to Fionn and tell him they are your eric fine. If you want to you can tell him too that it was you who killed Searbhan.'

'We will bring him one handful and no more,' they said, 'which is what he asked, and we grudge him even that.'

They thanked Diarmuid then, deeply and genuinely, before they left. And it was little enough for them to do since he had given them the berries to begin with, which they had not been able to get for themselves; and, although their lives were forfeit to him, he hadn't so much as mentioned the matter, but allowed them to go freely. So, bidding them farewell, the two knights went back to Allen.

When they had gone Diarmuid moved Grainne and himself into the Searbhan's house among the branches of the rowan tree, where they lived on the rowan berries from that onwards; finding, as it happens, that while the lower berries were as honey and mead compared with any other food, they were bitter compared with the berries on the topmost branches.

When the two young knights reached Fionn's castle they gave him the berries, told him that Searbhan was dead, and asked that he fulfil his promise to accept them into the ranks of the Fianna.

Fionn took the berries in his hands and smelled them three times. 'They are indeed the rowan berries of Tireragh,' he said, 'but they have passed through the hands of Diarmuid Ó Duibhne, for I can smell his touch. And as sure as I do,' he went on, 'I am equally sure that it was he and not yourselves who slew the Searbhan.' And he looked piercingly at the two young men who hung their heads in acknowledgment. 'That being so,' said Fionn, 'you will not get from me either the peace you want or a place in the Fianna; for, apart from not getting the eric I put on you, you have made friends with my enemy.'

Now, when all this was done and the young knights banished again to the life of an outlaw, Fionn summoned his most trusted troops and set off for Tireragh where he hoped to catch up with Diarmuid finally. They followed Diarmuid's track to the foot of the tree and found the berries without anyone to guard them whatsoever.

Fionn looked round and grunted at what he saw. He made the troops pitch camp some distance away and then, since it was noon and the sun was high and hot and they were dusty and tired, said: 'We'll camp here under the tree, and this is where I'll stay myself.' Then he added as an afterthought, but one that he could not contain nevertheless, 'for I'm certain that Diarmuid is above among the branches of the tree.'

Oisin looked at him in amazement.

'You must be truly blinded by jealousy,' he said, 'if you think that Diarmuid is a big enough fool to sit in a tree waiting for you when he knows you prize nothing more than his head.'

Fionn said nothing in reply to this, but he smiled the queer smile that had been growing in him lately and which sometimes worried those who knew him and loved him. However he called for a chessboard and men and himself and Oisin sat in the shade of the tree and began to play. Oscar and several more officers of the Fianna sat with Oisin while he played for there was none of them alone a match for Fionn and they were in the habit of playing him collectively. They played on for some time until there was one move which, if Oisin made it, would inevitably result in his winning the game. And Fionn said to him: 'One move, Oisin, and you can win the game, but I challenge you and all your helpers to make it.'

Now Diarmuid had been watching the game from the beginning and was following it closely; now he whispered to himself: 'If I was only below with you, Oisin, I could show you the move.'

Grainne, sitting near him, felt her terror – which had mounted bit by bit since the Fianna arrived below them – grow great within her and she put a pleading hand on his arm. 'What does it matter if Oisin win or lose a game,' she whispered, 'when you might lose your head?'

But already he had plucked a berry from the tree and, flinging it down, struck the chessman that should be moved; Oisin made the move and, in time, won the game and the Fianna who had gathered round and were watching the contest raised a great shout. Whereupon Fionn leaned back in his chair, his two hands on the table before him, and looked at Oisin with a smile on his face.

'I'm not surprised,' he said, 'that you won the game, Oisin, since you had the best help of Oscar, the skill of all these others and, above all, the prompting of Diarmuid Ó Duibhne from above.'

'Good Lord,' declared Oisin, 'has your jealousy no bottom to it that you think Diarmuid is up that tree waiting for you to kill him?'

And Fionn without changing his position, still looking at

Oisin, just raised his voice and said: 'Which of us is telling the truth, Diarmuid, Oisin or myself?'

'Yourself, of course, Fionn,' replied Diarmuid, 'for I'm here indeed in the tree,'

Then, looking up, Fionn saw them high above through an opening in the branches, and Grainne, seeing that they were discovered, began to weep and tremble in anger. Diarmuid put his arm around her and began to kiss her and comfort her.

Fionn seeing this merely smiled, for his jealousy had now become hate. He ordered the Fianna to surround the tree in several ranks with their shields interlocked so that there could be no escape and he warned them on pain of death that they must not let Diarmuid pass. Having done this he offered large rewards; armour and arms, rank and position in the Fianna, to anyone who would climb the tree and either bring him Diarmuid's head or force him to come down.

Then a man from Waterford, called Garbha, whose father had been killed by Diarmuid's father, stood up and said that he would try; and began to climb the tree branch by branch. But when he reached a spot close to the hut, Diarmuid leaped at him from above and sent him crashing to the ground with a kick. Then one after another nine men who had real or fancied grievances against Diarmuid; or men who were ambitious or covetous, tried to climb the tree after Diarmuid, but each of them was killed or sent hurtling to the ground to die there.

Meanwhile Aengus Óg had warning of the danger Diarmuid was in and he made his way through the throng of Fianna and fighting men as he had done before and to the hut in the tree and said that he would take Grainne away to a place of safety. But she would not go until Diarmuid insisted and even then it was with much reluctance that she allowed Aengus to wrap his cloak around her and take her in safety through the ranks of the Fianna below.

Then Diarmuid shouted from above down to Fionn: 'I'm coming down, Fionn. And be ready, for you can be sure that I'll kill a lot before I'm killed myself, and I have no fear of death to stop me. There was never a time or a place that I wasn't prepared to die for the Fianna and even for you in the past; well, if I have to die now it'll be dearly bought by that same Fianna.'

'He's right, Fionn,' said Oscar, 'now is the time for you to forgive him before there's more harm done.'

'I will not,' said Fionn.

With that Oscar, Fionn's own grandson, leaped to his feet and cried: 'Shame on you. Then I, Oscar, now take the body and life of Diarmuid under the protection of my knighthood and valour and I pledge my word that, should the heavens themselves fall on me, or the earth open beneath my feet and swallow me, I will not let any man harm him here.

'Come down, Diarmuid,' he cried, 'come down for you are no longer alone.'

Then Diarmuid, choosing the side where he had most concealment, leaped lightly to the ground beside Oscar and both champions faced the uneasy hosts of the Fianna. When Fionn saw Diarmuid his rage and hate boiled over and he seemed on the verge of apoplexy. But before he could summon his words Diarmuid and Oscar had passed through the silent Fianna, striking but a few blows here and there where the Clann Nephin tried to hinder them, like a pair of wolves through a flock of sheep, and when Fionn would have rushed to follow them the Fianna linked their shields together and held him back. Then Deirdru, who had climbed the tree, came down to tell Fionn that Grainne was not there either and he knew that he had lost all. He had lost the king's daughter, the trust of his companions and his own faith in himself which was the root of much. All this Grainne had taken from him when she passed him her goblet to drink at Tara so long before. And his heart was still unforgiving.

Meanwhile Diarmuid and Oscar had reached Brugh na Boinne where Aengus had taken Grainne and she died, as it were, a sweet death when she saw Diarmuid coming towards her bloody and torn from his encounter, but safe with her again.

DIARMUID AND GRAINNE REMAINED at Brugh na Boinne with Aengus for some time and, during that period, the king, Cormac, succeeded in making peace between the embittered Fionn and Diarmuid whom he had outlawed. Fionn agreed to lift the ban of outlawry and also agreed that he would not, without Diarmuid's permission, hunt across the land to which Diarmuid was now entitled; that is the barony of Corcaguiny in Kerry, that of Ducarn near Duoce Mountain in Leinster and that of Cos Corran which was given to Grainne as a dowry; and it was here that they built their great house, Rath Grainne; and it was here that Diarmuid prospered and grew rich in gold and silver and jewels; cattle and sheep and the produce of the soil.

Then, when they had lived there for several years, Grainne – out of boredom or of pride or of what, who knows – persuaded Diarmuid to do two things that he didn't want to do: to give a great feast, and to invite the Fianna to it. They spent a year preparing the feast and it was celebrated for more than a full month.

One night as Diarmuid lay beside Grainne he started up out of his sleep with such violence that she threw her arms around him in fear.

'What is it, little love,' she cried.

'A hound,' he said, 'I heard a hound baying.'

'But it is night,' she said, shivering in spite of herself.

'That is what I wonder at,' said Diarmuid, 'a hound that hunts at night.'

And she persuaded him to lie down again.

A second time he started up at the baying of a hound in the night, but Grainne kept him back with the song of her love and her fear; which she had sung when they fled together from Tara.

Sleep, my love, a little sleep
There is no fear abroad to keep
You from me, who owns my heart –
Oh, my love; my Diarmuid.

Sleep, as Fiach slept before
When from Conall of Craevroe
To the south he swiftly ran
With the daughter of Morann.

Sleep, as happy Fionncha slept
When he northward Slaine swept
To his bed in Assaroe
Where cautious Failbhe dared not go.

Sleep as Ann slept in the west
When softly to her lover's breast
By torchlight from her father's farms
She fled to Duach's loving arms.

Sleep, as proudly in the east
Dedaid slept when flight had ceased
With Coinenn, for whom his life he'd sell,
In spite of bloody, warring Deill.

Who'd separate my love and I
Must separate the sun and sky
Must part my body and my soul,
Oh soldier from the bright lake shore.

And he slept; but before the dawn broke in the east the baying in the night awoke him again from his slumber, and this time he made a song for her to show how distressed he was and to signify the urgency that was within him.

That roaring stag with stamping feet
That roves the night, he cannot sleep;
No thought of sleep within him stirs
Who tramples down the homes of birds.

The lively linnet does not rest
Leaping through tree-tangled tresses;
Making music in the night,
With hurried thrushes taking flight.

The slender duck is restless too
Swimming on from place to place;
She will not sleep or cease for rest
Drawing danger from her nest.

Tonight the curlew does not sleep,
His music's high above the deep
Rage that through this midnight screams;
He will not sleep between the streams.

Then Diarmuid left the bed and stood in the middle of the floor as if listening to something, but Grainne could not hear a thing. 'There it is again,' he would say, and she would shiver, as he stood there with his head to one side. Below in the yard his own hound Mac An Cuill ran about whimpering and trying to hide itself, shivering, beneath a cart.

'I'll go and find that hound I heard baying in the night,' said

Diarmuid.

'Oh don't go,' she said, 'don't go where I cannot see you today.'

But Diarmuid would not listen to her protests.

'In that case,' she said, 'take the Moralltach with you and the Gae Dearg, so that you will be prepared for any danger.'

But he laughed at her.

'What danger could there be in such a small matter, and anyway they are too heavy. I'll take Beagalltach and the Gae Buidhe instead.'

'Can we not talk today of the feast we will give to the king?' asked Grainne, 'and you can hunt tomorrow?'

'That is a good idea,' said Diarmuid, 'but today is a good day for hunting and tomorrow will not be a bad day to talk about the giving of a feast.'

And so he went off to the mountain and there, in the dawn, he found Fionn standing alone. Diarmuid gave him no greeting, but asked him where the hunt was and Fionn told him that some of the Fianna had left Rath Grainne during the night with the dogs and one of the hounds came across the spoor of a wild boar and both men and dogs followed it.

Even as Fionn spoke there was a faint baying below them. And Fionn went on: 'I tried my best to stop them for this is the boar of Benbulben who has been chased often, and as often killed men and dogs before him. He has already killed several of the Fianna this morning and, as he is tearing his way towards us, I think we would be wise to move to a safer spot.'

But Diarmuid would not leave.

'Leave the hill and the boar to the hunters, Ó Duibhne,' said Fionn, 'I do not want you here.'

'Why should I leave the hill,' said Diarmuid, 'I'm not afraid of a boar.'

'Then you should be,' said Fionn, 'for you are under *geasa* never to hunt a boar.'

Then Fionn told Diarmuid the story of what had happened so many years before in the palace of Aengus at Brugh na Boinne and of the curse that the steward had put on Diarmuid that night. When he had finished Diarmuid looked at the other man, standing there in the dawn light with a single hound, Bran, beside him.

'What you say may be true, if it is I don't remember it,' said Diarmuid, 'but in any case it would be cowardly of me to leave the hill before I had sight of the boar. I'll stay here, but would you leave Bran with me?'

Fionn didn't answer him, but, with Bran by his side, went down the hillside. Then Diarmuid stood with his own hound, Mac An Cuill, shivering beside him as the great boar came charging at him through the undergrowth. Suddenly it burst through the bushes, huge and black, its little red eyes glaring hatred in the dawn, its great tusks curving backward from black, foam flecked lips; the ground trembling under the razor-sharp feet of the heavy shouldered monster as it bore down on Diarmuid. Diarmuid unslipped Mac An Cuill, but the hound turned and ran in terror.

Then Diarmuid remembered what Grainne had said to him about taking his heavy weapons and muttered: 'Bad luck to him who doesn't heed the advice of a good wife.'

Nevertheless he slipped his finger into the silken loop of his smaller spear, the Gae Buidhe, and hurled it with all his might at the oncoming monster. The spear struck the boar between the little glaring eyes, but not a bristle, not a piece of skin, was cut, not a gash nor a scratch made in the terrible beast.

When he saw this Diarmuid guessed it was his end, but, drawing the Beagalltach in one, swift movement, and with a great battle-roar, he hurled himself at the oncoming monster and made a tremendous stroke at the broad neck with the full weight of his body behind it. But to no purpose for the sword splintered in pieces of the thick hide, while not a bristle of the boar was hurt, leaving only the heavy hilt in Diarmuid's hand. And even as he made the stroke the boar pitched him so that he fell across the humped back, and hurled him to the ground. Then the furious boar crashed through the brush and turned back again, rushing at Diarmuid, and gored and pitched and ripped him with his tusks until the hero was a mass of bleeding wounds both outside and in. Turning, the beast was about to renew the attack when, summoning his last strength, Diarmuid flung the hilt of his sword at him, driving it through the skull to the brain, so that the brute fell down dead on the spot.

Now as Diarmuid lay dying from his wounds, Fionn and the Fianna arrived and saw him beside the body of the boar.

'Oh my grief,' cried Oisin rushing to his side, 'to see you here like this, torn by a pig.'

'And mine,' said Fionn, 'that the women of Ireland are not here to see your beauty and grace torn away by a pig.'

'Fionn,' said Diarmuid, 'you speak with your lips and not your heart. You have the power to heal me if you will.'

'I am no leech,' said Fionn indignantly.

'It was given to you to heal a wounded man with a draught of water carried by your hands,' said Diarmuid.

'That is true,' said Oisin.

'And why should I do this for you, of all men?' asked Fionn.

'I'll only remind you,' said Diarmuid, 'of when you were surrounded in a thatched house by your enemies who threw firebrands on the roof and how I and a few of my men rushed out and quenched the flames and made a circuit of the place slaughtering your enemies before us so that you were safe. Had I asked you for a drink that night you would gladly have given it to me.'

'Unfaithfulness changes everything,' said Fionn, 'and the world knows how unfaithful you were to me when you carried Grainne from me in the presence of the men of Ireland.'

'Do not blame me for keeping the *geasa* under which I was pledged,' said Diarmuid, 'but remember how when you were treacherously invited to a feast by the king of Wales and captured I came to save you when he would have handed you over to the Romans; and how I kept the Welsh and the Romans at bay with my men until you were rescued, and all the other things I have done for you since I first joined the Fianna.'

Then Oisin, Fionn's son, said: 'I cannot allow you, Fionn, to withhold this drink from Diarmuid, and I say now that if any other prince in the world should think of doing Diarmuid such treachery there would leave this hill only whichever of us had the strongest hand.' He said this, his eyes flashing with angry fire, looking directly at his father. 'Do what I say and bring the water to Diarmuid.'

'I don't know where there is a well on this mountain,' said Fionn sullenly.

'There,' said Oisin pointing angrily, 'is one nine steps away from you.'

Slowly Fionn went over, the contempt of the Fianna lying heavily on his shoulder, and filled his hands with water. But he had not gone more than four paces when his jealousy overcame him again and he let the water slip, allowing it to spill through his fingers, saying that he was not able to carry water so far.

Diarmuid groaned when he saw this, and said: 'You let it slip yourself, Fionn, for I saw you. Hurry now, for I'm close to death.'

Fionn looked around guiltily and when he saw the stern faces of the others he returned to the spring and again took a handful of water; but again when he turned towards Diarmuid and thought of Grainne he let it slip through his fingers.

When the others, Oisin and Oscar and Diarmuid's other friends, saw this they lifted their spears and turned them against Fionn, and Oisin cried out: 'We will not allow this treachery.'

Then Fionn went a third time, and this time he carried the water to where Diarmuid lay. But even as the general of the Fianna stood above him with the life-giving handful of water, Diarmuid's spirit passed from him with a groan and he died.

There was silence, a stillness on the hilltop then. All the men of the Fianna, the officers and Fionn, stood as in a tableau still and immobile until Diarmuid's hound, Mac An Cuill, came through them and raised a mournful howl above the body of his master. Then Oscar looked across at Fionn and said: 'I wish it was you instead of Diarmuid that lay there, Fionn.'

But Fionn walked away from him, turning his back, and stood lonely beside the spring where he had gathered the water to bring to Diarmuid. And Oisin, his son and Oscar's father, looked at his lonely back and said: 'No draught of water can heal you, Fionn, or make you any different from what we now know you to be; an old, embittered and cunning man, caring for nothing but yourself – who was the emblem of us all.'

Caoilte looked a long time at Fionn, and then said: 'The strength of the Fianna will wither away because of this, Fionn. We can never hold you in the same esteem again, but as you have planted the acorn, let you bend the oak yourself.'

Then Oisin and Oscar and Caoilte and Diorraing covered Diarmuid with their cloaks and mounted guard over him. Then Mac An Cuill came to Fionn, who put him on a leash to lead him back to Rath Grainne, but Bran, his own hound, refused to come to him; and sadness covered the whole mountainside. So Fionn, leading the hound, and followed by the men of the Fianna except for the four who stood guard above Diarmuid, left the mountainside and made his way towards Rath Grainne.

Grainne herself was standing on the ramparts of her castle when she saw the chiefs of the Fianna coming towards her, Fionn leading Mac An Cuill, and a sudden fear that had been haunting her all that day went through her. 'If Diarmuid were alive,' she whispered in terror, 'it is not Fionn who would be leading his hound.'

And when Fionn came and told her that Diarmuid was dead she fainted and did not recover there upon the ramparts for a long time. But when she did and when she knew that what she had been told was true she raised a cry of grief that echoed and re-echoed in the glens and wilderness around, startling the birds in their nests and the wild beasts of the field and forest in their lairs. And then she ordered that five hundred of her people should go and recover the body of her husband with all the pomp and ceremony that he demanded, and so they went. But when they got to the mountaintop there they saw the hosts of the De Danaan with Aengus Óg at their head and their shields reversed as a sign of peace. And both armies, having viewed the dead hero, raised three mighty shouts of sorrow, so loud and great, that they were heard across the margin of the world and over the five provinces of Ireland.

Then Aengus asked them what they had come for and they said to carry the body of Diarmuid back to Rath Grainne, but he would not let them, saying that Diarmuid was his foster-son and he would take him with him to Brugh na Boinne.

'There I will preserve him,' he said, 'for although I cannot breathe life back into my foster-son again, I can breathe a spirit into him so that for a little while each day he can talk to me.'

Then he placed the body on a golden bier and, with Diarmuid's weapons raised before it, the people of the De Danaan, carried it to Brugh na Boinne.

When Grainne's people returned and told her what had happened she was grief-stricken and angry at first, but later she accepted the idea and lived alone and in peace with herself for some time. Meanwhile Fionn had returned to Allen with the Fianna, but his days there were gloomy and unhappy for the trust that had existed between himself and the Fianna was there no longer. But after a year of living like this, one day and without telling anyone where he was going, Fionn left Allen and made his way to Rath Grainne. When he got there Grainne received him coldly at first and asked him what he wanted from her.

'I come in peace,' he said, 'and to offer a place in the Fianna to your sons when they have grown.'

At first Grainne would not listen to him and turned away in disdain. But after some persuasion, when he pointed out the benefits it would be to her sons to get high places in the Fianna, her interest quickened.

'But who would guarantee that,' she asked.

'Yourself, Grainne,' he answered. 'For there is no man fitter for you to marry now than myself, and no woman fitter to be the wife of Fionn MacCumhal than yourself.'

Then Grainne turned from him in disgust and hatred. But the more she did, the more he persevered and impressed her at last with his sincerity and, odd though it may seem, his apparent humility. And at length she agreed.

And at last, after he had been away for some time, the men of the Fianna saw them both coming towards Allen across the plain and when they saw who was with Fionn they raised three great shouts of derision and mockery, and Grainne hung her head in shame.

But Fionn took her hand and led her into the great hall of his castle at Allen. But there was never the same spirit abroad in the Fianna after that, even though Fionn and Grainne lived together with mutual support until one of them died.

But that night at a banquet that Fionn gave, Oisin could not restrain the hurt that stirred in all of them, and his bitterness against the fickle woman, and he said aloud where it could be heard: 'I trust my father will keep her fast from this time onward.'

And so ends the story of Diarmuid and Grainne.

THE SICKBED OF CUCHULAIN

JUST AS THE STORY of the Children of Lir belongs to a time that is in the remote ages of man's memory, when gods and men walked the earth together and there was not that much distinction between the two, and that of Diarmuid and Grainne belongs to a time that is so close to our own that it can be measured in terms of time and of men such as are about us today, this story falls between the two. Conor MacNessa ruled Ulster with the aid and assistance of his noble lords, the Red Branch Knights of whom the most famous were Naisi and his brothers, Ainle and Ardan, the Sons of Usna; Fergus Mac Rí, true king of Ulster; Conall Cearnach, terrible in battle, and the youthful but mighty Cuchulain himself.

Now every year at Samhain, that is at the end of summer and at the beginning of autumn, the people held a feast for seven days; three days before summer ended, on Samhain itself, and for three days at the beginning of autumn. And on this occasion the festival was being held on Magh Muirtheimne, the plain of Muirtheimne, between the River Boyne and Carlingford Lough, which was the home and inheritance of Cuchulain ... and it is said that the place got its name from the words *muir*, the sea or a tide, and *teimen*, secret or concealment because at one time it was covered with the water of the sea until the Dagda himself caused the water to recede. But it is far more likely that it was a name given simply to the hinterland of that beautiful, deep and concealed lough itself.

Anyway, it was here that the festival was held at the time of which I write, and gay, splendid and joyful it was; with a great market and fair lasting for the week, a continuous feast of dancing, music, song and merry-making of all kinds, together with joustings and armed competitions among the knights.

Now, one evening, while Cuchulain sat in the shade of a tree – for it was still hot – playing chess, a great flock of white birds came and landed on the waters of the lough close by. They were strange and unusual birds such as had never been seen there before and the women who were there with Emer, Cuchulain's wife, at the lakeside talking to one another, began to say how much they would like to have these birds, until one of them, in the way that women do these things, said with an eye on Emer, 'If my husband was here he would catch some of those birds for me.' 'Or mine,' said another, and then another until they were all giggling among themselves and looking at Emer and nudging each other for Cuchulain was the only one near them at the time, apart from the knight he was playing who was an old man. Then Emer, proud within herself, but not for the sake of pride, beckoned Laeg, Cuchulain's charioteer, and said to him that the women wanted the birds and asked him to tell Cuchulain. Aloud she said, for she was a very true woman too, 'If anyone is to have these birds, then it is I who should have them first.'

Laeg went to Cuchulain and said: 'The women of Ulster would be well pleased if you brought them those birds there.' Cuchulain didn't answer him, but went on playing chess.

Then Laeg tried again: 'The women would like you to catch some of those birds on the lough for them.'

This time Cuchulain looked up in anger. 'Have the women of Ulster nothing better for me to do than to go chasing birds for their amusement?'

'It isn't right,' said Laeg, 'for you to speak against them like that. For it is on your account, and for love of you, that they have assumed one of their three blemishes.'

Now this was the truth; for the three blemishes of the high-born women of Ulster were lameness, stammering and bad eye-sight; the first was assumed by the women who were in love with Conall Cearnach, because of his limp, the second was assumed by those women who were in love with Cuscriadh Mian, the king's son, because of his difficulties in speech, and the third was assumed by those – more than either of the other two put together – who were in love with Cuchulain because in his battle rage a form of blindness, akin to that of a berserk, overcame him and distorted his features.

So, with bad grace, he growled at Laeg; 'Bring me my chariot – a fine thing it is for me to be doing, catching little birds for women!'

Then, angrily, he drove his chariot along the water's edge and hurled his curved, Egyptian sword so that it flew like a boomerang and returned to him; and the birds fell, their feet and wings flapping the water so that it was easy for them to be gathered up by Laeg. Then Cuchulain drove to where the women were and, with his anger still in him, he threw the birds at their feet and turned his chariot away without a word. He drove to where Emer was, but he had none of the birds left for her; and he did this deliberately because of his anger, but already was regretting it.

'You are angry with me,' he said.

'No,' she replied, 'why should I be angry with you? You gave the birds to those women, and it is to me as if it was I who had given them. You did right, for there isn't one of them who does not love you; and none in whom you have not an interest. But as for me, no one has any share in me except yourself alone.'

And she said this with a certain bitterness, for there was truth and love in it at the same time, and they do not always make a sweet mixture.

Cuchulain was sorry then for his anger and his infidelity to Emer with other women, and he said: 'Whenever in the future strange birds come to the plain of Muirtheimne, the two most beautiful will be yours ...'

Hardly had he spoken when they saw, sailing out of the distance and bearing down on them across the lake, two glorious birds, more beautiful than any of the others, and linked together by a chain of red gold. As they came, slowly and majestically, they made soft, sweet music that lulled all who heard it to sleep except those close to Cuchulain.

'There are your birds,' he said to Emer.

But she was afraid. 'There is something strange about those birds,' she cried, 'leave them fly on in peace.'

'Are you serious?' said Cuchulain in derision. 'Put a stone in my sling, Laeg.'

Laeg did so and Cuchulain fired, but for the first time since he had taken arms the cast missed.

'Well,' he said, 'that is a strange thing that never happened to me before.' And he fired again, and again he missed. And a third time he tried, and missed also. Then, in his anger, he threw his spear at them with true aim, but the spear suddenly deflected and passed through the pin feathers of one bird only.

Then, in his rage and frustration, Cuchulain took out after the birds and followed them until they rounded an outcrop of rock in the lake and disappeared. When he reached it they had vanished. And though he gazed out across the lake, and up into the clouds of heaven, there was no sight of them and he could not tell where they had gone. Then, suddenly, for no explicable reason, he felt unutterably weary and listless and he stretched out on the sward and, leaning his back against a pillar of stone, he slept. Then, as he slept, in a dream which was more real than any dream he had known before, two women came towards him. One of them wore a green cloak and the other a purple one folded in five folds. The woman in the green mantle carried a little sally rod in her hand and, laughing all the time, she came towards Cuchulain in his dream and began to strike him gently with it. Then the other did the same, laughing too, as if they played a game with him, and for a long time they did this, each of them in turn, and it seemed to him that whenever he was struck with one of the rods, the strength in his body departed from that place.

He lay like that until the men of Ulster found him and they were worried and upset because of the way he lay so still and entranced. And a group of them decided to waken him, but Fergus stopped them, saying that Cuchulain saw a vision. Shortly after that Cuchulain came out of his sleep and they asked him what had happened. But the weakness was still on Cuchulain and it was all he could do to ask them to carry him to the Speckled Hall of the Red Branch Knights. The Speckled Hall was one of three halls set apart from the king's palace at Emhain Macha. In the Speckled Hall they hung their weapons and stored their trophies and it was because of the glitter made by the reflected light of the sun off the gold and the bronze and the iron that that hall was called the Speckled Hall and it was there that they carried Cuchulain and laid him on a bed with his own weapons above his head. And he lay there like that for a full year with his friends and comrades keeping guard and watch over him. And at the end of that time, when Samhain had come round again, a stranger came and visited the Speckled Hall. Silently and unannounced he came and stood among them. He looked at Cuchulain and said: 'If the man lying there were in his health, he would protect all Uster. But, even though he is sick, he is still my protector, more so even than if he had his health, for it is to see him I came and I am sure that none here would injure me while he is unfit to protect me with his sword.'

'Welcome then,' said the men of the Red Branch Knights.

Then the stranger sang this song to Cuchulain, which none of those there could follow except the sick hero:

Cuchulain, there's no need to lie
In sickness as you do.
Aedh Abhra's daughters here will fly
And bring the cure to you.

Liban, who reigns as Leabhra's queen
On Crooagh's plain has cried:
'Lovely Fand must sleep or die
At Cuchulain's side.'

Cried Fand: 'How well that day will shine
When Cuchulain comes,
To him I'll offer all that's mine
And gold in mighty sums.

'If here with me Cuchulain lay
in sunshine or in dew,
I would his dreams by night and day,
Have made them all come true.'

To where Muirthemne's plain is spread
Liban will go from me;
At Samhain stand beside his bed
And cure his malady.

'And who might you be anyway?' demanded the Red Branch Knights when the stranger had finished this song.

'I am Aengus,' he said, 'son of Aedh Abhra and brother of Fand.' And then he left as he had come, without any seeing where or how. Then his friends crowded round Cuchulain and asked him what it was all about, but he was nearly as mystified as they, except that he understood the words of Aengus' song. And this was one of the first questions they asked him and when he told them that he did understand, they pressed him to tell them, which he did.

Then, when he told them, he asked King Conor what he should do, and the king replied: 'Cuchulain, for a whole year you have lain in sickness unable to speak or move for want of strength. Now, at Samhain again, you have made something of a recovery. And my advice to you, in the light of what Aengus has said, is to go again to that pillar stone and see if Liban has a message for you.'

So Cuchulain was carried in a great cart to where the pillar was against which the sickness descended on him a year before, and when he arrived there he saw the woman in the green mantle there before him.

'It is good that you are here,' she said to him.

'Little good it has done for me,' said Cuchulain, 'since I came last year. What brought you then?'

'It was to do you no injury that we came,' she said, 'but to seek your friendship. I've come from Fand, the daughter of Aedh Abhra and my own sister. Her husband, Mananaan MacLir has released her, and she has turned her love on you and will not live without you. My own name is Liban and I am the wife of Leabhra the Swordsman, King of Moy Mell. He has asked me to seek your help against Senach the Spectre and Eochaid Euil and Eoghan of the Stream, who have declared war on him with all their unearthly hosts.'

Now Cuchulain knew of Fand, who was beautiful beyond the beauty of all women of the world, with an unearthly loveliness. Because her face and person were perfect and flawless she was named Fand, which means 'tear', for there was nothing else so wonderful and flawless with which she could be compared. And she lived with her sister and her husband, Leabhra, in their country of Moy Mell.

Nevertheless Cuchulain replied: 'I am in no fit state to go to war. But let Laeg go with you, and he can bring me back a report of what he sees.'

'That weakness will not last you long,' said Liban. 'And soon you will have your strength back again, greater than before. Meanwhile, let Laeg come with me if he will.'

Then, taking Laeg under her protection, she brought him to the plain of Moy Mell by secret and enchanted ways. During the journey she looked at the charioteer and teased him: 'You would never make this journey, Laeg, if you were not under a woman's protection.'

Laeg didn't think the joke amusing, and replied with dignity: ''Tis not a thing I have been accustomed to doing, putting myself under a woman's protection.'

Then, without thinking, Liban half aloud murmured the

thought in her mind: 'It is a great pity that it is not Cuchulain who is under that protection.'

'Indeed,' replied Laeg angrily, 'it would be a great deal better for me if it was.'

Eventually they reached the shores of a great expanse of water and a bronze boat, small and light, bobbed about waiting for them. They entered it and it took them to an island off the shore and so to the door of Leabhra's palace. Before the palace were armed men and Liban spoke to one of them and asked him where Leabhra was, for she knew the king would be gathering his troops for the impending battle.

And, indeed, that is exactly what the officer said he was doing; but was able to add that he was at that very moment on his way back to the palace. Even as he spoke there was the distant rattle and thunder of a war chariot coming at a gallop and in an instant it swept up to the palace gate and was hauled to a stop by the straight, towering, stern-faced warrior who held the reins with stiff-muscled arms.

Lightly tossing the reins to one of the officers nearby, he jumped down without looking to see if he caught them, and strode towards Liban and Laeg. At his side hung the huge and terrible two handed sword from which he took his *nom-de-guerre.* He was frowning now, and worried looking, as Liban went forward to greet him.

Glancing doubtfully at Laeg, Leabhra – for that is who it was – asked: 'Has Cuchulain come?'

'No,' she replied, 'but Laeg is here, and he will surely come tomorrow.'

Leabhra made no reply to this, but his disappointment rose and added to the frown on his face.

She laid her hand on his arm. 'Don't worry,' she said, 'Cuchulain will be here. You are the strongest and the wisest: your law is just and so are your battles, you cannot fail.'

But Leabhra turned away from her a trifle impatiently in his worry and said: 'Proud words, Liban, are out of place this day. My enemies have immense armies ranged against me and it isn't boasting of my ability I feel like, but lamenting my weakness.'

'Look,' she said, to turn his mind away from such thoughts, 'there is Laeg, and Cuchulain will be here tomorrow.'

Then Leabhra, remembering his duties, greeted Laeg: 'Welcome,' he said, 'for the sake of him you come from and of her you have come to see.'

And at that Liban said to Laeg: 'Will you go now and see Fand?'

Laeg agreed, having paid his respects to the king, and Liban brought him through the palace to Fand's quarters. And as they passed through the palace he looked out of a high casement across the plain and there, in the dim distance, he saw the armies of Senach the Spectre, Eochaid Euil and Eoghan of the Stream assembling, silently and in masses, filling the distant plain. More and more of them he saw, advancing and filling the distance; their spears glinting in the sun and their banners waving against the sky; but, although there were countless numbers of them, there was no sound of armour and horses; no clashing of weapons and rasping of metal as they came onward noiselessly; the only sound to be heard was a low, soft wailing like that of wind in the trees of the forest.

'Tomorrow,' said Leabhra, 'there will be battle, and we cannot stand before that host unless Cuchulain comes.'

'He will surely do that,' said Laeg.

Then, having greeted Fand, Laeg returned to Cuchulain and told him all that he had seen and heard. Immediately Cuchulain's strength began to return to him and his mind was strengthened in him for the news that Laeg brought.

****

Then Cuchulain said to Laeg: 'Go to Dun Dealgan (which was where he had his castle) and see Emer for me. She has been waiting now for a year. Tell her what has happened, that I had a fairy sickness, but that I am getting my strength back now. Ask her to come to me.'

Laeg did as Cuchulain asked him and went to Dun Dealgan where he found Emer in great grief not knowing why she had not heard from her husband ... although in those days, it seems, such was the enlightenment of the people that for the most part wives were not expected to be curious about their husband's whereabouts especially when they were on some knightly errand or other; and the probability is that because they didn't worry, there was nothing for them to worry about.

At all events it was not like that with Emer, and possibly she had more justification for her attitude than most women of her time, for already half the noblewomen of Ulster were openly in love with her husband and even in those liberal times when a man – or a woman – could openly acknowledge a deep and pure love without fear of social ostracism if it did not conform to certain rules; even in those times the wife of a great and distinguished man might well be jealous in spite of her love for him and his for her.

When Laeg told her what had happened to Cuchulain, she was bitter and angry. 'Shame on you,' she cried, 'and shame on the men of Ulster. If it was one of them – aye, or yourself, indeed, master Laeg – who had been bewitched with a sleeping sickess, my Cuchulain would not have rested until he had found some cure. But not one of them would think it worth their while to do the same for him. If it was Fergus, his foster-father, Cuchulain would have gone through the earth for him; or Conall Cearnach, he'd have scoured the earth, or Laoghaire, or any of the others, he wouldn't have stopped night or day until he had the power to heal him. But they do nothing for him when he's struck down, except stand around his bed, you tell me, looking sorrowful and waiting for him to cure himself. It would make you sick. Friends indeed!'

Then, having spent her anger on Laeg, she instructed him to take her to the Speckled Hall at Emhain Macha as quickly as possible that she might be with Cuchulain when he recovered.

And when she arrived and saw him, still weak, but conscious, her tenderness and pity and love turned in her bosom; but her distress and the memory of the past year made her angry with him all over again that he should languish like this under an enchantment. And, in her typical womanly jealousy, she upbraided him unjustly for something he wasn't guilty of at all (at that time at any event), but loving him the greater all the while she did so.

'Shame on you,' she cried, 'to lie there like a schoolboy for a woman's love.'

And so she taunted him and provoked him and gradually his spirit returned, though whether from her anger or from the lifting of the enchantment by Liban is not known; at all events he improved and greeted Emer.

Then again he went to the place where he had seen Liban the year before, and she was there again before him. He spoke to her and greeted her, and she welcomed him and pressed him to come with her to Moy Mell to assist Leabhra in the battle. But Cuchulain hung back. Then, said Liban, 'Fand waits for you with the world of her love to offer you.'

But Cuchulain still resisted. 'I will not go at a woman's call,' he said.

'Well then,' said Liban, 'let Laeg go and confirm what I have told you.'

'Very well,' said Cuchulain, 'let him go with you.' So Laeg went with Liban across the Plain of Speech and past the Tree of Triumphs, over the festal plain of Emhain and the festal plain of Fidga until they reached the palace of Leabhra where Fand was. And she asked: 'How is it that Cuchulain did not come?' To which Laeg replied: 'He didn't care to come at the summons of a woman; moreover,' he said, 'he wanted to know if it was indeed from you that the message came and wanted to know all about this place.'

'It was from me,' said Fand, 'and now return and bring Cuchulain quickly for the battle is tomorrow.'

Then Laeg returned to where he had left Cuchulain, who asked him: 'How does it look to you, Laeg?'

'Good,' replied Laeg, 'there is happiness and a battle before you,' and he told him what he had seen.

While I was on this great journey
A wonderous township I did see –
Though all I saw seemed normal there –
Where I found Leabhra of the Long Hair.

There he sat upon a hill
His armoured troops surrounding him;
His glittering hair, with colour dappled,
Was tethered by a golden apple.

He looked at me before he spoke
From his five-folded purple cloak,
'Come, Laeg, and we will go within
And meet my regent, Failbhe Finn.'

Into the palace me he brings
Where three hundred serve the kings;
So mighty is their palace great,
That all reside within its gate.

The couches are scarlet and golden and white
Jewels for candles disseminate light,
The couches are banded about a great hall
And there's room, and to spare, there for them all.

Westward of the palace gate
The dying sun's rays illuminate
A stable full of dappled greys,
Another too, as full of bays.

While eastward from the palace grow
Three crystal redwoods in a row
Whose branches ring with singing birds,
The sweetest sounds I ever heard.

And in the palace court I sought
That tree of tinkling silver wrought
Which will accompany anyone
And glitters gaily in the sun.

Sixty trees whose branches meet
Drop fruit in plenty at their feet;
Enough to feed three hundred each
With fruits more pleasant than the peach.

Within the palace there's a maid,
More lovely than I ever prayed
To see in Erin: With golden hair,
She's beautiful and skilled and fair.

A woman all mankind might seek.
A wonder 'tis to hear her speak.
The hearts of all she talks will break
With love and longing for her sake.

She looked at me awhile and said:
'Who is this youth, where was he bred?
If you are from Muirtheimne too
Come here and let me look at you.'

Slowly, for I moved in fear,
To her side I ventured near
Conscious of the honour done.
'Where,' she asked, 'is Dechtire's son?'

Long before you should have gone
When those that lived there urged you on,
That, like me, you might have seen
What dreams are real, what might have been.

Were all of Ireland mine to give
I'd give it all, if I could live,
Aye, and Bregia's kingdom too,
Whence I returned in search of you.

'Then you think I should go,' asked Cuchulain.

'I think you'd be a fool not to,' said Laeg, 'everything there is wonderful and there is danger too, for they are threatened with war immediately.'

Then Cuchulain and Laeg returned with Liban and journeyed over the Plain of Speech, beyond the Tree of Triumphs, across the festal plain of Emhain and that of Fidga until they came to where Leabhra and his chiefs and officers waited for them. And a great and tremendous welcome was given to Cuchulain. But he did not wish to waste time in ceremonies for he knew, from what he had heard, that the battle was imminent and, though he acknowledged his welcome graciously, he did it briefly, and then, turning to Leabhra, he said: 'Let us go and take a look at the enemy.'

So Leabhra mounted into Cuchulain's chariot with the champion from Ireland and together with a few picked men, they set forth to observe the enemy dispositions. When they reached the great plain not far from Leabhra's palace it was covered as far as the eye could see with the black tents of Senach the Spectre, and from the pole before each tent hung a black pennant. Among the tents they could discern black-clad warriors moving or riding blood-red horses with fiery manes. Over the lot hung a mist, low over the tent ridges, so that the full extent of the host was obscured, and from out of the mist came the low moaning sound of the demon host.

When Cuchulain saw this frightening assembly his spirits

revived within him and his blood began to run hotly and boil for action. 'Come on,' he said to Leabhra, 'let us circle them and see how many they are.'

But, although he drove his chariot in ever widening circles, the black-clad enemy sprang up before him wherever he turned to go, behind them as innumerable as the blades of corn in a field, or the stars in an autumn night; grim and gaunt they faced him on their blood-red steeds. It seemed to Cuchulain that the smell of blood was already in the air, but instead of daunting him it gave him all the more courage and anger.

Turning to Leabhra and his officers again he said: 'Leave me now, and take your troops with you, for this battle I must fight alone.'

Reluctantly the king did as Cuchulain ordered him to, because he said he would not fight at all unless he did it his own way. And when they saw him left alone to face the demon hordes, two ravens, the spirits of the Morrigu who were allied with Senach, fluttered and cawed about the hosts trying to tell them that it was Cuchulain that stood before them. But they laughed at the birds' antics, saying: 'It must surely be the madman from Ireland who is there alone.' And they chased the ravens away so that there was no resting place for them in the plain with the moaning laughter of Senach's troops.

All that night Cuchulain stood with his hand upon his spear watching the enemy. Then, as dawn broke, his battle-rage came upon him and his whole aspect changed and altered terribly. It is said of him that one of his eyes retreated into his head so that it could hardly be seen, and that the other extended forth so that it was as big as a fist; that a column of red blood sprang from the top of his head and that his body became so hot that it burned those who came within feet of it; and with all that his rage and fury and strength were that of a hundred men. Such was the change that came over the noble youth in his fury.

Just as dawn spilled gently over the hills to the east, one of the enemy chieftains, Eochaid Euil, left his tent to bathe himself in a nearby stream; he removed his tunic and, as he did so, Cuchulain hurled his spear and transfixed him where he knelt. Then, without pause, and in the wild ferocious rage of his battle fury, he leaped amongst them and killed them right and left. Thirty-three men he killed outright before Senach the Spectre attacked him himself and tried to rally his men; but the battle did not last for Cuchulain slew him with a terrible blow of his sword and, as he did so, the army of Leabhra fell upon the demon hosts and drove them in confusion from the field. But still Cuchulain would not stop and he pursued the fleeing soldiers cutting them down as he did so, so that dead and dying lay behind him like a bloody path across the plain wherever he went. Then Leabhra tried to stop the fight for he was sick of the slaughter, and called on Cuchulain to stop. But to no avail. For his battle-fury was still on the hero, and Laeg turned to Leabhra and said: 'Go easy, Leabhra, that he might not turn his fury on ourselves for he has not fought himself out,' and Laeg was frightened for he knew well the terrible wrath in Cuchulain.

'Then what will we do?' asked Leabhra.

'Go and get three huge vats of water,' said Laeg, 'and bring them here. I will persuade him to go into them. The first vat into which he goes will boil over; no one will be able to bear the heat of the second vat after he comes out of it and after he has been in the third vat it will have but a moderate heat, and that is how we will bring him to his senses again.'

So this was done. Laeg persuaded Cuchulain, with no little danger to himself from the hero's bloody and dripping sword, to enter the three vats. And when he emerged from the third he was himself again, hardly more than a boy. And they took him and bathed him, and scented him and gave him fine clothes to wear and after that brought him to Fand who was waiting for him.

When he came before her, refreshed and scented; his hair bound and oiled and swept into a golden ball on his head; his bearing proud, yet youthful too, she thought that she had never seen anyone half so wonderful before and her heart went out to him. And he, in his turn, when he saw Fand, knew that he had never in his life seen a woman so beautiful as Fand. She asked him to sit beside her, and her musicians and maidens sang a song of praise for Cuchulain that she had made for him. And after that she asked him to tell her of the battle, which he did, but with a modesty that belied his feats. And then, with darkness drawing in and the jewelled lamps throwing out their rays, she dismissed her women and her musicians and Cuchulain slept with the lady.

He stayed with her for a month. But at the end of that time he felt a desire to return to Ireland and, though he loved her, he told Fand this. But she was upset and terrified that she would lose him and tried to keep him with her, but to no purpose, for he had his mind made up to return to Ulster and the Red Branch Knights.

'I am a hound of war,' he said to Fand, 'not a little dog to play about his mistress' feet; I must go and stand before the enemy and battle for my country and my king.'

When Fand saw that he could not be persuaded to stay with her, she was sad, but bade him a gentle and loving farewell; all those who had befriended him were sad at his going and Leabhra, in particular, came and thanked him for his help against the demon hosts. Having thanked Cuchulain Leabhra asked Liban to take him back again to Ireland. Before he went Fand looked at him with great love and tenderness and said: 'Tell me where and when I may meet you again and I will be there.' And they agreed that their meeting place would be the Strand of the Yew-Tree's Head.

And so Cuchulain returned to Ireland and he and Laeg were greeted warmly by all their friends in the Red Branch and by Emer; and he told them all about what had happened except that to Emer he said nothing about Fand. But she got to learn about her and about their meeting place at the Strand of the Yew-Tree's Head.

The more she learned the more her hatred and jealousy grew and then, one day when she knew that Cuchulain had gone to keep his rendevous with Fand, she took fifty of her women with her and arming each of them with a strong, sharp dagger, she set out to kill Fand. Silently they crept to the place where Cuchulain and Fand sat in the shade of a yew tree. Cuchulain and Laeg were playing chess and were unaware of what was going on. But Fand, whose senses were keener than those of either, heard the women approaching and then saw them and immediately realised their intention.

'Look, Laeg,' she cried.

'What is it?' he asked sharply, jerking up his head.

'Behind you,' said Fand, 'Emer and her women coming through the undergrowth. Cuchulain, they are armed and against me I don't doubt.'

Cuchulain turned and saw the women led by Emer and saw that Fand was right into the bargain.

'Don't be afraid,' he said to Fand, helping her to her feet. 'Get into my chariot and I will protect you. Emer will not harm you as long as I am here.'

Then, turning to Emer, he said: 'Put down your knife, Emer. I cannot fight you back and you would not kill me in spite of your rage. It would be ironic if I were to be killed by a woman when I've been so victorious on the battlefield.'

'Then tell me,' she cried in anguish, 'why have you shamed me and dishonoured me before the women of Ulster and all Ireland? What have I done that you have turned away from me and loved another woman, and a fairy woman at that?'

'Emer,' said Cuchulain, 'it may be true that I have broken my vow to you; but where is the gravity of the fault? How could I not love Fand too? She is fairer than the fair, more beautiful than the beautiful, intelligent and talented and a fit wife for any king and moreover has a mind that is as keen and able as the best. There is nothing under heaven that a wife would do for her dear husband that Fand has not done for me. Therefore do not lay too much blame on us. And as for yourself, where else would you find anyone who has loved you as I have, or who shows you so much reflected honour?'

Emer laughed scornfully at him. 'In what way is she better than I am,' she asked. 'Men are all alike. What's red seems fair and what's white seems new. Men worship what they can't have, and what they have seems nothing. We lived happily together, Cuchulain, and would again if you only loved me.'

'Indeed,' said Cuchulain, 'I do love you, and always will as long as I live.'

'Then,' said Fand unhappily, 'I must go.'

'No indeed,' cried Emer, 'it is better that I should be the one who is deserted.'

'No,' said Fand. 'It is I who must go.'

A terrible sadness and loneliness seized Fand then, and her soul was great within her, for it was a terrible shame for her to be deserted and returned to her home; moreover the mighty love that she had for Cuchulain was tumultuous in her. Then she made this lament:

My heart is turning in me,
Yet I must go my way;
My love remains behind me–
If I could only stay.

Nothing could be sweeter
Than your loving hand,
I would choose it rather
Than my native land.

Emer, gentle lady,
I set your husband free;
Although my arms release him
Longing stirs in me.

Then she lifted up her lovely face and Emer saw teardrops, so well fitting her own name, welling in her eyes.

But now a strange thing took place. Mananaan, who had been Fand's husband and who had released her, learned that Fand was in danger from the women of Ulster and that she was likely to be left by Cuchulain whom she loved. Thereupon he came from the east to help her. Mananaan was old, so old that no one knew his age except himself. He was kingly and majestic, but feared too by men, for his moods were terrible and variable, though he could smile benignly when it suited him. But now, when he saw Fand's great distress, he came swiftly to help her, invisible to men, but not to her. And as he passed her she felt his presence and looked up as he passed. But for a moment she did not know him, for he had shed his years and the man she saw was young and strong, with a noble gentleness upon his face.

Then she cried to herself, looking into her heart, and said: 'Oh God, here is Mananaan. Once he was dearer to me than the world we shared, yet today, though his voice is music to my ears, no love and exultation fills my heart, for the pathway of love may be bent astray and its knowledge depart. Oh Mananaan,' she cried, 'when we lived together in the past our life was an unending dream. It seemed as if nothing could divide our love. I know that no one save myself can see you and that you can understand all; but that is no help to me now. Being a woman I am helpless now that the man I love has left my side.' Then, turning to Cuchulain, she said: 'Cuchulain ...' but could say no more for her grief overcame her.

Then Mananaan said to her: 'Fand, what will you do? Will you come with me or stay here until Cuchulain comes to you?'

Then in anguish Fand looked at him, her love turning like a live thing inside in her bosom, and she said: 'Dear lord Mananaan, I do not know. Either of you is a greater man than any woman could wish for, and neither of you is better than the other. Yet he has betrayed me and besides that he has a wife to love him already while you have none. Therefore, Mananaan, I will go with you.'

Then Mananaan stretched out his arms to her and she went to him. And Cuchulain, seeing her go, as he could not see Mananaan, cried out: 'What is happening, Laeg? Where is Fand going?'

And Laeg, who had the ability to see the great one, said: 'She is going back to Mananaan since you do not love her above all else.'

Then Cuchulain gave three great cries of grief and rushed about in despair, so wildly and madly that he did not stop until he came to the desert of Luachra. And he lived there for a long time, eating no meat and drinking no wine and sleeping by the highway that goes to Tara of the kings. Then Emer went to Tara and spoke to the king about Cuchulain and what had happened to him in his grief for Fand. And the king sent out his physicians and doctors to cure him and bring him back to health and to Emhain Macha. But Cuchulain had so lost his wits that when he saw them he ran from them at first and then tried to kill them, until at length he fell in a fit from weakness and begged a drink from them. This they gave him, but with it they mixed a drug which dulled his memory and sent him into a deep sleep. When he woke from it the memory of his passion was gone, though there lingered a deep sorrow in him. And the physicians gave a similar drug to Emer to help her to forget her jealousy, and with her it was more successful and her natural joyousness returned. But she was troubled to see Cuchulain so sad.

Then Mananaan, who learned of the trouble between Emer and Cuchulain, shook his cloak between Cuchulain and the beautiful Fand so that from both of them the memory passed away as though it had been a dream, and they thought of each other no more.

And that is the story of the Sickbed of Cuchulain.

Folktales of the Irish Countryside

Kevin Danaher

Nowadays there is a whole generation growing up who cannot remember a time when there was no television; and whose parents cannot remember a time when there was no radio and cinema. It is not, therefore, surprising that many of them wonder what people in country places found to do with their time in the winters of long ago.

People may blink in astonishment when reminded of the fact that the night was often too short for those past generations of country people, whose own entertainment with singing, music, dancing, cards, indoor games and storytelling spanned the evenings and into morning light.

Kevin Danaher remembers forty of the stories that enlivened those past days. Some are stories told by members of his own family; others he took down in his own countryside from the last traditional storytellers. Included are stories of giants, of ghosts, of queer happenings and of the great kings of Ireland.

ENCHANTED IRISH TALES

PATRICIA LYNCH

Enchanted Irish Tales tells of ancient heroes and heroines, fantastic deeds of bravery, magical kingdoms, weird and wonderful animals. This illustrated edition of classical folktales, retold by Patricia Lynch with all the imagination and warmth for which she is renowned, rekindles the age-old legends of Ireland, as exciting today as they were when first told. This collection includes: Conary Mór and the Three Red Riders, The Long Life of Tuan MacCarrell, Finn MacCool of the Fianna, Oisín and the Land of Youth, The Kingdom of the Dwarfs, The Dragon Ring of Connla, Mac Datho's Boar and Ethne.

DEFIANT IRISH WOMEN

EDMUND LENIHAN

Defiant Irish Woman tells the story of five Irish women who were unusual in a variety of ways – mostly because of their ruthlessness, political cunning or merely because they rebelled violently against the repressive mores of their times.

In our time when attention is being paid to more aspects of woman as individuals and to their role in society than here-to-fore, it may be appropriate to pause a moment and question the generally-held view that Irish woman in previous ages were voiceless, subservient creatures, merely part of that silent anonymous mass of humanity that has had precious few chroniclers.

Edmund Lenihan in telling the stories of their lives and the legends that grew up around them, ensures that we will not forget the prominent part played by these women in our Irish heritage – Aoibheall the banshee, Máire Rua McMahon, Lady Betty, the Roscommon hangwoman, Moll Saughnessy and Alice Kyteler.